THE SPIN I'M IN

FOR THE LOVE OF FIBER ~ BOOK 1

KATE BOWMAN

Print ISBN: 978-1-7334674-1-4

A determined widow faces the challenge of a new life to regain the confidence and independence of her youth, but finds that life, unlike knitting, doesn't always follow a pattern.

PRAISE FOR 'THE SPIN I'M IN'

"If you like stories about women starting over, whether they want to or not, *The Spin I'm In* will pull you in from page one. Martha, a widow, leaves her old life behind when she moves to Wisconsin and takes up spinning, and lucky her, meets Riley, a sheepshearer. It's not always an easy journey, and Riley's young son, who struggles with Asperger Syndrome, proves challenging, but Martha could be on her way to a richer, fuller life than she's ever imagined. Readers drawn to novels about quilting and knitting circles will love Bowman's book that features a group of avid spinners."

~Virginia McCullough, Author, Ghostwriter and Writing Coach

To my husband and family for never giving up on Mom's dream.

ACKNOWLEDGMENTS

A special thank-you to my daughter, Molly Bowman Johnson, for her fantastic cover. Her talent amazes me. And to my son, David Bowman, photographer extraordinaire for his work in photographing said cover.

And thank-you to all my WisRWA friends, especially Gini Athey, Shirley Cayer, Virginia McCullough, and Nancy Sweetland for their encouragement and helpful critiques. Go WisRWA!

And of course a big thank-you to my fantastic spinning group, who taught me much more than how to spin wool.

And last but not least, a thank-you to Maria Connor who somehow put this all together.

1

IF IGNORANCE IS CONSIDERED BLISS, I'D BEEN LIVING in paradise.

On a beautiful spring morning in suburban Chicago, reality dug its bony fingers into my chest and wouldn't let go. My neighbor had just cut his lawn, filling the air with the sweet smell of fresh cut grass, and I stood in the doorway, breathing in the scent before walking out to the mailbox. The yellow daffodils I'd planted just before Robert's death waved in the gentle breeze. How long had they been in bloom?

Reaching into the mailbox, I pulled out the stack of envelopes. Another batch of unpaid bills. I shuffled through them half-heartedly, pulling out a folded sheet of typing paper stuck in-between the pile. Curious, I unfolded it.

YOU OWE ME. I'LL BE AROUND TO COLLECT WHEN THE TIME IS RIGHT.

The bold, slash-like letters jumped out at me, bringing to the surface fears I'd managed to suppress for months. I dropped the envelopes, and they fluttered to the ground. Was the note meant for me? No. Couldn't be. Someone had put it there by mistake.

I stood rigid for a moment, shocked into paying attention to my surroundings for the first time in months as the fog of denial lifted. I couldn't be sure of anything anymore though, could I?

I looked up and down the street. The mailman was long gone and the street bare of pedestrians. I bent down and picked up the envelopes. Was I over-reacting or finally facing reality?

I forced myself to remember how my Barbie-doll world had crashed at my feet in a heap of lies and betrayal. No more denial. A whimper escaped through my dry lips.

Life as I knew it was gone, if it ever existed at all.

Walking back into the living room, I paused on my way to the kitchen for a second cup of coffee. Or was it my fourth? I didn't know, and I didn't care. Clearly, life had given me another major jolt. As if Robert's death wasn't enough, now I was left to carry his secrets. Anger rose like bile, bringing me back to life and energized. Time for me to begin my own life.

"I *hate* that couch." I said the words out loud. It was the first honest thing I'd said to myself in years. That blasted couch looked as blah as I felt—beige and lifeless—no warmth, no color, no softness to give comfort. Just cold and indifferent, like the rest of the furniture Robert chose, and I hated. There. I finally admitted it.

This room is as dull as dishwater. Too neat, too perfect, nothing to show the heart and soul of Martha Carey, the woman I used to be before my marriage. I tossed a few of the aqua pillows on the floor and scattered the neat stack of coffee-table books around the glass-topped chrome table. Had anyone ever opened one of those books? After throwing a few newspapers on the floor with the pillows, I stomped over them. *Yes!* I smiled for the first time in months.

I continued on to the kitchen, desperate now for a caffeine fix, my mind reeling with the need for change. The morning sun glared off the stainless-steel appliances, granite countertops, and glass cabinet doors. I blinked in defense. The ceramic tile floor turned my bare feet cold.

My kitchen could pass for an operating room.

When had I become emotionally numb, sleepwalking through life these past years, putting everyone else's needs before mine without a murmur? Always trying to be the perfect wife and mother, never questioning, never making waves. I clamped my hand over my mouth in horror. Had security become my only goal? I had become the woman my husband wished he'd married. Now, that life had disappeared.

I stared down at my bleach-stained navy sweats. They hung on my middle-aged body like a mis-shapen sack. Had I even combed my hair? I didn't have to look in the mirror to know gray roots showed at the base of my scalp and my skin hadn't seen makeup for weeks. *Martha, you're a fifty-year-old loser.*

My words echoed back at me through the cool morning air wafting in through the kitchen window. Sometimes the truth really does hurt. I couldn't remember when I'd last been to the salon, something that never would've happened while Robert lived.

Robert's heart attack months ago left us shocked and unprepared. I'd put my dreams and ambitions aside long ago for a husband who had all the answers. And I loved him for it. Most of the time, anyway. Robert was supposed to protect and provide for the girls and me always. Instead, his loss and the aftermath left me totally unprepared to cope. *Was it my fault? Had I driven him to another woman?* I wrapped my arms across my stomach, shaking my head in denial. No. I refused to believe it. If that were true, my life was nothing but a sham.

Robert's sudden death left me with so many questions, some of which I would never have the answers for. His death also left me with a few cold, hard facts. All our savings had disappeared, and I was left with a mountain of debt. Why hadn't I taken an interest in our finances? I would have at least been aware of what I now faced. The money had to have gone somewhere, like to poor investments.

By the time I'd met Robert in college, I'd realized I was only a small fish in a big pond. I may have been one of the brightest, even one of the prettiest and most ambitious in my small town high school, but the competition on the university campus was overwhelming. To be noticed by a man like Robert was absolutely thrilling. He was everything I admired: sophisticated, intelligent, handsome, and he knew his way around people. Together, we would conquer the world. Too late, I discovered the plan was for me to be the woman behind the throne.

The phone rang, and I searched the caller ID. Of course, my eldest daughter, Brooke. Calling for her daily update.

Brooke had taken over where her father left off, calling daily to give me advice on everything, from how to spend my time on up to what I should cook for dinner. I'd been too lethargic and dazed these past months to pay much attention, going through life like an android from "Star Trek: the Next Generation." Smiling, agreeing with everything she and everyone else said, listening but not hearing.

Thank God, my youngest daughter, Lexie, moved on with her life after her father's death, returning to her home and teaching job in New York with her yuppie husband. The term is passé but too bad—Donald is a walking cliché.

"Hi, Mom. How did you sleep?"

What was with Brooke's fixation on my sleep patterns? It had become a daily question.

"I slept fine." The words rolled off my tongue like baby Pablum. A force of habit.

"What are you doing today?" She gave that deep sigh she'd perfected as a teen. "You're so lucky, getting to enjoy this beautiful spring weather while I'm moldering in the city."

Who did she think she was kidding? She'd hot-footed it out of our Chicago suburb the day she graduated from high school and never looked back.

"I'm going shopping for a new couch," I said. I blinked in surprise. Did I say that? One more bill to add to the pile. At this point, it didn't seem to matter.

"What? Why would you do that?" The horror in her voice was palpable. "That couch is a Rotola Italian Leather. I know people who would kill for it." Brooke was her father's daughter, all right.

"I want an overstuffed red couch with bright pillows. The room needs color."

Silence. And then another sigh.

"Dad loved that couch. He always napped there on Sunday afternoon."

Was she trying to make me feel guilty? Of course, he loved it. It was beige, unobtrusive, and practical. Robert wasn't anything if not practical.

Loving him didn't mean I'd been blind to his faults. Well, obviously I'd been blind to some, as I knew now. But I couldn't tell my daughter. She'd adored him.

"He's been gone for months, Brooke. It's time we got on with our lives." I cringed after those clichéd words left my mouth and wanted to call them back. If only I could give her a hug. Even if she were here, it would be difficult, though. Brooke's personal space must never be violated. She'd established that rule in her early teens.

"There's nothing wrong with the couch," she said. "It's like new."

"There is something wrong with it. I hate it. I have since the day your father brought it home."

"You have to be practical about these things, *Mother*. It's made of hand-selected Italian leather and very valuable."

"I know that. I still hate it. If you love it so much, take it. It's yours."

Brooke's shocked intake of breath told me this child of mine hadn't a clue as to who I was. Not the real me who had hopes and dreams of my own. Or at least who used to. To her, I was simply Mom, someone who blends into the background and keeps the family peace.

"Mom, take a deep breath. Don't do anything rash. I'll be out to see you on the weekend."

She'd adopted that condescending tone soon after her father died, and it annoyed the hell out of me, even in my fog of lethargy. Usually, I bit my tongue, knowing her heart lay in the right place, but today I couldn't seem to stop.

It was only now I realized that for a long time, inside, I'd been angry.

Very angry.

Don't get me wrong. I love my daughter to death and would gladly give up my life for her. But there were times she made liking her damn difficult.

"Brooke, I'm a grown woman and can make my own decisions."

"Just wait until I get there, okay?" she soothed. "We'll talk about it then."

"I won't be home this weekend." I was on a roll.

"Oh? Where are you going?" she asked.

I visualized her professionally shaped eyebrows raised in surprise.

"I'm driving up to Wisconsin for a little getaway and plan to visit Aunt Suze on the way."

Silence again. She must have been weighing the pros and cons of my staying home and tearing the house apart or going to Milwaukee and being influenced by my freethinking sister. There had always been tension between my sibling and my husband, and the kids had picked up on it at a young age.

"A weekend away is probably just what you need. Have a good time, and give my regards to Aunt Suze." I heard the rat-a-tat of her long fingernails beating impatiently on the table. "Call me as soon as you get home."

When had Brooke become the mother and I the daughter? I wasn't ready for that stage of life, not by a long shot. The girl needed a husband and family of her own to worry about. My chest closed up like a steel safe, locking my breath inside. *Just breathe in and breathe out.* I set the phone down with exaggerated calm.

As the numbness of the past months continued to recede, anger boiled up to take its place.

Anger at myself. Anger at Robert for keeping secrets, no matter his intentions.

Things had to change.

This is good. I'm starting to feel again. What I wanted now was to be left alone to make my own decisions about my future. Was that so difficult to accept?

I'd begin by buying a new couch. A bright red one.

It didn't take long to change into my suburban outfit of camel-colored dress slacks, white blouse, and navy blazer, backcomb my hair a little to hide the roots, and apply makeup in an attempt to cover the dark shadows and new wrinkles around my eyes. I'd learned the secret to good service was dressing like you could afford it.

Twenty minutes later, I pulled into the lot of the largest furniture dealer in the area. I couldn't waste my time in a place where you dithered over fabric samples and design. I was buying the couch today before I lost my nerve. Never mind the dance going on in my stomach.

It only took a minute before a clerk noticed me and hustled over.

"Can I help you?" she asked with a smile so wide I could see fillings.

"Yes. I want to buy a red couch."

"Red?" She blinked. "A red couch. Any particular style you had in mind?"

"No, it just has to be red and comfortable."

"Uh-huh." She scanned the showroom." We have a pretty plaid."

"No, it has to be red and in stock. And I want it delivered today."

Did I really say that? I thrust out my chin in defiance of the conventional niceties that had ruled my life for so long. No salesclerk would stand in my way today.

"Why don't you look around while I check our stock listing?" she said, carefully drawing back.

I swear I wandered through an acre of furniture before I spotted it. I ran my hand over the soft denim-like fabric and plopped down, getting comfy. It was overstuffed, wide enough so you could curl your legs up comfortably beside you, or even lie down and sleep in comfort. A soft red with brass-button trim, it had five multi-colored pillows along the back. In other words, it was perfect.

"I'll take this one," I told the clerk when she finally found me.

"Give me your address, and I'll check the delivery schedule," she said as we returned to her desk. She flipped through a manila folder. "I'm sorry, but we deliver in your area on Friday and Tuesday."

"It has to be delivered today. I'll be out of town on Friday."

"What about next Tuesday?"

"No, it has to be today."

She warred between the customer is always right mantra and her desire to tell me exactly where I could take my business. The desire for commission won out. "I'll see what I can do," she said with a smile so tight I thought her cheeks would crack.

Was I being totally unreasonable? Maybe I should just forget about it and let them deliver on schedule. The old Martha reared her wimpy head, but I managed to squash down the feelings.

The clerk returned a few minutes later. "It'll be there this afternoon."

"Perfect." I'd met the demon of self-doubt and triumphed. I'd figure out how to have the old couch delivered to Brooke later. Hopefully, it would soothe any hurt feelings. On the way home, satisfied warmth nestled in the pit of my stomach.

It lasted until the deliverymen set the new couch in the living room. It looked like a mutt at the Westminster Dog Show. Lovable but outclassed. Kind of how I felt about myself in this house.

That's when I realized I'd only taken the first step in the rehabilitation of Martha Carey LeBeau.

I'M TOLD THERE ARE ONLY TWO SEASONS IN THE STATE of Wisconsin.

Winter and construction.

Following the Tri-state Tollway North from Chicago, I swung onto Interstate 94 that Friday afternoon. I made it through the Milwaukee traffic and construction with hands clenched on the wheel and the classical music station out of Madison playing full volume. When the sign for 43N and Green Bay appeared, I knew I'd soon be home free.

I pulled up in front of my sister Suze's modest brick home in Whitefish Bay, a suburb north of Milwaukee. As difficult as it would be, I needed to talk to her.

We'd been close as children, but in the decades since my marriage, things had changed. We'd taken such different views of our roles as wife and mother. That's why I'd always steered clear of any deeply personal discussions, knowing Robert would feel I was being disloyal.

But now I needed my sister to make sense of these emotions surging through me.

Suze flew out the door to meet me, her athletic body still graceful after all these years. She wore her hair in a silver bob, having sworn off color years ago. It had to do with her whole women's lib thing.

Thank goodness I'd had my roots done, or she might have made some snarky comment.

"I'm so glad you didn't have to work today," I said in the midst of her bear hug.

Suze's husband was a schoolteacher, and she'd always worked at least part-time to supplement their income. She could never understand why I had to give up my career for Robert. It was a bone of contention between us. I was the first in my family to get a college education, and it broke her liberated heart to see me *waste* it.

"What's the matter?" She put her hands on my shoulders and stared me down like a mother would an unhappy child. "You look upset."

"Everything's just..." I swallowed the rest of the sentence. The practiced line had almost slipped through my lips again. I'd discovered early in my married life that any dissatisfaction I voiced could ruin the day for my family. Mothers weren't allowed to be unhappy. They were the cheerleaders of the group, always seeing the cup half full. Time to get real. "Crappy."

No use pretending with my sister. Her eyes saw right into my soul, knocking down all the barriers I'd erected during my marriage. We had grown up together and shared too much to even try to fool her now. Suze was my lifeline to sanity, especially since both our parents had passed away a few years back.

Making friends hadn't come easy for me since my marriage. I'd never been close to my neighbors.

Robert was only interested in socializing with coworkers. The only thing the neighbors and I had had in common were our kids. With their children now grown, most of my neighborhood acquaintances had moved to careers and condominiums in the city. I was just now realizing how lonely my life had become without friends.

"Let's go in and have a cup of coffee." Suze herded me into the house.

If I were lucky, she'd have made my favorite cookies. Suze was like that. She could switch from "I Am Woman, Hear Me Roar" to nurturing female in a flash.

As soon as I stepped into her kitchen, a wave of nostalgia rose in my throat. It was like going back in time. A time when I was loved and appreciated as the spoiled youngest child—pretty, precocious, and guaranteed to succeed.

My grandmother's favorite teapot, the one with yellow and blue flowers, sat in the center of the Formica table, on top of the tablecloth Gram had hand-embroidered years ago. Everything in the room was yellow and white and happy, and the contrast between my life and my sister's couldn't have been clearer than at that moment.

"I always loved that teapot," I said with a catch to my voice.

"I told you it was yours when we cleaned out Gram's place."

"No, it would've just been put in a cupboard if

I'd taken it. Robert said it was too 'kitschy' for our decor."

She didn't say anything, and I was thankful. Robert's opinions had a habit of rubbing Suze the wrong way. Instead, she got two mugs out of the cupboard and poured us each a cup of coffee. She motioned for me to sit down and set a plate of cookies between us.

"Hey, you made chocolate chip." Did I know my sister or what?

"You sounded like you needed some."

When the tears formed, I blinked them back. Why was it that having my daughter try to take care of me made me so angry and yet when my older sister did the same, I was touched?

"Okay, spill it. Something happened to jolt you out of your apathy. It's about time."

Leave it to Suze to come right to the point. "If you felt that way, why didn't you say something?" I asked.

She shrugged. "I figured you were still grieving, and everyone has their own timetable." She bit into her cookie while watching me closely.

"Brooke and I had a little dust-up the other day." Safer to talk about that than my other problems.

"What did my darling niece do to get you so shook up?"

"She made me so damn angry." I had to take a deep breath to calm myself. The weight of her condescension burned like acid in my gut.

"What did she say?" Suze asked.

"It wasn't so much what she said. It was her attitude. She was as patronizing as possible, talked to me like I was in my dotage. It got me to thinking about how I'll spend the rest of my life." I looked down at the half-eaten cookie in my hand.

How could I explain these new emotions jumping all over the place? One minute I felt my life was over since I'd lost Robert, and the next I had a terrible urge to get rid of the past and start a new life, one more of my choosing. And then there was the whole ungodly mess of my financial situation.

"So how *are* you going to spend the rest of your life? Tell me what you've been thinking," Suze said, reaching over and patting my hand.

I don't think I ever loved her more than at that moment. She became my mother, my confessor, and my friend, all rolled into one. But still, I held back. Out of some misplaced loyalty to Robert, I guess. I couldn't voice my suspicions about him until I knew for sure. And even then, I doubt I could. What would it do to his children and to my own self-esteem?

"I need a reason to get up in the morning. Does that make any sense at my age, or am I too old to be looking for a change?" If I was with anyone but Suze, I'd be ashamed of the pleading in my voice.

"Well, glory be to God, you finally woke up and realized Martha Carey is alive and kicking. Now, get rid of the guilt I hear in your voice. Staying in the house Robert loved and doing things exactly the way he wanted is not going to bring him back. That life is over. Accept it."

"But the kids. They don't want things to change."

"Of course, they don't. That's the nature of the beast. You're not a person to them. You're their mom. Especially those two. They've been the focus of your life since the moment they were born."

"Yeah, well, I wanted it that way," I said, sudden heat rising in my face.

"Do they ask your opinion when they want to make a change in their lives?"

"Are you kidding? They might've asked Robert's opinion, never mine. Not since they were children, anyway." I swallowed the sudden lump in my throat.

Suze gave me a funny look, and I realized I'd said more than I intended. For so many years, I've squashed down those feelings of resentment. It surprised even me when they popped up.

"You've got a lot of years left to fill, Martha. Don't chicken out now that you finally woke up to reality."

Suze was right. But then, I wouldn't be here if I wasn't already on the path from my past to a new kind of freedom.

"Enough about me," I said, grabbing another cookie. "What have you been up to?"

. . .

I LEFT MY SISTER'S SOON AFTER THAT, NOT WANTING to drive in the dark down strange roads. I'd decided to head up toward the Door Peninsula—maybe stop for the night in Shoreview. It was a picturesque little town on Lake Michigan, near Grandma Carey's old farmhouse. We'd visited there often when I was a child, and the place held happy memories. Maybe there I could find some answers.

The sky stayed sunny and bright, and the temperature was unseasonably warm. For the first time in years, I felt content. A few minutes later, after getting out of the heavy traffic and exhaust fumes, I went so far as to open the moonroof and change the station to classic rock. The fresh smell of early spring rushed through the car confines, filling me with forgotten energy.

I turned up the radio volume. The Boss—Bruce Springsteen—singing a remake of "Born to Run" blasted out of the speakers. He was still at it after all these years. And sounding damn good.

A feeling of freedom zinged through my veins, as though I was on the cusp of some life-changing event. I could go either way—back to my old life as the grieving widow or on to some grand adventure. The siren call was out there if only I knew what it called me to do? A new career? I had to do something, and soon.

Who was I kidding? Any marketable skills I'd had were woefully out of date. That old dejection started creeping insidiously into my soul, like an early evening fog.

I hadn't taught school since Brooke's birth. Robert wanted me to be there 24/7 for the kids and was willing to work extra hard to make it possible. By the time they were in grade school, he'd begun traveling several days a week, sometimes even weeks at a time. In those days, work schedules weren't geared to accommodate working mothers.

Just as I arrived in Shoreview, my stomach growled with hunger. I gazed down the hill onto the harbor. Boats of all sizes and shapes were anchored there; several entering the channel into Lake Michigan, preparing for an evening catch or cruise. The downtown streets were lined with renovated nineteenth-century buildings that housed shops, restaurants, and commercial businesses. Under the clear early evening sky, the town sparkled clean and fresh.

No Holiday Inn or other large hotel marquee blinked on the horizon, and my heart sank. For the first time, I'd left home without making reservations. Another daring deed, something the Robert I knew never would've considered chancing.

Turning onto a side street, I noticed a lovely Victorian B&B nestled among the older homes lining the residential area. It was painted yellow, with white gingerbread trim, and the rooms had a view of the lake. A large VACANCY sign swung on the well-manicured lawn. Luck was with me. I slammed on my brakes and pulled into a parking spot.

The elderly owner was warm and friendly as she showed me to my room, so different from the cool green, white, and masculine brown of my room at home. This room was a riot of color—flowered wallpaper, white provincial furniture, and touches of lace. I had stepped into a princess's room.

"I keep this room for my female guests," she said with a twinkle. "Sometimes we need a little pampering, right?"

I plunked myself down on the soft bed. "This is lovely."

"I'll leave you to settle in. We don't serve dinner here, but there is a pub a few blocks away that serves good food."

After relaxing for a few minutes, I went in search of the pub.

The place was crowded, the air heavy with the smell of fried food. A country-western tune played low in the background. I asked the waitress to seat me at a small table back in the corner. It gave me a clear view of the room, and I could watch the other diners without being conspicuous, a favorite pastime I'd developed since dining alone. Had I met any of these people when I spent summers with Gram? Doubtful.

Since it was Friday, I ordered the perch plate, a

Wisconsin tradition. The fish was lightly breaded and delicious. Of course, if Robert were here, I wouldn't have ordered the fries—or the second glass of wine. He'd believed in moderation in all things—or so he'd said. Somehow, that made the second glass of wine more enjoyable.

I was told to pay at the bar, so after leaving a sizable tip for my over-worked waitress, I made my way through the now crowded tables to the bar area. The place was jammed. Patrons lined the dark mahogany bar, perched on stools, talking to each other or staring into the mirrored back of the bar. There, short glass shelves lined with fancy booze bottles broke up their reflection, making their faces appear disjointed.

"Excuse me," I said to the bartender when I finally caught his eye. "I'd like to pay my bill."

He looked up from the tray of drinks he mixed. "I'll be with you in a moment." He had the wind-burned complexion and sunburned scalp of a commercial fisherman, probably his trade when the catch was prolific.

I reached into my oversized purse for my wallet, pulling out a fifty. But I managed to drop the bill on the bar floor. I bent down to retrieve it and touched another pair of warm fingers already covering the cash. I jumped back and looked up into a pair of the deepest blue eyes I'd ever seen, the corners crinkled in a friendly smile.

"Here you are, miss," he said, pushing back the

silver-streaked black hair that had fallen across his high forehead as he handed me the bill.

Inexplicably, my breath caught in my throat, and after a breathless *thank-you,* I turned back to the bar. Only in my haste, my gigantic purse hit the tray of drinks, knocking several over onto the tray.

"Oh, I am so sorry," I squeaked out.

The bartender sighed. "Don't worry about it. Things like this always seem to happen when Riley's around."

"I'll take care of the extras, Frank," a deep male voice said from behind.

I looked up into the mirror then and flushed. Those blue eyes watched me, the corners crinkled up in laughter now. It was then I noticed that every head had turned to watch my reflection in the back mirror. I felt the heat rise up my neck and looked away.

"That won't be necessary," I told the bartender. "Take it out of here," and I pushed the fifty closer. Flushing even brighter, I grabbed my change and hurried out of the bar.

Thankfully I didn't meet the owner when I returned to my room at the B&B. I dropped my clothes in a heap on the floor, exhausted after the long drive and day of emotional turmoil. I pulled back the rose-patterned quilt and crawled between the sheets of the lace-canopied bed. What had my days of self-discovery netted so far? I'd pissed off my daughter, rediscovered a closeness to my sister that

I'd missed for years, and made a total fool of myself in front of strangers. Not a bad beginning.

After an early breakfast at the B&B, I drove out into the countryside, a burning need to see my grandmother's old farmhouse hot in my chest. It'd been sold long ago, and I didn't know if I'd be able to locate it. Without an address, my GPS wasn't of much value.

I left the highway and drove down some county roads—past red barns, old farmhouses, and cows grazing in the pasture—with happy memories of summers spent with my grandmother floating through my mind in a gauzy haze. Old feelings of being loved just for being me surfaced.

After driving quite a few miles, I realized nothing looked familiar. I should've brought a map. But I'd been so sure I could find the place. I never imagined I'd forget the way. The house could've passed through several hands by now, so no use asking the locals.

Just when I was about to give up in despair, I saw a familiar-looking brown frame home in the distance. Could it be Gram's? In my memories, it was white clapboard, but the structure was the same. Red and white rose bushes climbed up the trellis on the side of the porch. I had a sudden memory of their sweet scent filling the air on a summer afternoon while I drank Kool-Aid and ate

Gram's freshly baked chocolate chip cookies. Is that where I'd developed my love for them? Funny how smells can bring those old feelings to your gut as quick as a sucker punch.

Sheep and alpaca grazed in the field next to the road. I parked my car to get a better view. When I saw the lambs, I had to get out. I'd always had a weakness for baby animals. Watching them cavort between the ewes brought a smile to my lips and lightness to my heart.

I hadn't been this close to farm animals in years. The sheep gave me a baleful glance but soon went back to munching grass. One of the alpaca came up to the fence and eyed me curiously. The longing to touch his wooly head almost overcame my common sense. I backed away slowly so I wouldn't frighten him and climbed into my car.

Just as I turned the ignition key, the thought struck me without warning, but so pure and clear, I knew it to be true. This is what I wanted, what I'd always wanted—to be out in the country, on my own little piece of land with a few animals. I'd had the dream for so long, knowing it was impossible because of Robert's work. Now, it was within my reach. My heart pounded, and my stomach churned. The idea grew and gathered strength, and with it came a sense of relief. This could even be the answer to my financial problems, and my escape from whoever sent that note. And I'd found it after only one day of searching. Surely, my life could find new meaning here.

I LEFT SHOREVIEW WITH A COPY OF THE LOCAL REAL estate ads tucked in my bag. I didn't say anything to Suze when I stopped for a break late that afternoon. I knew I should slow down and take a deep breath. Decisions shouldn't be made this fast. But the seed had planted itself in my brain and mushroomed with all sorts of possibilities.

Robert's voice played in my head. *Are you nuts? You don't know the first thing about farming. Just because you spent a few weeks on a farm as a kid doesn't mean you know how to take care of livestock.*

He would've been right, of course. But that wouldn't stop me from looking for a nice little place, close to the highway. A place that didn't need much work—maybe a little painting, redecorating, that sort of thing. It would be fun. Shopping therapy was close if I got too lonely. What could possibly be lonelier than the place I lived in now, with neighbors I neither knew nor saw?

It could work. I should make a good profit off the sale of my house, even with the second mortgage. We'd lived there over twenty years, and the original loan was paid off. Hopefully, I could pay off most of the debts and find a job to make a mortgage payment if necessary. That would give me enough financial security to start my new life.

I decided not to tell the girls about my plans just yet. Better to wait until it was a done deal, or they'd exhaust me with their arguments against it. Lexie would be surprised. Brooke would be furious. That gave me a sense of satisfaction on some level. Sheesh! I was going to hell in a hand basket, as Gram would say. What happened to the nice person I used to be? Taking out the resentment for my and Robert's mistakes on my daughter had to stop before I damaged our relationship permanently. As long as possible, I'd have to straddle the dual role of doting mother and independent woman.

But now, I knew which would win out.

I DROVE BACK AND FORTH TO WISCONSIN SEVERAL times during the next month, scouting the Shoreview area. It was on my third trip up that I stopped to see Suze, much to her surprise. I'd finally found an exciting listing and made an appointment with a realtor to see it that afternoon. Suze's expressive face revealed her thoughts about the appointment.

"Are you sure you want to do this?"

"You said to find what would really make me happy, and this is it." Just saying it aloud gave me a tremendous sense of freedom and strength. I'd follow through on this life-altering decision I'd made all on my own.

"Well, I'm coming with you. You don't want to make such a decision based on emotion alone."

"Now you're sounding like Brooke."
I blinked at her withering look.

W<small>E MET UP WITH THE REALTOR IN HER</small> G<small>REEN</small> B<small>AY</small> office. "I think this is the place for you," she said. "But it doesn't have a lot of land, only twenty acres."

Who did she think she was talking to? My lot in the suburbs measured fifty by one hundred feet.

We drove about twenty-five miles along the highway, getting close to the village of Shoreview, then turned off on a side road. As soon as the realtor pulled into the yard, I knew I had found my new home. I'd never be able to explain the sense of déjà vu filling my soul at the moment. I'd been here before, whether in my dreams or a past life, I didn't know. But I knew this was where I belonged.

It was a two-story log home, older but cared for lovingly. A porch wrapped around the front and side, and a quaint iron swing with brightly colored pillows was suspended from its ceiling. The logs glistened like warm honey in the afternoon sun. A fieldstone chimney climbed the outside of the living room, and visions of a warm, crackling fire on a cool fall day filled my head. This wasn't a house. It was a *home*.

Hopefully, my home.

We walked around the property. An old stone-and-timber barn stood behind the garage. Lilac bushes in full bloom surrounded the doorway.

"The previous owners kept a few animals as pets," the realtor commented as she led us to the front door.

"This is exactly what I want." I'd made up my mind, and no one was changing it this time.

My sister poked me in the side. "You haven't even looked inside or negotiated a price."

"I don't think you'll find it unreasonable," the realtor said. "The owner's been transferred, and they've already moved to Milwaukee."

I could hardly contain my excitement as she opened the lockbox hanging on the door. She walked in first and threw open some windows. "It's a little musty after being closed for a few weeks." She reached for her cell phone and moved toward the door. "I'll make a quick call to the listing realtor and tell her you're interested."

Birds chirped, and the sweet scent of lilac drifted through the open window. I had to fight back tears. The fieldstone fireplace dominated the living room, flanked by double patio doors with a breathtaking view of the countryside. The perfect spot for my new red couch.

We walked across the dark oak flooring and gazed out the patio doors. The ground sloped away from the house in the rear. Part of the land was wooded, and ducks swam in a small pond at the bottom of the hill.

It was the home of my childhood dreams—a fairytale home. "Can you imagine what this would sell for in the Chicago area?" I pinched my sister in my excitement.

"There's a problem," the realtor said apologetically, walking back into the room and hanging up her phone. "An offer was made on the house late last night, and we can't move forward until the owner decides whether or not to accept it."

My heart plunged into my shoes. No. God wouldn't put my dream so close I could taste it and then snatch it away. Would He?

2

THE DRIVE BACK TO CHICAGO TOOK FOREVER. MAYBE because I gripped the steering wheel so tightly that when I finally pulled into my garage, I had symptoms of carpel tunnel.

Had the owner accepted the previous offer? The question ate at my gut all the way home.

I'd stopped in the realtor's office before leaving town and made my formal offer—just in case the gods of fate were with me. The realtor and I knew it was high enough to be accepted. I wasn't taking any chances, even if it meant using up a good portion of the small inheritance Gram had left me in one fell swoop. It was the only money in my name only, and Robert hadn't been able to touch it.

The next days were spent on tenterhooks. I was in danger of wearing a path through the kitchen as I walked back and forth, drinking coffee and wringing my hands. It was several days later that the realtor left a message on my cell with the good news. My offer had been accepted.

I walked into the living room in a daze. Should I throw up with excitement or lie down in panic? I did neither. Instead, I sat on my new red couch with a glass of wine and stared into space, faced with the enormity of the step I was about to take.

It had taken most of Robert's life insurance policy to pay for his funeral and some of the mysterious credit card debts. I refused to even think about that demand note in the mailbox. After making the down payment on my dream home, I wouldn't have much cash until I sold this house. And there was no guarantee there, either. For once in my life I was going to give up security for self-fulfillment.

I had done what would have been unthinkable not long ago. I took a big gulp of wine.

What were the girls going to say about my leaving their home? Especially Brooke. The image of her reaction made the hairs on the back of my neck stand at attention. Look what happened when I said I wanted to get rid of the couch. Sheesh. I still couldn't believe she'd called Lexie about it.

Whining to myself wasn't going to accomplish anything. I wanted a new life, and by God, I was going to get it. After a few minutes, I got up and phoned a local realtor. The house should sell for a pretty price, at least double what they were asking for the country place. It sat right smack in the center of a prime market, all upscale homes on the Burlington northern train line that carried commuters into the city daily.

The agent assured me she'd be out first thing in the morning, and the eagerness in her voice was reassuring. I had started the ball rolling. There'd be no stopping it now.

Calling the girls was another matter. It took a few days to get up my courage. I called Lexie first; dealing with her would be easiest. My girls were not only different in looks but personality as well. Lexie had hazel eyes and the warm brown hair of my youth, while Brooke had the cool blond looks and temperament of her father.

Lexie took the news with grace, as I'd expected. But then, she'd never been hung up on precedents like her sister. After a few moments of silence to digest the news, she had only one question. "But Mom, what about all my things?"

I wanted to ask, *Are you talking about the jumble of junk in the closet you haven't looked at in years?* Only, I walked on thin ice here. No use stirring up trouble.

"You'll have a few weeks to come and get anything you want to keep," I assured her.

"Oh, Mom, I'm so happy for you. This is your chance to start a new life, isn't it?"

"I'm hoping so," I said, swallowing the lump in my throat.

Brooke, well...she was Brooke.

"You did what?" I could hear her hyperventilating over the phone. "You put the house up for sale without telling us? Mother, how could you?" Her voice squeaked in a way I've never heard before.

"Brooke, listen to me. I'm looking for something meaningful in my life—"

"Meaningful? What do you mean, meaningful? You're sounding like some aging hippie. I'm coming out there right now."

Oh, well, I had to face her at some point. Might as well get it over with before she had too much time to stew in her self-righteous juices. Lord only knows how many reasons she'd come up with if I didn't get in a few words in my own defense. I waited out on the patio, desperately searching for some logic behind my decision that I could throw her way.

She arrived at the house in record time. How she'd managed speeding down the Eisenhower Expressway at that time of day without getting a ticket, I'll never know. As I watched from the patio, she stormed through the house. She was a woman on a mission, and I was it.

"Mother," she said, drawing out the word in that Mother Superior voice that never failed to make my hackles rise, "you can't make a major lifestyle change like this without taking time to think it over." She was at least five inches taller than me and took full advantage of it, trying to intimidate me, I suspected. She had her long blond hair in a business-like twist, and her blue eyes snapped their displeasure. "You're being completely irresponsible. What if you find out you hate it there? Then what will you do?"

"Well, at least I'll have tried, won't I?" I took a deep breath that was supposed to calm but didn't. Why hadn't I stuck with that yoga class years ago? But she probably wouldn't have liked my "om" while she talked anyway. "I refuse to spend the rest of my days in regret. If I don't like it, I'll sell the place in a few years and find somewhere else to live."

She narrowed her gaze, eyeing me like I was some kind of a crazy person inhabiting her mother's body.

"I can't believe you're doing this." Frustration radiated out of her like laser points.

"You're focusing on the negative here. Have you even looked at the pictures of the new place?" I spread the photographs out on the patio table. We were still sitting out in the back yard. I had hoped a glass of Chablis would calm her down. A quart would've been more in order. "Just look at the gorgeous land. Can you imagine waking up to that beauty every morning?"

Brooke barely gave the pictures a glance. She was in her righteous mode, and nothing was going to change it. "It's very nice right here. You have a beautiful patio—lots of privacy." She swung her arm out dramatically like she was in a forensics class. "What are you going to do out there in the boondocks when the road is snow-covered and icy?

You could be stuck in the house for days. How beautiful will it all seem then, huh?"

"The house is on a county highway, and they're always plowed, not like the city streets here. And the neighbor has a side business of plowing driveways, I'm told." I stared directly into her eyes without flinching so she'd know I wasn't backing down this time.

"Well, Mom. I really don't know why you bothered calling me. It sounds like you've already made up your mind about everything, and it's a done deal."

Her face flushed with hurt and anger. What could I say to comfort her? My children were the most important things in my world. Only, they had their own busy lives now. After giving them and their father almost thirty years of love and caring, I'd had to let them go, and it had been damn hard. Now, it was time for them to do the same for me.

"Brooke, we've had a good life here, but that's in the past. If I don't make a change now, it will never happen. I called to share my excitement with you. Can't you be happy for me? I have to start a new life...on my own again."

Chagrin crossed her face. "I just don't want you to make any rash decisions. Without Dad here..."

"Your dad isn't here. And he won't be ever again." This time I didn't try to soften my words. She had to face reality. "From now on, I'll be making my own decisions. Get used to it."

She flinched as if I'd struck her. I reached out to touch her shoulder, but before I could, she rebounded.

"What about finances? Have you even given that a thought? I know this house is paid for, but what if it doesn't sell? Your little nest egg will disappear fast if that happens." The daughters don't know about the second mortgage or unpaid bills.

"Why wouldn't it sell? It's in prime condition, and in a perfect location." I sounded as though I tried to convince myself as well as her. "You're looking for problems where there aren't any." Oh, God, if she only knew the half of it. I had to turn away to hide the guilt. But I was determined to protect my girls.

Brooke wasn't giving an inch. She wore her anger like a shield. She'd always resisted change, even as a child.

Brooke left in a huff a few minutes later, leaving me with plenty of time to stew over my decision. Was I doing the right thing? Only time would tell. Doubt and excitement warred in my soul. But I'd never know if I didn't try, and staying in this house wasn't an option.

Later in the week, I went out to the mailbox, filled with the usual angst. I shuffled back into the kitchen, clutching the bundle of new mail with both hands. I had already glimpsed the credit card logos on two envelopes, and my stomach muscles clenched. Hadn't I just paid those bills? I flipped through the stack half-heartedly and stopped when I found the folded sheet of white notepaper. *Oh, no.* After setting the rest of the mail on the kitchen counter, I unfolded it.

YOU'LL HEAR FROM ME SOON. LAST
WARNING.

There was no signature again. No way to identify the bold scrawl. Who was it meant for? This was crazy. I crushed the plain white paper in my palm, ready to throw it in the trash, but a niggling memory just at the edge of my consciousness stopped me. There was something fluttering there. I tried desperately to remember. Something that happened at the wake.

Too zonked out on the sedatives Brooke insisted I take and the shock of Robert's death to think clearly, the whole episode of the wake and funeral were surreal. Finally, a memory came back to me in bits and pieces.

The vague image of a well-dressed man in a dark suit, black hair slicked fashionably back, heavy gold and diamond rings flashing on both hands, and the mention of a loan.

Was the note from him? Trepidation ran coldly up my spine. Who was he, and how would I ever contact him? Was it even legit? Should I call the police? I'd gone through Robert's papers after the funeral in a frantic need to find out how all our money had disappeared. There were no receipts, only copies of his expense account. When the credit card bills and bank statements showed the many cash advances, most in the areas where Robert traveled on business, I assumed they were work related. Only, the amounts didn't match his expense account. Not by a long shot. That's when the idea of his having an affair surfaced and when I went back into shock. No drugs needed.

I'd call the police. They'd know what to do.

"I'm sorry, ma'am, but we need more to go on. Do you have a name or a signature on the note, anything to give us a clue?"

"No, only the blank paper the notes were written on."

"Could it be a prank from one of the neighborhood kids?"

"No, it's more serious than that, I'm sure." I found myself babbling on about my husband's recent death and the debts left behind, etc.

"I'm very sorry about your loss, ma'am, and I'll file a report. Let us know if anything else occurs. Take care now."

With that, he hung up. Was I making a big deal out of nothing but a prank? Self-doubt warred with relief. Still, the thought of leaving my old neighborhood gained new momentum. I now had this fear to add to my list of reasons. Whatever was going on, I didn't want any part of it.

. . .

FOUR WEEKS LATER, I FOUND MYSELF FOLLOWING A moving van containing all my earthly possessions down the street as my neat suburban home—a large FOR SALE sign planted in the front yard— disappeared in the rearview mirror. I still couldn't quite get a handle on my feelings. One minute I thought I'd stroke out from the excitement, the next my stomach was tied in knots of fear. *What the hell was I thinking?*

I looked up and met my own eyes in the rearview mirror. Even I could see a sparkle there that had been missing for years. It was the affirmation I needed. *Okay world, here I come.*

I soon lost sight of the van on the Illinois Tollway. I couldn't drive that slowly; it went against my nature. How many times had Robert told me early in our marriage to "slow down, you're too impetuous." I smiled, remembering.

"Oh, Robert. What would you have to say today?" I heaved a great sigh.

No, I won't think about that now. This is my new beginning.

Hours later, after stopping to sign the final papers at the bank and picking up the key, I pulled into the yard of my new home.

The minute I saw the house, my fears disappeared like downy dandelion heads blown on a summer breeze for childhood wishes. How often does a person have one of those wishes come true? I sat in the car for a moment, just to savor the sight.

This was the home I'd dreamed of owning while sitting on my beige couch on a cold winter's day, perusing the *Sunday Tribune* Magazine Section. Before getting out of the car, I gave myself a pinch to make sure it was real.

The logs gleamed in the early afternoon sun, welcoming me home. I walked up the steps and across the wraparound porch, touching the warm wood. The fireplace was as beautiful outside as in, obviously built by a master craftsman. I peeked in the patio doors before walking back to the front door. Soon, this place would be filled with my possessions, and I would be a part of it. I took the key out of my purse and opened the front door with shaking hands. The aromatic odor of the cedar paneling flooded my senses. I had actually done it—purchased a home all on my own. Should I laugh or cry?

I walked through the empty rooms, deciding which furnishings would go where. The red couch already had a perfect spot, looking out the patio doors with a view of the pond. I glanced at my watch. Just when I decided the movers were lost, a truck rumbled into the driveway.

It wasn't long before the truck was half unloaded. My daughters now possessed most of the minimalist furnishings of our former home, and I'd sold quite a bit on Craigslist. The cash came in handy. I only kept things that fit in with my new decor. Who needed Mother LeBeau's fine china and

Waterford crystal in the country? The girls could have that, too. It didn't fit my image of the life I planned to lead. Simple and rustic. Well, not too rustic. Maybe a life of simplicity was the better choice.

That's when Brooke called. She'd given me tearful orders that morning to call by six o'clock. In the excitement, I forgot. It was now six-thirty.

"Mother, why didn't you call? I've been so worried." Her voice had that whiny, angry sound adopted by the mother of teenagers. Like I'd probably sounded, actually. You know how people say they hear their mother's voice coming out of their mouth when they talk to their children? Well, my voice was coming out of my child's mouth all right, only instead of a grandchild, the criticism was aimed at me.

"Calm down, Brooke. Everything's going well." It was like she'd reattached the umbilical cord since her father's death. I had to find a way to cut it again without being ruthless. "The movers are leaving— gotta go. We'll talk tomorrow." And I hung up on her for the first time ever. I had to admit I was glad not to see her reaction.

THE MOVERS LEFT, AND I WAS ALONE. MY RED COUCH sat cozied up to the stone fireplace like it had been there forever. If only I felt the same. My footsteps sounded hollow on the hardwood floors, and the curtain-less windows made me feel exposed. That was before I realized there wasn't anyone around to peer in. This isolation would take some getting used to.

As dusk fell, I decided to take a quick walk around my new property. I'd only given a cursory look at the weathered gray outbuildings, which I assumed had belonged to some long ago farmer.

I'd just stepped into the barn when a rustling sound came from inside one of the stalls. I quickly backed out, slammed the door, and latched it. Tomorrow, in the light of day, would be soon enough to explore the barn.

Suddenly, it was far too quiet, and the thought of being alone in the dark countryside was daunting. How ridiculous was that? My chances of being attacked here were about a thousand times less than in the Chicago area. For the past year, I'd had no problem living there alone.

As I turned to leave, a woman driving a red minivan pulled into the driveway. I ran up to the house, curious. I didn't know anyone around here.

She stepped out of her van—petite and blond, dressed casually in khaki Capri pants and plaid camp shirt—carrying a casserole dish, a loaf of fresh bread that smelled divine, and a bottle of red wine. My stomach rumbled, reminding me I hadn't eaten lunch.

"Hi. I'm Carol Schneider, your nearest neighbor." She gestured with a shrug across the field toward an older brick home that I had to squint to see. Being my closest neighbor here was a lot different from the suburbs. "Welcome to the area. I understand you moved here from Chicago?"

"That's right." My first clue that everyone in the area already knew all about me, even though I'd never laid eyes on any of them.

"I brought supper, thought you could probably use a little something after a busy day. I still remember when we moved into our home. I told Sam —that's my ex-husband who left me for his slutty young assistant—that he'd have to take me out of there feetfirst next time. I'm sure there were days after that he would've liked to."

I winced at the pain in those words.

"I teach fourth grade in Shoreview and have three sons, so my life is pretty crazy. But, now that summer's coming, I'm feeling as free as the kids. Meeting the new neighbor was one of the first fun things on my to-do list."

I had to take a breath for her. My God, I'd learned more about her in three minutes than I'd discovered about my suburban neighbors in ten years. Wouldn't Robert just about croak?

"Come on in."

"I have a cheesecake in the car. Take these while I get it." She thrust everything in my arms.

I knew then I was going to like this woman. She'd already found my weakness. We walked into the house, navigating between the half-unpacked boxes and a kitchen in complete disarray.

"Please pardon the mess." I sighed as I set the food on the kitchen table.

She gave a sympathetic nod. "Are you sure you're up for company? My boys are at a game with their father, so I'd be glad to help you get settled if there's any way I can."

I could've hugged her, even if she was a stranger. "That would be great. I've just realized being alone in the city isn't quite the same as being alone in the country."

"The rumor is you're a widow."

I nodded in agreement, her blatant curiosity catching me by surprise.

"How long has it been?"

"Almost a year, but it seems like forever some days." I forced a smile.

"Yeah, I've been divorced about that long. Thank God, I have my teaching job to keep me sane and busy." She pulled a corkscrew out of her pocket. "My ex picked a good time to leave. Raising three boys can be a nightmare. Especially when it won't be long before two of them have a driver's license." She smiled wickedly while pulling out the cork. "I just hope the jerk and his bimbo have a whole passel of kids in the next few years. Serve him right."

I didn't know how to reply to that after all the years of Robert insisting all family matters stay private. There was something so warm and friendly about this woman and her openness, though. It made me want to confide in her and set me to wondering if my reticence hadn't been the cause of the distance between me and my former neighbors. Not that I was about to spill my guts about my reasons for moving here. Not by a long shot.

"What a beautiful table. It fits in here perfectly." She walked around my new maple table, running her hands over the smooth, light-colored wood. "And I love these chair cushions."

Her comment brought a big smile to my face. "Thank you. I bought them just before I left Chicago." Another bold act.

I'd found the cushions, along with the table, on Craigslist at an unbelievably low price, hoping they'd fit into the décor of the log home. The cushion fabric was a print of clear blue cotton with small red cherries. They were one of the first things I'd unpacked. I doubted anyone could ever understand the pleasure I had choosing those cheery cushions—so different from the furnishings in my other house.

"Let's eat. I'm famished, and your dinner looks wonderful." She'd even brought paper plates and plastic cutlery.

After a nice dinner of ham casserole, salad, fresh bread, and, of course, the cheesecake, along with some comfortable chatter, she helped me with some unpacking. An hour later though, I'd had it. It'd been a long day, and I was starting to feel the effects. Or maybe it was the wine.

"I don't know about you, but I'm ready to quit. I think I'll just make up my bed and call it a day." I said the words with a smile, hoping she wouldn't think me rude. But I had to keep remembering to assert myself. That's what this change was all about, right?

"Of course. You must be exhausted. Let me help you make up the bed."

We went upstairs, and I unpacked linens from a box in the hallway and set them out. I'd replaced my king-size bed with a double brass one. It looked so cozy against the log walls of the room. Very up-scale country.

I spread the white cable afghan I'd knitted long ago across the foot of the bed when we finished, running my hands over the soft wool. It'd been stored in a closet for years, and spreading it across my bed was a real marker to me of being in my own home.

"What a beautiful afghan. Did you knit it?"

"Yes, years ago."

"I'm a knitter too. I find it so relaxing after a hectic day."

"I'm afraid I wouldn't qualify as a knitter anymore. I haven't done any since my daughters were little."

"You'll have to join our Wool Gathering group and get back into it. We get together to knit and spin every few weeks and share a potluck dinner. One of the gals gives spinning lessons if you're interested in learning a new craft."

"I don't think I'm ready for that. I just want to take my time and get acclimated before joining anything."

"You'll like it, I promise. Everyone is very nice, and we're always anxious to meet new people."

"I'll think about it. I have no idea what my schedule is going to be like." It was an obvious cop-out, but I couldn't come up with a better excuse that fast. I didn't need the pressure of deciding right now.

"Well, remember, you have an open invitation. We're a pretty fluid group, just show up whenever we can. There's a core group of us who are pretty faithful though. I think you'd find it a lot of fun."

They say the same thing about bungee jumping off a bridge, don't they? I wasn't going to sign up for that either.

I WAS JUST ABOUT READY TO CRAWL INTO BED WHEN Suze called.

"So, how did it go?" she asked.

"The movers finished by six thirty, and I managed to get a few things unpacked."

"Great. Do you feel like company? I thought I'd drive up for lunch tomorrow."

"As long as you bring the food, it's a date. I haven't gone grocery shopping yet."

"What'd you do for dinner?"

"You'll never believe this. One of my neighbors brought dinner and wine and then stayed to help me unpack." I still basked in the glow of Carol's friendliness. "Turns out, we have a lot in common. She invited me to join a local group that meets to knit and spin wool."

"Now that sounds right up your alley. Remember how fast you picked up knitting when we were kids?"

"That was a long time ago, Suze. I don't think I'm up to the task these days."

"What did you tell her?"

"I said I'd give it some thought."

"Sheesh, that sounds very enthusiastic."

"Give me a break, will you? I just moved in today."

After hanging up and crawling into my new bed, I thought about our conversation. Maybe I had been too quick to turn down Carol's invitation. I pulled the covers up closer to my chin. Exchanging my king-size bed for a double one didn't make it any less lonely.

I looked up at my bare windows. It was so dark, not a streetlight for miles. An owl hooted in the distance. At least, I think it was an owl, and then a shrill dog's bark sounded close by. Or was it a coyote? Yikes! This silence was killing me. I needed to hear jets descending for O'Hare or at least a siren or two. And then, thoughts of that those bizarre notes crept back in and played havoc with my peace of mind. But whoever had written it wouldn't know where to find me, would they? Surely, by this time they'd have realized their mistake.

It was going to be a long night.

3

EARLY THE NEXT MORNING, AS I LEANED DOWN INTO the bottom of one of the tall packing boxes, intent on grabbing the last of the Fiestaware plates, the doorbell rang. Who the heck would come visiting at this hour?

It couldn't be Suze already. My sister would no more leave her home at five in the morning to visit me than Brooke would wear a polyester pantsuit with shoulder pads. I opened the door with trepidation.

"Hi." A tall, angular woman dressed in jeans and a blue denim shirt stood on the porch, clutching a wicker basket decorated with gingham ribbon. She wore her dark hair pulled back into a tight ponytail, and her face was devoid of makeup. Her dark brown eyes radiated friendship.

"Hello," I answered, making an effort to keep the

big city suspicion out of my voice. Judging from her expression, however, I didn't quite succeed.

"I'm Sue Ellen Johnson, and this is my husband, Tony." She gestured to a tall, stocky man behind her, dressed in jeans and a football jersey. "We're your nearest neighbors." She pointed in the opposite direction than Carol had the night before.

What kind of neighbors came calling at eight in the morning? The glow of country living dimmed a bit.

"I baked some blueberry muffins this morning and thought I'd bring them over while they were still warm." She thrust the basket in my direction. "That's when they're best."

"Thanks," I said, hoping she wouldn't recognize the phony brightness in my voice. I ran a hand through my uncombed hair and tried to look welcoming. "That was very thoughtful of you." Taking the basket out of her hand, I clutched it to my chest. This wasn't the way I'd planned to meet the neighbors.

I finally remembered my manners and opened the door wider, gesturing for them to come in even though the new me wanted to slam the door and say, *Come back later.* "Please, come in."

"Carol said you're from Chicago." There was no denying the smirk on her husband's face. "You a Bears' fan?"

Luckily, I'd been to Green Bay often enough to know better than to make a wisecrack about the longstanding feud between the teams at this point. His wife stomped on the toe of his work boot.

"Don't even start," she warned before turning back to me. "We're really happy to have you here. I missed having close neighbors. Ella—she's the woman who used to live here—hated to leave the place. It was her dream house."

"I fell in love the moment I saw it," I said, some of the tension I'd been holding in leaving my body.

"Carol said you live alone?" Her brow wrinkled. "It can be lonely out here, especially for a city person used to close neighbors."

"I've gotten used to being alone. My children are grown and off on their own," I said. For some reason, her husband's face lit up at the news.

"I have just what you need," he said, smiling broadly "I left her out in the car." He went back out the door.

"Don't mind him. He had to look you over before he'd part with her."

Part with her? Should I be intrigued or scared? Visions of chainsaws and hatchets ran through my mind. Did they really live next door? What could he possibly be getting out of his car?

"Can I offer you a cup of coffee?" I asked. My hands shook a bit as I dug around for a mug.

"No, we can't stay long. We just finished the milking and have other chores to do. I wanted you to have the muffins for your breakfast today, is all," she said.

Well, that was good to hear. I relaxed a bit. Dare I hope that meant early morning visits wouldn't be a common occurrence?

"You're making the place real cozy." She gave the kitchen an approving glance. "Ella would like it. She was a great cook, although she spent a lot of her time outdoors with her animals. Good therapy, she always said."

"What kind of pets did she have?" Maybe I would get a few later when I was settled in and knew exactly what I wanted.

"Well, let's see. She had several sheep and a few angora goats. And of course, the black Lab and barn cats. Oh, and a few chickens."

"Didn't that keep her awfully busy?" I couldn't imagine making such a commitment at this time in my life. Unless it would bring in some income, of course.

"Ella didn't mind," she said. "She enjoyed the animals, especially the sheep and goats and working with their fiber. She was into all kinds of crafts—knitting, weaving, you name it."

The door opened, and Tony came in, carrying a black-and-white puppy. "This is what you need for company. She's the last of our finest Border collies and will make a great watchdog. Comes from good stock."

I gazed down at the small wriggling creature and took a step back. "Oh, I don't think so. I've never had a dog of my own."

"You've never had a dog?" Sue Ellen asked, her eyes wide with amazement.

You would've sworn I'd said I never had a bath, the way they gaped at me.

"My husband was allergic." It was an outright lie but the first thing that came to my mind. In a way, he was allergic. Allergic to pets making a mess in his home.

"You really should have a dog if you're going to live in the country." Tony thrust the puppy at me again. "Just hold her for a minute."

I took another step back. Everything inside of me screamed this was not a good idea, yet I'd carried a secret longing for a puppy since childhood. But a dog was far from self-sufficient. It had to be walked and cleaned up after. Not on my list of things I wanted to do at this point. "Maybe when I've been here awhile and get to know what my life will be like."

"She's the runt of the litter. No one wanted her." His smile was positively angelic.

Our eyes met as he handed the dog over again. How had he pegged me so fast for the sucker I am?

I glanced down at the pup. Her face was white on one side and black on the other. Warm brown eyes pleaded to be loved. The hitch in my heart told me I was hooked. Of course, having a dog in the country would be easier than in suburbia. I could feel myself weakening.

"I really don't know much about caring for a

puppy," I said, all the while cuddling the warm creature and feeling trapped. What would happen to
the dog if I didn't take her?

"What's to know? I brought some puppy kibble.
Just put her in a box with a blanket and a dish of
water tonight, and she'll be fine."

"You don't have to keep her if you don't want her.
Don't feel obliged," Sue Ellen said, patting the pup
on the head. "I'm sure we can find another home for
her. We just thought she'd be good company for
you. You can keep her in the barn if you don't want
her in the house."

Like that was going to happen. "I'll give it a try."
I sighed, knowing it was already too late. Robert
would've been horrified.

Then I remembered. This was *my* home. I could
do whatever I wanted here. If I wanted a dog, by
God, I'd have one. Still, I had to ask.

"I can give her back if it doesn't work out, right?"
They both nodded a bit too enthusiastically for my
peace of mind. Should I have had them put it in
writing?

SUZE ARRIVED EXACTLY AT NOON. ALWAYS PUNCTUAL,
that's my sister. I had visions of her driving aim-
lessly down country roads to fill up the last fifteen
minutes.

"I hope you're hungry for a cheeseburger and
fries. I couldn't resist when I passed Dad's favorite

hamburger joint." She waved a paper bag under my nose.

A heavenly smell had followed her into the room. I snatched the greasy, white bag out of her hand. "Omigod, are these the ones with the pat of melted butter?"

"Yup, you're in dairy country now, baby."

"The table's set. What would you like to drink?"

"Coffee. Maybe it'll dilute some of the grease flowing through our arteries." Suze turned toward the door again. "I brought you something. Consider it a housewarming gift." Her voice drifted over her shoulder as she stepped onto the porch, but I was too involved with the burgers to care.

The door hit the wall with a bang just as I poured the coffee, and Suze came back in, carrying a spinning wheel. I immediately recognized it as Grandma Carey's. I hadn't seen it for years.

"Where in the world..." I was too surprised to be coherent.

"I've had it stored in my attic and completely forgot about it until our conversation last night."

"I'll put it in the living room next to the fireplace." I ran my hand over the smooth wood of the wheel and gave it a spin as I had so often done as a child. "Do you think it still works?"

"Why wouldn't it? Although the bearings probably need oiling."

"It's a wonderful conversation piece."

"Conversation piece, my eye. Gram would want

you to use it. And after your neighbor telling you about the spinning group, I think it's a sign."

"A sign of what? That you've lost your marbles?"

"Gram always said you could do anything you put your mind to. She had complete faith in your abilities." With a sigh, she touched the wheel. "I always envied that."

"I was just a kid and full of unrealistic confidence." I smiled at the memories of sitting with Gram and telling her all about my grand dreams for the future.

"Oh, give the rest of us some credit, please," Suze said and curled her lip.

I wasn't about to make a list of my many failures at this point. I wanted to enjoy this time with my sister. I set the food on the table and grabbed a bottle of ketchup from the fridge, happy now that I'd taken the condiments and staples from my kitchen.

"Let's eat. I'm starving," I said, putting out the napkins.

We'd just sat down at the table when the puppy started whimpering.

"What's that noise?" Suze frowned in confusion.

"It's a puppy," I managed to say with a straight face.

"A puppy?"

"Don't ask. I'll tell you all about it later," I said.

But Suze was not to be deterred. She put down her burger and walked over to the living room where I'd prepared a crate with a water dish and old blanket tucked in the corner.

"Oh, he's darling." She reached down into the box and lifted the pup out, all the while cooing and petting her. The collie responded by licking her face and cuddling into her neck when Suze held her close. "What's his name, and where'd you get him?"

"It's a she and I didn't name her yet. My neighbor brought her over this morning. Thought I needed company." I rolled my eyes in feigned disgust.

"Well, isn't that perfect? You were always pestering Mom and Dad for a dog after we lost Rex, remember?"

Rex had been our family dog when I was very young, a gentle golden retriever. He'd died of old age when I was eight, and my father had refused to replace him. Mom had said he couldn't ever again face the trauma of losing a beloved friend.

I'd forgotten about that. Maybe it was a good thing Robert put a ban on all pets. My girls had never had to go through the trauma of that loss. Of course, they'd also missed out on the unconditional love given by a pet. It got me to thinking. Was that what had been missing in my life—unconditional love? My daughters loved me, of course, but they had moved on with their lives.

AFTER SUZE LEFT THAT AFTERNOON, I WENT OVER TO

the wheel, running my hand again over its smooth surface. I remembered my grandmother telling me she'd ordered the wheel from New Zealand, a place that sounded so exotic to my young ears. It had intrigued me then, and I was still intrigued.

Maybe I let Gram and the rest of the family down. That familiar weight pressed on my heart at the thought. They'd been so proud when I graduated from college. I'm sure they had big dreams of a career for me. I knew they weren't crazy about my marrying Robert right after graduation, although a word was never said. But when you're as close to your family as I'd been, there are some things you learn through osmosis.

I decided to call Carol and make plans to go to the Wool Gathering group. Going just once couldn't hurt.

SUZE AND I HAD SPENT A LOT OF TIME PLAYING WITH the collie that afternoon, watching her antics as we rolled a ball of yarn around the floor. I could see a trip to the pet store in the near future for doggy toys and treats.

"Don't think I'm going to spend all my time taking care of you," I told the pup as I settled her back in her box that evening. "I'm a free woman now—able to do what I want, when I want—with no one to tell me what to do or think. There'll be no tying me down again. Got that? And I'm not going to name you for at least a week. Just in case things don't work out."

Was it my imagination or had a sly smile crossed her black-and-white face?

After getting up three times because of her whimpering during the night, I began to wonder if I'd ever really be able to change. I'd let complete strangers talk me into taking this dog out of guilt. Why couldn't I stand to see anyone, even an animal, unhappy, without trying to fix things? I was hopeless.

Finally, I gave up and let the dog snuggle next to me in bed. We both slept soundly the rest of the night. I had to admit, having that warm body next to mine gave me comfort. I missed the warmth of another human in my bed more than I'd realized.

CAROL WAS AS ENTHUSIASTIC AS MY SISTER OVER THE spinning wheel.

"It's a sign," she said. "You were meant to spin. One of the women gives lessons for a nominal fee. I'll pick you up Friday evening, and we'll go together."

There didn't seem to be any way of getting out of this spinning thing.

So, one week later, I found myself reluctantly following Carol down the gravel driveway of a newly renovated farmhouse to my first Wool Gathering.

Memories of the evenings spent with Robert's colleagues had surfaced earlier that day. I'd had trouble fitting in with the sophisticated, well-heeled women married to his business associates. Would this be any different?

After our first few years of marriage, he'd coached me beforehand, making sure I was up to par on important topics. Not a great confidence booster, but he knew how inadequate I felt when thrown among the movers and shakers of the Chicago business world, and he wanted to help me feel at ease. At least, that's how he explained it. I always suspected he just didn't want his colleagues to think he'd married a naive woman. Especially when early in our marriage he'd jokingly referred to me as *the little woman*. We'd had quite a row after that evening. That was before I'd learned, in the name of family peace, to ignore his feeble attempts at humor.

Would these women ask how I got interested in spinning? I could answer that. I'd tell them about Gram and the time spent at her farm watching her spin. And at one point in my life, I'd been a knitter. That gave us some common ground.

We could always discuss children. I had two of those, even if they were adults on their own now.

But if they started talking about crops and farm animals and milking cows, I would be completely out of my element and just stay out of the conversation as I had many times before.

I didn't want to come off as a wealthy Chicago suburbanite, but I knew I couldn't pass myself off as a local, even if my grandmother had lived in the area. I now lived in a no-man's land, caught between two very different lifestyles and didn't seem to fit in anywhere. What was I doing here?

Sheep and a llama grazed in the side pasture of the farm, no cows in sight. The setting sun bathed the low clouds in pink and violet. What a beautiful bucolic scene. The sun managed to color even the wool of the animals with a golden hue.

As Carol opened the door, my nerves jumped around like olive oil in a hot skillet. What would these women think of a city girl like me wanting to join them? Sheesh, I felt as insecure as my first day back in high school.

We were meeting in the home of one of the members. According to Carol, they took turns hosting. There were nine women talking and sipping wine when we walked through the open kitchen door.

They greeted Carol enthusiastically, and she introduced me as the new neighbor who'd bought Ella's house. All were dressed casually—tee shirts and jeans seemed to be the norm, with an occasional denim skirt and blouse. *Granola eaters*, Robert would've called them. My khaki pants and cotton sweater fit right in the mix.

But more importantly, their smiles were open and friendly.

They set out the buffet after a few minutes, and we all filled our plates and stood around, talking and mingling while we ate. Several of the women made an effort to include me in the conversation.

As the talk flowed, I discovered several of the women were teachers, a few were young stay-at-home moms, one was director of the Women's Domestic Abuse Center, another a writer for the local paper, and one in the running for Town Chairman. A very diverse group in many ways but all connected by their love of working with fiber. Not at all what I'd expected.

"What made you decide to move here?" an older lady named Lucy asked, her voice laced with curiosity. She was the owner of a Scandinavian gift shop, I'd been told.

"I guess it was a longing to get away from the traffic and noise...you know, a chance to breathe in that fresh country air."

Oh, good grief. That was really lame, especially since the neighboring farmer had just fertilized the surrounding fields. No one looked impressed. Did they think I was being sarcastic?

"What do you do?" asked one of the younger women. "I mean...do you work outside the home?"

I blinked as that old feeling of inadequacy rose up to bite me. "I've been a stay-at-home mom since my first child was born," I said, looking around desperately for Carol.

I should've seen this coming. Of course, they

would ask the same question I always got at Robert's business events. Why would they be different? Why had I assumed that, like me, they'd all be housewives?

"How old are your children?" she asked.

"Twenty-five and twenty-three."

She raised an eyebrow. "I see."

But, of course, she didn't see. She assumed, just like the old cliché, that for the past twenty years I'd sat around eating bonbons and reading romance novels.

I wasn't about to explain that I was married to a control freak who wanted me at his beck and call 24/7. Would she be interested in hearing about the countless last-minute dinners I'd prepared for visiting executives? Or the numerous weekends spent with Robert while he entertained clients, interspersed with business trips where I was expected to accompany him to all company events—all in the name of supporting my husband's career? I think not.

"I've managed to keep myself busy." Even I felt the frost in those words and wanted to take them back. Too late. She backed up, gave me a weak smile, and started a conversation with the woman next to her.

Oh, yeah. I really knew how to make friends and influence people, didn't I? I searched the room for Carol. *It was none of their business anyway.* Most likely, they'd learned all kinds of things about me before I'd ever entered the room. Small town people were just too nosy for their own good.

Even though I felt like *persona non grata* now, I couldn't help but get enthused about knitting and spinning as they described their latest projects, remembering the hours spent with my grandmother. She'd been so patient with me as I struggled with the yarn and needles, and I'd treasured each square of the colorful fabric I'd knit. By the end of the summer, I'd had enough to make a doll blanket. I would never forget my pride in that project.

"C'mon, I want you to meet Joan. She's the best spinner in the group and will give you lessons if you're interested."

I hadn't noticed Carol come up behind me, but she grabbed my arm and pulled me across the room toward a gray-haired woman sitting in a straight-backed chair, an aluminum walker at her side.

"She was a writer for the local newspaper but had to quit when she had a stroke a few months ago," she whispered. "It's slowed her down some, but she keeps teaching—needs the money. Are you interested in lessons?"

"I guess so."

"Joan, this is the new neighbor I told you about. She wants to learn to spin," Carol said when we reached her side.

"Great." Laugh lines crinkled out from her pale blue eyes, and she nodded vigorously. She grasped my hand with her right one, the other lying limp in her lap. I surmised she no longer had full use of it. "I'd love to teach you." Her speech was a little slurred but understandable.

"She brought her wheel," Carol said. "We'll bring it over after we finish eating."

"That'll be good," Joan said with a soft lisp. Her smile was warm and friendly, and that did a lot to restore my confidence.

Just as my worries about fitting in began to fade, I noticed a tall blonde, her hair piled carelessly on top of her head and wearing a mini denim skirt, glowering in my direction from across the room. She must've come in late. I glanced behind me. No one else was in her line of vision. When I peered back at her, she sauntered over, disapproval in every thrust of her hips.

"I hear you're from Chicago," she said. My ears picked up a thinly veiled hostility in her voice. "Life here must seem pretty boring compared to Chicago, huh?"

"Not at all. I'm having a great time." That ended the conversation as far as I was concerned. I took a slow sip of my wine.

"Oh, come on. You can be honest," she drawled, her smirk looking anything but friendly.

What had provoked this attack? I looked around for Carol once again, but she was engrossed in conversation with another teacher. The woman had an annoying habit of disappearing when I needed her most.

"I met people like you when I worked summers up in Door County."

I blinked in surprise. "What do you mean, people like me?"

"Chicago people who like to lord it over the locals."

Now, I was ticked. Who did she think she was, lumping me in with every tourist who'd done her wrong? A few months ago, I would've cowered in front of this onslaught. No longer. I narrowed my eyes and looked directly at her.

"Listen, I'm sorry if you've had a bad experience with tourists, but it has nothing to do with me." I strained to keep my voice low and pleasant. It wouldn't do to get involved in a catfight on my first foray into local society. Before she could answer, Carol's hand settled on my shoulder.

"Let's find a seat next to Joan. We'll get you set up for your first lesson," she said.

"Who was that young woman talking to me?" I whispered as we walked away. "She doesn't seem too happy I'm here."

"Nancy?" She waved her hand in dismissal. "Did she say something about you being from Chicago?"

"Yeah, and it wasn't a compliment."

"Ignore her. She got her heart broken as a teenager and never got over it." She shrugged and rolled her eyes. "Some rich kid acted like he was crazy in love with her all summer, then went back to his girlfriend in Chicago in the fall and dumped her. Her dysfunctional family didn't help. She'll warm up to you when she realizes you're staying."

Carol didn't seem concerned, so I tried to put it aside, but the episode left me feeling different and exposed. "Let's get your wheel in and set it up," she said.

A few of the women were already seated with their knitting, looking comfortable. I gave Carol a questioning look. What was I supposed to do now? I was a little uneasy about her asking Joan to help me.

"Go get a chair," Carol directed as she dragged my spinning wheel over to where Joan sat. "Sit down, and Joan will get you started."

Joan reached into a basket at her side and handed me a ball of fluffy gray wool.

"Don't panic," she laughed after looking at my expression. "We all felt the same way when we started."

As I sat avidly watching, she explained in her halting fashion that the wool in the ball was called *roving*. It was a sheep fleece that had been washed and carded into fat strips, so the fibers of wool were opened and aligned in the same direction, making it easier to spin. She had me feel the softness and springiness of the wool. Already, I could visualize a pair of warm mittens.

"This is a natural fleece from my own sheep, not dyed. It still has some lanolin in it, making it more rain-resistant, like the wool used to make Aran sweaters."

First, she had me help her tie a piece of bright red yarn, about three feet long, tightly to the bobbin and threaded it through the orifice of the wheel. "This is called a 'leader' string," she said.

Using her right foot, she began to very slowly pedal the wheel. As the leader string started winding around the bobbin, she laid the wool roving in the palm of her left hand and gently pulled fibers from it with her right hand to wrap around it

"Wool has the wonderful property of 'grabbing' onto the yarn," she said.

I watched in amazement as she continued to gently pull on the roving. By this time, the leader string had disappeared onto the bobbin.

The wheel turned rhythmically as her right hand continued to grasp the roving resting in her left palm, pulling back and forth as the wool was drawn toward the wheel, twisting on its own now, forming a beautiful strand of gray yarn on the whirling bobbin.

"Just watch me for a while, and then you can try your hand at it. The most important thing to re-member is that it's supposed to be fun."

I sat mesmerized, watching the resulting yarn wind around the spindle. After a while, she set the wheel in front of me and guided my hands.

"That's it, just take your time, and you'll develop

a rhythm that works for you. You'll need to use both hands for a while, but after some blood, sweat, and tears, you'll all of a sudden 'get' it. It's difficult at first because you're trying to coordinate three things: your feet and your right and left hand, all doing different things and at different speeds. It's simply a matter of practice and coordination."

After an hour of fits and starts, I was ready to quit and admit defeat. It seemed I lacked the required coordination. I stopped trying and just listened to the conversation of the others.

"Are you going to the Lake Front Festival on the weekend?" the woman sitting next to me asked.

"I haven't heard about it," I answered.

"Oh, you should come. Some of us are giving demonstrations on spinning and weaving. Are you a knitter?"

"I haven't knit in years, don't ask me why. I just got away from it."

"Have you ever knit with handspun yarn?"

When I shook my head no, she looked at me with pity. "Wait until you spin and dye your own yarn. You'll never want to buy the machine-spun stuff again. It just doesn't have the character."

I studied the mess of fiber in my lap. She had to be kidding. This was character? It looked more like disaster.

"We're joining together and running a booth. I have several baby sweaters and blankets to sell."

"I'm bringing my homemade soaps and lotions," another added.

"I'm bringing some of my sheep to be sheared. I kept a few in their wool this spring for the occasion. That'll be something new for you to see, I'll bet."

I relaxed a little more. Maybe they didn't see me as an unfriendly snob after all.

"Wait until you see the shearer," Carol said, fanning herself with a newspaper. "Be still my heart."

"Is it Riley?" another asked, her eyes lit with expectation.

"Oh, yeah." She rolled her eyes and gave a deep sigh. "And I'm telling you all right now, I get the front position by the fence."

"That's what you think. It's first come, first serve," Joan said while smiling crookedly.

Carol made a half-hearted swipe at her with the newspaper.

"I just want to watch the warm-up ritual," sighed another. "That physique of his would make a much younger man envious. I'll never understand how Brandi could cheat on him and leave the way she did."

"I'm afraid I can't make it this weekend," I said, sorry now that I'd made plans.

"Too bad. It's really something to see when Riley shears."

I couldn't help but laugh quietly to myself, wondering who this guy was that they found so exciting. If I hadn't promised Suze I'd visit this weekend, I'd be tempted to go just to have a look. For the first time since Robert's death, I found myself interested in checking out a man. Just out of curiosity, of course.

I picked up another ball of wool and tried wrapping the end around the leader string again. The wheel took off at an alarming speed, first going forward and then backward. I reached over to stop it with a frustrated sigh.

"You know what I told myself when I started spinning?" Joan put her good hand on my arm. "Years ago, a woman had to spin, or she didn't have yarn to knit sweaters or weave into cloth. Even children learned. I know they had quite the incentive, but I figure if everyone could do it then, surely I can learn, too. Don't give up. It just takes practice."

When it was time to leave, they discussed who would host the next meeting.

"I have an idea."

I'd studiously avoided Nancy all evening but looked up when she spoke. She sent a sly look in my direction. "Why don't we have the next gathering at Martha's? Then we can all see her new home."

Did that mean I was now considered a member of the group? I thought I'd have more time to make that decision.

"I've been dying to get inside of that place," she continued, the smile on her lips never reaching her eyes. "Unless, of course, you've decided you don't care to join our little group?"

I didn't have the nerve to say I wasn't sure, at least not to their faces, and she'd guessed it.

It was like high school gym class all over again, being taunted by one of the jocks. Anger formed a tight knot in my throat, cutting off any reply. Didn't life ever change?

The other women looked at me uncertainly. Carol came to my rescue.

"Maybe we should give Martha a chance to get settled first," she said.

I gave Nancy my most angelic smile. "You're all welcome to come to my home. I'd love for you to see it." This time. the jock was not going to win.

"Super," Carol said. "Martha's it is, next time." Everyone nodded in agreement.

As we were driving home, Carol gave me a questioning look. "What was that all about in there?"

"What do you mean?" I asked.

"I don't know. You just didn't seem like the same woman I've been talking to these past weeks. Was it my imagination or were you very uptight?"

So, she'd noticed. Had everyone else? "I have a problem meeting a whole group of strangers at once."

She gave me an assessing look. "You're afraid, aren't you? To have us all over, I mean."

"Don't be ridiculous. Why would I be afraid of hosting a group? Lord knows I've done it often enough in the past." Only this time, Robert wouldn't be there to fill in any hostess gaffes, a small voice whispered.

Who was this person I'd become? I jumped back and forth between two personalities like Jekyll and Hyde, from strong, independent woman to meek, eager-to-please Martha. Would the real Martha Carey LeBeau please stand up and state her wishes?

4

A WEEK LATER, I PUT THE DOG CRATE, PURCHASED ON Carol's advice, in my bedroom one afternoon, turned the radio on so the collie wouldn't be lonely, and took off for Green Bay and some shopping therapy. There were several small items I needed for the house, and I'd convinced myself the selection there would be greater.

The truth of the matter was that as much as I loved my new home, all the peace and quiet was dragging me down. I needed to be among crowds and noise for a while. The dog was a great diversion, but come on, she couldn't provide that much social interaction. Her care wasn't nearly as time-consuming as I'd feared.

The mall was as crowded as I'd hoped. Meandering from shop to shop, picking up the few kitchen items I wanted, a sudden surge of enthusiasm gripped me. Just having all these strangers smile at me, as if I, Martha LeBeau, really mattered, did wonders to boost my confidence in my new life.

I finished my shopping and decided to have dinner in the mall rather than eat alone in my kitchen again. I dawdled over cheesecake and coffee, letting the sounds of happy chatter and laughter soothe my loneliness. I'd made a few friends, and that was good. It would be some time before I felt free to call them just to chat, though. *Could I ever become the carefree person I longed to be?*

When I got home, I hurried up to the bedroom, guilty as hell for leaving the pup alone for such a long time. I opened the door, calling to her in a soft voice. *Oh, rats.* One look inside, and I wanted to slam the door and run back to the mall.

My prized knit afghan hung over the foot of my bed as usual, but the dog had managed to get a large piece of it through the wire spacing of the crate door and was chewing on it like a prize bone from the butcher shop. I couldn't prove it was because the classical station was playing Ravel's "Bolero", but it looked like she clamped down with a bit more ferocity as each beat intensified. Her sharp little teeth had torn a hole in the afghan by the time I managed to stop jumping up and down and screaming in frustration.

Devastation pulsed in my throat. That afghan was the one thing of beauty I'd produced from my

Gram's teachings. I slammed my finger on the off button of the blasted radio and picked up the pup.

"How could you?" I moaned and dropped her unceremoniously on the floor while I inspected the afghan. Sure enough, the yarn was ripped through in several places. I felt like crying as I shepherded her out into the yard. The bloom was definitely off the rose.

The dog ran off into the woods without so much as a by-your-leave. When she came back, she wriggled her whole body with joy at seeing me there, waiting.

I bent down to pick her up, caught between anger and frustration as she covered my face with kisses.

"Well, you are just a puppy, I suppose." I sighed and berated myself for not checking closer when I'd put her crate in the room. "C'mon, it's been a long day. I need some sleep."

THE NEXT MORNING, AFTER TAKING HER FOR A SHORT walk, I went into the kitchen to make coffee, stepping between the chew toys and doggy bones.

Things got suspiciously quiet. I looked around the room but didn't see the collie. That's when I heard the gnawing sound and walked into the living room. And that's where I found her, busily chewing away on the leg of my beloved red couch.

Okay, I admit it. I fell over the edge. Did frustration with my life, or the lack of one, add to it? Or was it simply because I hadn't had my morning coffee?

Whatever. I picked her up, got in the car, and drove to the Johnsons'. I'd had enough.

I pulled into their driveway with a screech of tires, slamming on the brakes so hard it should've set off the automatic airbags.

Picking up the pup, I marched toward the barn, righteous indignation fueling every step. How dare they talk me into accepting this home-wrecker? Within twenty-four hours, she'd damaged two of my most prized possessions. The afghan that held a memento of my past and the couch that proved I'd stepped into my new future.

Nothing would deter me. Only what I wanted mattered now, no more worrying about what other people thought was best. I knew it sounded selfish, but I couldn't help it. There'd be no backsliding.

Sue Ellen stepped out of the barn before I even reached it.

"What are you doing here so early in the morning? We're still milking." She looked quizzically at the pup. "Is she sick?"

"No. I'm returning her."

"What happened?"

"It isn't working out. You said I could return her, right?"

"What did she do to get you so worked up that you're here before seven in the morning?"

The pup was trying to lick my face and whimpering, but I was having none of it. I hardened my heart. It was time we parted ways. I hated to rat on her, but Sue Ellen deserved to know.

"She's ripped holes in my prized afghan and chewed the leg on my new couch. All within twenty-four hours."

Sue Ellen sighed. "I told you to keep her in the barn." We walked through the door and into the cavernous barn. "Put her in that pen in the corner. I have to get back to milking."

I leaned over the gate and set the pup down on the straw-covered floor. She looked awfully small and alone.

"Can't she come with you?" I asked with that familiar guilt intruding.

"It'd be too dangerous. If she runs under the cows and scares them, they're likely to kick her. We lost one dog that way already."

"Sue Ellen, where the hell are you?" Tony called from deep inside the barn.

"I gotta go. I'll talk to you later."

I could hear the pup whimpering, and I walked over to the pen to say goodbye.

"It's your own fault, you know. If you hadn't behaved like that, we could've gotten along."

She cocked her head to one side as if trying to understand what I was talking about. I looked down into her adorable black-and-white face and my heart squeezed with regret.

I ran out the barn door before I could change my mind and drove off as fast as I'd arrived.

When I got home, the coffee had finished brewing, and I poured myself a cup and sat down at the table. The house was unbearably silent.

I got up and turned on the television, winding my way again through the doggy toys and chew bones for the last time. I'd clean them up after I drank my coffee. *If only she hadn't chewed the couch leg.* I had an unnatural attachment to that piece of furniture.

I looked at the couch leg again. Definite teeth marks and tiny chips of wood on the floor. It would take more than Old English Scratch Cover to disguise that mess.

The local news was on, and I half-listened as I started making breakfast. Who was I kidding? I'd lost my appetite. Instead, I opened the packages I'd brought home from the mall the night before.

Wouldn't you know the first bag held the little red-and-black plaid coat I'd bought for the collie? The plaid would be perfect for her breed. I'd bring it over to Sue Ellen.

Yeah, right. Like she'd put it on her to run around the barnyard. I set the coat down and stared around the semi-orderly room.

What was the matter with me? Hadn't I wanted this home to be different? So what if there were a few nicks in the couch leg? Wasn't this the freedom I'd been fighting for? Should I give up the companionship of my dog so my house could be perfect?

I set the cup down and grabbed my car keys.

The pup was still alone in the pen when I arrived at the farm. She lay in the corner, looking sad and confused. As soon as I opened the pen, she ran over to greet me, her fat puppy body writhing with joy.

"Hopefully, we've both learned a lesson this morning, missy," I said as I picked her up and cuddled her to my chest.

Sue Ellen came into the barn then. "You're back," she said with a grin.

"I changed my mind."

"Why am I not surprised?"

IT WAS A FEW WEEKS LATER WHEN I STRETCHED MY limbs and took a deep breath of the scented breeze wafting through the open window. My bed felt so warm and cozy. The English rosebush planted below was in its second bloom, and the sweet lushness of the blossoms surpassed even those of June.

I began to mentally run through my plans for the day, a habit I'd tried to develop after Robert's death. It was supposed to give me a reason for getting out of bed.

My eyes snapped open. The Wool Gatherers were meeting tonight. Here. I vaulted out of bed.

What was I thinking when I offered to host the

meeting? I was the outsider, new not only to the area but to this whole way of country life. I hadn't just stepped out of my comfort zone; I was about to leap into shark-filled waters.

Granted, the women I'd met so far were friendly enough. At least they were when I kept my size sevens out of my mouth. Except for that snide bitch, Nancy.

I grabbed my robe, pulling it on and whining all the way down the stairs. What did I have in common with these women? The yarn I'd been spinning lay in a lumpy, bumpy mess on the floor. Contrary to what Joan had said, I hadn't suddenly "got" it. As time went on, the whole idea had soured.

Even following a knitting pattern would be a stretch after so long a time. And as far as raising my own animals? Please, direct me to the local yarn shop and a helpful clerk. Or better yet, the sweater bin at Macy's. Why had I become so determined to complicate my life?

I knew what was happening but couldn't seem to stop it. That same freaky fear I'd had since marrying Robert, that I'd say or do something stupid when I met new people, loomed over my head like a water-filled balloon, ready to burst at a moment's notice.

I plugged in the coffee pot, still complaining to myself.

The pup picked that moment to grab onto my

pajama leg with her sharp little teeth and start shaking it for all she was worth. "Stop that."

She gave me a disgusted look and growled for the first time. Had I even embarrassed her with my timidity?

"Okay, okay, I get it," I said, raising my hands in defeat. I had to be more adventurous and learn to take chances if I was going to make it in my new life. My god, even the dog knew it.

Wait a minute. Hadn't I already proved myself in that area? I stood a little taller and looked down at the pup. "Give me a break, dog."

I'd bought a house all on my own, moved to an area where I knew no one, all the while facing financial insecurity because of my actions. If I could do that, why the hell was I worrying about entertaining a group of women in my home?

LATER THAT AFTERNOON, WE WERE OUT IN THE BACK yard, and I watched the pup scamper among some fallen leaves, chasing the orange-and-black Monarchs and pale green moths that fluttered their delicate wings in a seasonal ballet in front of her.

After these weeks together, we'd definitely bonded, two strangers trying to get along in a new world. Only she seemed to face hers much more fearlessly than I.

Watching her, a name came to me in a flash of intuition. Maeve. I'd name her after the Irish warrior queen. We would grow together. She would be my protector while I grew, for the second time, into my own person.

I picked her up, and looking into her soft brown eyes, I walked to the front yard. "Maeve," I whispered. "What do you think?" She licked my nose in agreement.

"Okay, Maeve it is." I put her back down, and she stood a little taller, assuming the stature of the queen she would grow to be. She cocked her head regally, listening intently to all the sounds around us. That's when she took off down the driveway after a passing car.

"Oh, hell." I'd learned in the past weeks she'd try to herd anything that moved, a bad habit of her breed.

I raced after her, the sound of a speeding pickup in the distance giving me extra momentum. I finally caught her, just as the truck whizzed past the two of us where we stood on the side of the road. I carried her back into the house, my body shaking.

"You stupid dog, do you want to get killed?" I was overreacting, but I couldn't stop yelling. My heart continued to pound, and a cool sweat misted my back. Already, I was too attached to the animal. My dad had been right.

Maybe spinning would calm me down. Lord knew I needed the practice. I sat at the wheel and tried to think positive thoughts. *Think about Gram.* Remember how peaceful she seemed on those long ago summer afternoons, sitting on the porch with this very same wheel.

I picked up the roving, pulled out a strand, and wrapped it around the leader string, determined to do it right this time. I started with a slow treadle, not easy for me. The barbed wool fibers grabbed onto the string, and I pedaled as slowly as I could, trying to keep control of the wheel while the wool twisted into yarn.

It seemed to be working. I actually got some yarn around the bobbin. It was uneven, of course, but not as lumpy and bumpy as the previous stuff. It actually resembled yarn, in the loosest sense of the word. A feeling of satisfaction settled over me. Maybe I could do this, after all.

Just as I got into the rhythm of the wheel, the phone rang. It was my Chicago realtor with her weekly update.

"I've got bad news."

My heart dipped to my shoes at her ominous tone.

"What happened?"

"Your house was broken into sometime during the night. Your neighbor noticed the open patio door when he walked his dog this afternoon and called the police. I'm on my way to meet them right now."

"I'll get down there right away." My mouth was now dry enough to spit cotton. Could this be tied in to those strange notes in my mailbox?

"No, it's pretty late in the day. It'd be better if you waited until I call back so you'll have an idea of what damage has been done and how to deal with it."

I set down the phone and looked over at the spinning wheel. Now that I had the perfect excuse for bailing out on the meeting, I found I didn't want to. I needed to see friendly faces. People who weren't involved in my past life, and who wouldn't judge me for leaving it behind. Hopefully, these women would do.

NANCY WAS THE FIRST TO ARRIVE THAT EVENING, wouldn't you just know it? I had to fight the urge to slam the door in her face.

"Come in," I managed. She handed over a large bowl of salad while giving me a smile so sweetly fake that I almost went into a diabetic coma.

"That looks delicious." I attempted a cordial expression and turned back toward the kitchen. "Make yourself at home."

Arranging the dishes on the counter gave me something to do while she strolled into the living room and picked up knickknacks and pictures for a closer look.

"Your decorating style is sure different from what I expected."

"Thank you," I said. I'd be darned if I'd take it as

a put-down. Her glance scanned the room like a heat-seeking laser. What did she expect to find?

Chewing the carpet would be more fun than making small talk with the woman. Just as I was ready to bite the bullet and try for light conversation, the door opened and Carol came in. I felt my face relax.

"Are you okay?" She set a casserole dish on the counter and looked at me.

"Nancy's here," I muttered.

"Enough said." She winked knowingly and joined Nancy in the living room.

I tried relaxing breaths as the others arrived, determined to put thoughts of my other house out of my mind for the time being. They were friendly but reserved at first, standing around in small groups, watching me expectantly.

"How about we get started?" Carol grabbed the tray of appetizers I'd prepared and began passing them around, effectively breaking the ice. Was she my new Robert?

As if I wasn't already socially challenged, images of the vandalism to my house kept popping into mind. What kind of vandalism were we talking about? Visions of the scene I could be facing tomorrow were driving me crazy. I only half-listened to the conversation around me. I should've canceled this get-together.

"I'll get the drinks," I muttered. It would be better to keep my shaking hands busy.

Nancy, of course, still watched me from a distance with snapping eyes. At least she kept her thoughts to herself while the others admired my home. I wouldn't let her attitude get to me. I was going to be part of this group, even if it meant putting up with her. What better place to find my real self than with these women, unhampered by past expectations?

"Where's Joan?" someone asked.

"Probably waiting for Carl to drive her over." Lila and Carol exchanged a look.

"I offered to pick her up," one of the younger women said, "but she said she had a ride."

"Carl wouldn't like it. He wants to drop her off and pick her up," her friend Lucy said with a shrug.

"Can you imagine losing your independence that way?" Sue Ellen asked. "Especially someone as self-sufficient as Joan. It must drive her crazy."

Just as I carried the tray of drinks from the kitchen, I heard the knock on the door. Joan stood on the porch with her walker, a basket of wool, and her spinning wheel beside her. As soon as she stepped in the door, a black pickup pulled away.

"Hi, Joan. So glad you could make it," I said, reaching for the wheel.

The entire room gave a collective sigh of relief when they saw her. I looked at Carol questioningly, but she just shook her head.

We were in the kitchen later, setting the food

out, before I had a chance to get an answer to my unasked question.

"What's this about Joan?"

"It's her husband. He's a jerk."

The phone interrupted us. It was the Chicago realtor.

"The lock's been broken off the patio door, and there's some strange graffiti painted on the bedroom walls," she reported. "That's all we can see at first glance.

"I'll be there early tomorrow," I said. It didn't sound as bad as I'd feared, and the weight in my chest lightened.

"It could be a lot worse," she said. "When you get here tomorrow you can give things a thorough going over,"

"You're right. It could be a lot worse."

After assuring her all would be taken care of as soon as I got there, I hung up the phone, only to face the stricken looks of Carol and a few others standing close by. They pretended they hadn't heard my conversation, but it was no good.

"That was the realtor. My house in Chicago was broken into some time during the night," I told them. "It hasn't sold yet, so it's been sitting empty since I moved here."

"Oh, Martha, that's terrible," Carol said.

"Was there a lot of damage?" Joan asked with her halting speech.

"No. As far as they know, a broken lock on the

patio door and some graffiti on the bedroom walls. All the furnishings were already gone." My emotions tumbled about like dice in a roulette wheel, from relief to anger. "I have to drive down there in the morning."

"I'll go with you," Carol said. "My ex can watch the boys. You shouldn't have to face that house alone. Having someone break into your home is very traumatic psychologically, even if they didn't steal anything."

"I won't be alone. I'm sure my daughter will meet me there." Oh, God. Brooke. I didn't even want to think about how she'd react to the break-in. I'd have to check it out myself before calling her.

And as much as I would've enjoyed Carol's company on the trip, I didn't want to get into sharing all the family angst with her. After all, I barely knew these people, and I wasn't ready to share my personal life with them. Old habits are hard to change.

"Should we leave so you can get ready for tomorrow?" Lila, one of the younger women I'd met earlier, asked.

"No, please stay. I can't do anything about the house tonight. I need to get my mind off it, if possible."

After dinner, we gathered in the living room and settled into an evening of knitting, spinning, and small talk.

"Your place is so warm and comfortable," Lila said. "I'm so glad we got a chance to meet here."

Several others agreed, and I basked in their compliments while hoping they wouldn't notice the chewed leg of my new sofa. As much as I tried, I couldn't seem to quite get over the habits learned from my years with Robert.

"So, how was the festival?" I asked, changing the subject.

"The turnout was wonderful. Of course, the gorgeous weather had a lot to do with it. A perfect day to be along the lake front, wasn't it?" Sue Ellen smiled in satisfaction.

"I sold quite a bit of my handmade soap."

"And the handspun yarn went pretty fast," Lila said.

"And what about the sheepshearer? Was he worth the trip?" I asked as I pulled up my spinning wheel.

"Whoo-hoo, you missed it, Martha. It was worth the entrance fee for that alone." Carol grinned broadly.

"It's a good thing John was busy with the kids. He doesn't appreciate it when I stare at other men." Lila blushed. "Not that I usually do—only Riley."

Their lighthearted banter did the trick as I sat and carefully threaded the yarn through the orifice of my wheel with the threading hook.

"How's it going?" Joan asked.

"I don't seem to be making a lot of progress."

"Have you been practicing?"

"A little," I admitted. I showed her the lumpy

yarn on the spindle. It didn't look as good to me as it had earlier in the day. "It's pretty bad, isn't it?"

"It looks like the work of a beginner. You'll get better with more practice."

"I'm seriously beginning to doubt that. Maybe I should just stick to knitting." Oh, how I hated that whiny tone in my voice, but I couldn't seem to make it go away. Had this all been a huge mistake? Should I be in Chicago, trying to live the life my children wanted and expected? Was the break-in a message from beyond? Or something more sinister.

"What you need are a few sheep of your own. That'll give you the incentive to spin," said Lila.

"Yeah, nothing like bags of wool taking up all the space in your house to give you that incentive," Nancy said. "That's why you won't find sheep at my place." She smiled slyly. "Of course, you have a lot of room here, and a lot of time on your hands, right?"

"I'll wait a bit on that, thank you." All I needed were more animals to join the dog from hell. Besides, I didn't have the money to buy sheep at this point. Not until the other house sold. I just wanted to get through this night and be on my way to Chicago to assess the damage.

Then I realized I would have to ask the Johnsons if I could leave Maeve with them while I was gone. This was exactly the type of dependency I'd been trying to avoid. Here I was, up to my neck in it again.

5

I STOOD IN THE CENTER OF THE CHICAGO KITCHEN the next day and stared at the empty cabinets. This room had been the heart of my home when the kids were little. The place where we worked together on their homework, did crafts, and ate after-school snacks. That was before Robert surprised me with a complete renovation, turning the room from a family gathering place into a model of cool efficiency.

He'd expected me to be thrilled, of course. It took some time to convince him my lack of enthusiasm was due to shock and not disappointment. Why make both of us unhappy?

The place looked hollow and foreign and smelled antiseptic and damp now like the windows hadn't been opened since the cleaning service left. According to the realtor a few interested buyers had been through when the house had first been put up for sale but the market was slow at this time.

I'd called Brooke earlier that morning out of guilt and given her the news. She'd taken it as only Brooke would.

"Well, Mother, what did I tell you? A house sitting empty like that is an attractive nuisance, isn't it?"

I don't know which was more upsetting, the vandalism or my daughter's lack of empathy.

"I'm leaving for Chicago right now to assess the damage and file the insurance report," I'd told her.

"It's a good thing you have neighbors close by. Something you don't have in your new place."

Leave it to Brooke to kick me when I'm down. I sighed. "Goodbye, Brooke."

"Wait," she said, her tone a bit mollified. "I'll meet you at the house this afternoon."

"Don't come until I call you," I said. A bad feeling had settled between my shoulder blades and wouldn't leave. "I may be at the police station."

I stood in that cold kitchen, face-to-face with my past life. I no longer identified with the person who'd lived here. Why didn't I feel a tug on my heartstrings? What did that say about me? Had I become totally unfeeling? Leaving my past wasn't as simple as I'd hoped.

The heels of my sandals clicked on the ceramic floors as I walked through the kitchen and down the hall to the living room. Nothing had changed. The white walls and aqua carpeting were as cold and indifferent as I remembered. I'd worried the vandals had stolen light fixtures or broken the plumbing, causing a flood. Graffiti on the white walls I could handle, or so I thought.

I went to look at the patio door. There was a makeshift chain across the opening where the lock had been broken. I'd expected feelings of violation to surface, but strangely, I didn't feel anything but anger. It was as if the break-in had happened to someone else. Some person removed from me.

That was until I went upstairs, opened Brooke's bedroom door, and read the words splattered across the white walls in vivid red paint. I CAME FOR MY MONEY.

I slammed the door shut and moved to Lexie's room.

I'LL FIND YOU WHEN THE TIME IS RIGHT in the same shade of vivid red greeted me. I stood frozen in place for a moment and then started to shake uncontrollably. Who was this person and what money was he talking about? I needed help. *You need to get a grip.* I went downstairs to call the realtor. She said she'd contacted the police.

Just as I was dialing the number on my cell, I saw Brooke's car pull up in front of the house and broke the connection. I'd left the garage door open, so she knew I was already here. *Damn. Couldn't that girl ever follow directions?* I ran upstairs to make sure the bedroom doors were closed. Even if the break-in itself hadn't affected me emotionally, anyone who saw this would feel threatened. I had to shield Brooke until I knew who this person was and what money he referred to.

Brooke's bedroom had been her refuge during those turbulent teen years—the one place she could call her own. She was bound to check on it unless I could head her off. It struck me then that maybe she tied the loss of this house with the sudden loss of her father because Robert had been so much a part of everything in it. She stomped through the garage door as I made my way down the steps.

"Hi, honey," I said, reaching for her. But she walked right past my open arms, darting from room to room in her haste to assess any damage.

She turned back to me, a wounded look in her expressive eyes. "Who would break in here and why?" she asked. "Was it just kids?"

"The police are looking into it."

This was, and would always be, her family home, at least until she married and had a family of her own. She may have moved to a condo, but she still had a deep connection to this place. It was her lifeline to her father and her childhood. I had to keep her out of those bedrooms.

"Let's check the bedrooms." She started toward the stairs.

"I already did. There wasn't anything left up there to steal."

"I guess you're right," she said, her shoulders slumping.

She looked around the house again before walking out toward the patio. "What about the patio door?"

"A locksmith is coming today to fix it."

"This is such a beautiful place. I don't know how you could've left it like you did." Her wistful words touched my heart.

"Brooke, this is no longer home. It's an empty shell. You don't need it to keep your memories alive. It's time to move on and make new memories in a new place."

I was her mother and wanted her to feel wherever I lived would always be her home. The house was just a shell. She didn't need it to keep her memories of her father alive. When would she realize that? Would she ever transfer those feelings to the farmhouse? I got my answer soon enough.

"This was a disaster waiting to happen, wasn't it?" She turned to me, her face crumbling in a mixture of pain and anger. "But I guess you don't care about that, do you, Mother?"

"Brooke, please. I know you're upset, but don't say things you'll later regret."

"You're right. I've said all I can, and it fell on deaf ears."

"C'mon, let's go to Gino's and have a pizza." It had been our family's favorite eating spot, and the one place I could count on to cheer her up when she was a teen.

"I can't. I have dinner plans tonight. I'll be late as it is, but I wanted to be here when you came."

"Thank you for that. It's times like this when you need family." The slam passed right over her head. She was too much into her own feelings to notice mine. "I had hoped we'd have dinner and a quiet evening together."

"Are you going to spend the night? I brought an extra key to my condo."

"No. I may stop and visit Suze on the way home."

"Well, I might as well leave then." She glanced down at her bracelet watch and walked slowly toward the door. "Goodbye, Mom." A quick kiss on the cheek and she was gone.

I watched her drive away and said a prayer of thanks that she hadn't seen the paint-smeared walls of her bedroom. At least I'd been able to save her a little heartache. She mustn't know what her father was mixed up in until I could get things sorted out. Only I didn't know where to turn for information. The lawyer who'd handled our finances seemed as clueless as I was. The only information he could give me was about the second mortgage on the house.

The realtor showed up soon after with a locksmith in tow and the news that the police would be there shortly to question me and finish their report.

I took the opportunity to ask the realtor a few questions about the traffic through the house. During our last telephone conversations, she'd sounded evasive. Selling the house quickly was imperative now.

"Things are really bad in the housing market at this time," she said, looking everywhere but at me.

"But you told me this would be a quick sell. Hasn't there been even one offer?"

Her expression told me she was working up to more bad news.

"Actually, only one couple went through this week."

I could feel my face fall.

She rushed on. "Don't worry, things will pick up. People like to be in a new home for the holidays. We haven't missed that market. And if nothing turns up then, there'll surely be a pickup in spring."

Dear God, Brooke was right. While I'd been sitting in my little Martha world, pondering my navel and searching for myself, the outside world was about to come crashing down around me. That familiar wave of acid rose up from my belly.

"But this house in its perfect location should've sold in a matter of weeks."

"As I've said, the market has changed drastically in the past months."

One of the local policemen arrived then and interrupted our conversation.

"What does this mean?" He gestured to the graffiti.

"I honestly have no idea," I said, close to tears. The realtor was dealing with the locksmith, and we were alone in Lexie's room. I told him about the experience at the wake and note in my mailbox.

"Do you think there's a connection?" I asked.

"It's a possibility," he hedged. "But of course, we can't be sure. Do you remember his face?"

"Vaguely. I'd taken a sedative at my daughter's insistence, and it hit me pretty hard. I'm not in the habit of taking drugs." I closed my eyes and brought a shaky hand to my forehead.

"Why don't you come down to the station and look through the books of known criminals in the area. Maybe you'll recognize him."

"Can we keep this quiet? I don't want my daughters seeing their dead father's name dragged through the mud if it's anything to do with him."

"Oh, I think so. It was only minor vandalism after all. I wouldn't leave a forwarding address at the post office though, just in case."

AFTER THE LOCK WAS REPAIRED AND A PAINTER called, I left the house and drove over to the police station. A fruitless trip as it turned out.

Then a stop at the post office to remove my forwarding address and get a P. O. box number. I'd send Brooke the key, and she could send the mail in a large envelope weekly.

Then it was back on the road to Wisconsin and my new home, my mind vacillating between the horrors of the threatening graffiti and the depressing words of the realtor.

I stewed over those words all the way to Milwaukee and Suze's home. My nest egg had already depleted so far as to be almost non-existent. I could only make a few more house payments without taking out an interim loan. Would I even be eligible? The thought was enough to bring on a migraine. Thankfully, I wasn't prone to them. Just your regular old pounding tension headache.

I had to look for work, at least a part-time job, to tide me over until the house sold. But what could I do? I'd been out of the workforce for years and didn't have any marketable skills. I'd been too busy making the best Halloween costumes in the neighborhood and learning to stuff herbs under the skin of a roasting chicken. As far as my teaching qualifications, I could've graduated in the Stone Age compared to the technology out there now. I slapped the steering wheel in frustration.

I had to make this work. Going back to my previous life was both impossible and inconceivable. Selling the country house would be even more difficult than selling the one in the Chicago area. I was caught in a vice of my own making. The realization that I had to begin a job search immediately hit me like a sucker punch.

Forget visiting with Suze. She'd probably read the guilt from my secrets like she always had. I'd just head on home. What a wonderful word.

Home.

The word immediately conjured up pictures of relaxing on my red couch in front of a glowing fire, Maeve curled in my lap and a mug of warm tea in my hand.

Would I ever be able to relax like that again?

It didn't take more than a few days combing the want ads to discover the only jobs available in the area were waitressing and childcare. No. I wasn't that desperate. At least not yet.

I brought up the subject of my job search at the next Wool Gathering, and it opened up the floodgates of concerned opinion.

"The problem with living in a small community is that most jobs aren't advertised. People usually hire by word of mouth," Lila said.

That explained the lack of job openings advertised in the local paper.

"If someone needs a job, they tell their friends and family, who spread the word," Joan agreed. "And if someone needs an employee, they ask their friends for recommendations. It's a system that works pretty well around here."

"I heard that the school district is short on paraprofessionals. Maybe you'd qualify for that job." As usual, it was Carol who threw me a lifeline.

My ears perked up at the news. I hadn't told anyone I'd been a teacher at one time in my life and didn't mention it now. It was so long ago that qualifying for a teaching license would take a lot of time and effort, and I needed a job now. If I told them, they might look at me like Suze, wondering what the heck I'd been doing with my life since the girls grew up. I didn't have an answer. Unless they wanted to learn how to make a perfect tray of canapés for a family brunch.

"Do you know what the qualifications are?" I asked.

"I could call a friend who works for the school district office and find out for sure if there's an opening. She'd know. I'm sure they'd love to talk to you." Carol's voice carried her usual optimism.

"That'd be great," I said, all the while my stomach was tying itself into familiar knots at the thought of a job interview. Going back into the education field had never been on my radar screen. Way too much of a long shot. I was totally unprepared. The thought was enough to make my scalp sweat.

Then again, it could be the answer to my prayers. I offered up another quick one, just in case. I'd always loved being a teacher, and maybe this was a way to get back in the field without all the responsibilities that came with the profession.

"Not to change the subject, but have you thought anymore about getting a few sheep of your own?" Lila asked. "I just happen to have two young ewes with beautiful wool that I haven't been able to sell. I'd be willing to give them to you. I'd hate to see them go to market; their wool is so beautiful, but my husband gave me an ultimatum. He says we've taken over his farm."

My mind was so befuddled with the job issue that even the wild idea of raising and selling animals as an income seemed a possibility. I paused for a moment, caught in a dream. Why couldn't I try being a farmer? I could remain totally independent that way. I could even spin wool and knit for extra cash. Thankfully, common sense took over before I could get carried away with my bucolic dreams. An actual cash-paying job was what I needed.

"I don't think I'd have the time to take on more animals if I go to work," I said.

"Raising sheep is not that much trouble, especially if you only have a few," Lila continued undeterred. "They make wonderful pets."

I gave her a blank look, speechless for a moment and overcome with memories of the morning the Johnsons brought Maeve. Been there, done that.

"I'll have to think about it."

"Why don't you come out to my place and see them?"

Whoa, I was beginning to know myself well enough to realize that could lead to disaster. "Maybe after I have this job thing settled." But I could feel myself weakening. After all, they were free, and it was part of the dream, wasn't it?

SEVERAL DAYS LATER, I STOOD AT THE PATIO DOOR, a mug of tea in my hand, and watched the September sun set behind the green pines, fiery sugar maples, and brilliant yellow birch on the edge of my field. A cool evening fog settled in the lower spots of the field, swirling upward in the breeze. My heart ached with that familiar fall melancholy—a deep longing for some nameless person or experience. Or was it a longing for a return to my youth, where every day was a new adventure? The phone rang just as I took my final sip.

It was Carol. "You're in luck. I just got a call from my friend at the school office. They're in desperate need of a paraprofessional to help in the elementary school, second grade, I believe. Get your butt down there right away."

"Thanks, Carol. You may have just saved my life."

As nervous as I was, I didn't have a choice. I couldn't go back to my old house. The police hadn't turned up anything on the break-in, and there was nothing more to be done. I'd spent the week in a panic, alternating between convincing myself that the house would sell soon or that I'd made the biggest mistake of my life.

I drove into town early the next morning after spending an hour trying on and discarding outfits. What did teachers wear in the classroom these days? Were they as casual as the students? Good grief, I hoped not. I finally decided on a pair of dress slacks, a classic white blouse, and a colorful scarf. All the way there, I silently repeated my qualifications. I had no reason to be nervous. I reached the district office before convincing myself, however. Wearing a forced smile, I managed to ask the young woman behind the reception desk for an application.

"And you are?"

"Martha LeBeau."

"Superintendent Kyle would like to speak to you before you leave," she said. "He's been expecting you."

Ahh, I had become one of those persons recommended by friends. I did a mental shrug. *Whatever it takes.*

She picked up the phone after I handed her the completed forms. The young man who came in at her call was a surprise, with his mod haircut and casual khaki pants and plaid shirt. I'd expected someone older, more my age, I guess. My first impression was that he was too young for the job. Was that age discrimination in reverse?

"Good afternoon, Ms. LeBeau, Jason Kyle." He

extended his hand." "I see from your application that you're a former teacher." He studied the forms without really listening to my reply to his greeting.

"I also see you haven't been in the field for more than twenty years." He frowned.

"Is that a problem for this position?" Now, I almost wished he'd say yes, it was a problem, and let me off the hook. I was beginning to have second thoughts about the job.

"Well, no..." He looked up and scanned my face with assessing gray eyes. "Although, I think you'll find things have changed quite a bit since you were last in the classroom. Not only with the curriculum, but with the way we handle students."

Did he think I'd been living in a vacuum these past twenty years? "I'm aware of that. I had two children go through the public school system."

"We usually have special-needs children in the classroom. That's where we would need the most help. The teacher can't give them the extra attention often needed. It takes a lot of energy some days." His eyes narrowed. "Think you can handle that?"

"I know I can." Something about him reminded me of Robert's attitude, and I could feel my hackles rise. I'd learned a lot about my energy levels and myself in the past few weeks and felt more alive than I had in years. When it came to having enough energy to deal with children, in that area, I had total confidence. It was the other aspects of the job that concerned me. Would I be up to the challenge?

That familiar flutter rose up my throat. I needed this job badly, and I'd better not wimp out now. The hours were perfect, and no one loved children more than I did. I could do it.

"As I said, I've raised two children of my own, so I'm very aware of their high energy levels, and I've always prided myself on being especially attuned to their needs." I hoped I sounded more confident than I felt.

His raised eyebrow and long measured look didn't raise my confidence level.

"I know my teaching background doesn't look all that great." I rushed the words as he looked at the forms again. "But if you'll give me a chance..."

"Well, you did come with a good recommendation from one of our long-time teachers... How soon could you be available?"

"As soon as you need me," I replied.

"We need someone today, but that's not possible. Before we can go ahead with any new hires, we need to do a background check. We don't take any chances these days."

"All right." There wouldn't be any problem in that area. Not with the white-bread suburban life I'd led these past years.

"One more thing. If we do offer you the job, you'll need to attend in-service classes on working with special-needs children. I know there is one child in the second grade class with possible Asperger's syndrome. It's a difficult condition to diagnose definitively, so we're going on the assumption that that's his problem. He does well with schoolwork but has trouble socially, from what I've been told. The teacher could use extra help. She's new and pretty stretched as it is. If I'm not mistaken, a class begins next week. Are you available for that? The district will reimburse you for your time, of course."

I assured him I was definitely available and left with a bounce in my step. Holy camolie. I'd expected to be put on a waiting list with other applicants and wait weeks or months to be called. This was so different from the way things worked in the large city school district I'd been involved with before.

WHEN THE CALLER ID REGISTERED THE LOCAL school district that late September morning, my heart did a flip.

"Ms. LeBeau, are you ready to tackle the paraprofessional job?" I recognized Mr. Kyle's voice immediately.

"Yes, of course." It'd only been a few days since I'd finished the training offered by the district, and I'd assumed it would be a few weeks before I'd get a call. I should've realized things like the background check worked much faster since everyone was on the internet.

"Great. We'll expect you in class on Monday."

After a little more discussion about my duties I hung up the phone, and the doubts began once more. Was this really what I wanted? I'd never worked with special-needs children.

But I'd learned so many things in those classes, from what to expect behavior-wise and how to handle the occasional meltdown. Most importantly was how to remain calm, no matter the situation.

I thought of Brooke and her condescending attitude and straightened my spine. I'd never know if I didn't give it a try, would I? How many times had I said that to my girls? Kids were kids, no matter the circumstances. The superintendent seemed to think I'd learned what I needed in class. It was one more challenge. That's what my new life was all about, wasn't it?

Only time would answer the question, *was* I up to the challenge?

6

It was a bright October morning when I arrived at the grade school, armed with a head full of new knowledge and an excitement to get started. I found a parking spot easily enough in the lot behind the small limestone building and made my way through the rear door. I had to be buzzed into the building and came face-to-face with a new reality. Things had definitely changed.

Entering the sixties-era building, the familiar smells of wet sneakers intermingled with newly waxed floors and cleaning solution greeted me like old friends. Not everything had changed. After stopping in the office to pick up the class list and other forms, it was easy enough to find the classroom with the sign, Ms. Adele Brice.

Class had already started when I walked quietly

in the room and took a seat in the back. I could observe all the children from that vantage point.

Halloween witches and goblins, along with bright orange pumpkins and colorful paper leaves, hung around the chalkboard, adding a child-like charm. The room had large windows with a view of the clear October sky, and I sensed a feeling of welcome and acceptance in the place. Watching the students as they worked, I hoped to get a feel for the dynamics in the room before being introduced.

One of the girls quickly caught my attention. Her tiny face overwhelmed by saucer-sized brown eyes, her dark brown hair in high ponytails above shell-like ears, she listened intently to the group reading at the front of the room. Another dark-haired boy with swarthy skin stared out the window, caught up in his own dreams. Then there was the tall blond boy, whose size made him seem much older, more intent on fooling around with his neighbors than doing the work at hand. In other words, it was much like the classrooms where I'd spent my early teaching career.

Wouldn't they be surprised to learn how nervous I was? Thank goodness for those weeks of classes I'd just completed. Without them, I'd be a basket case.

A young woman stood at the front of the classroom, dressed casually in charcoal-gray slacks and matching sweater, her shoulder-length hair a riot of auburn curls. Obviously, the teacher. Good lord, she looked so young.

The six students in the reading group were seated around her in a semi-circle. She looked up at me as I took my seat and gave a forced smile. As soon as she finished speaking to the group, she sent them to their desks and came to the back of the room and introduced herself.

"You must be Ms. LeBeau," she said, extending her hand. At my nod, she continued. "I understand you'll be observing my class today."

"Yes, and if there's anything I can do to help, please let me know." The eagerness in my voice sounded juvenile, but I couldn't control it. I wanted so badly to succeed.

A spasm of irritation crossed her face. "Why don't you just watch for today, and we'll take it from there tomorrow?"

Whoa. What was this all about? I thought I'd be welcomed with open arms, but apparently, Ms. Brice didn't feel she needed help.

She turned to the class and clapped her hands for their attention.

"This is Ms. LeBeau, children. She's going to be working with us this year. You can go to her for help whenever I'm busy working with others."

I gave what I considered my friendliest smile and a wave as they all turned in their seats to stare at me. Most of them smiled and eagerly waved back. I couldn't help but notice the one child who never turned or raised his head from the paper he worked on.

"Okay, class, back to work." Ms. Brice wasted no more time on making me feel welcome as she walked to the front of the room without a backward glance.

I looked over the seating list I had in my papers and identified the students in need of extra help. It only took a moment to see the boy who'd been so intent on his work was Jake O'Connor, the child with possible Asperger's syndrome. I studied his behavior discreetly.

A good-looking boy with thick black hair and bright blue eyes, he seemed to hold himself apart from the others, and they, in turn, gave him a wide berth. Except for one other boy who whispered in his ear and poked him whenever the teacher was otherwise occupied. It may have been Ms. Brice's plan for the day, but it was darn hard to remain a casual observer.

An hour later, things began to fall apart.

"Pull out your workbooks, class, and turn to page seven. I'll work with reading group B while you complete page eight."

Ms. Brice had them working on their letters, and Jake was having a difficult time. His little face red with frustration, I watched him erase and rewrite until the paper ripped.

That same teasing boy whispered something again, and Jake looked around the room as though aware of his surroundings for the first time. His face flushed with embarrassment. I couldn't stand it any longer and went over to his desk.

"Hi, Jake. Can I help you with anything?"

He didn't look up or answer me.

I decided to try again. "Are you having a problem?"

"No," he shouted.

Ms. Brice looked up from the book she'd been following with the reading group in the front of the classroom. I felt my own face flush. This was not going according to plan.

"Maybe we could work on it together," I whispered.

"I can do it myself," he shouted, never once looking in my direction.

"Jake's just dumb," the other boy told me.

That set Jake off, and he crumpled his paper and threw it on the floor, his little face pinched with frustration.

"I can so do it," he shouted.

Ms. Brice sent me a disapproving look and got up from her chair.

"Jake, what did we say about shouting in the classroom?"

At that, the child hung his head, looking miserable. Ms. Brice gave me a look reminiscent of Sister Margaret Mary, my own second-grade teacher. I could still feel the sting of those rebuking looks whenever I did something stupid. Like now.

The day went downhill from there, and I drove home in a deep funk. When I reached the quiet of my own home, I took off my shoes and opened Maeve's kennel. She jumped all over me in her excitement, and I realized she needed to get outside.

Now.

I opened the door and followed her out as far as the porch, bare feet and all. I sat on the step, chin in hand, waiting while she relieved herself, feeling dejected and useless. Whatever made me think I'd be good at this job? Obviously, I sucked at handling kids with special needs. It would take a lot more than a few classes to get me up to speed. Should I do everyone a favor and quit? Waitressing began to look good. But there was that matter of a contract I'd just signed.

Sitting there, resting my chin in my hand, old feelings of inadequacy seeped into my head, pushing out all the new confidence I'd worked so hard to acquire. Had anything in my life really changed?

Carol's van pulled into the drive. Oh, great. Now I could tell her what a failure I was at this job, too. It wasn't bad enough that I'd embarrassed her in front of her spinning friends with my stupid attitude. Now, she'd hear from the other teachers how lousy I performed in the classroom.

"Uh-oh. By the look of things, your first day didn't go so well," she said, walking toward me.

"I suppose if you consider the teacher seems to

hate my guts and the student who needs my help the most is completely turned off by my presence in the classroom, you could say that."

"Oh, c'mon, it can't be that bad."

"You had to be there." Maeve had finished exploring and run back to the steps, crawling all over me while licking my face with abandon. At least I still had one friend in the world.

"Come on inside, and I'll tell you the whole sad tale."

We went into the kitchen, and I made us each a cup of tea. After relaying the miserable details of my day, I felt a little better.

"Give Addy some time. She's a fairly new teacher and very good from what I hear. Maybe it's hard for her to give up some of the control of her classroom. Who knows? She'll come around once she realizes how much of a help you are to her and the kids."

"From your lips to God's ear," I mumbled.

IT ONLY TOOK ONE VISIT TO LILA'S FARM TO CONVINCE me that raising sheep for my own wool was the way to go. After all, I was a working woman with a salary now, and I could afford to spend a little on something that brought me pleasure. I wished Robert could see how I'd changed. Lila was a very convincing saleswoman and I a willing consumer, especially after seeing the young ewes, all white and fluffy, prancing about the barnyard. I suspect she knew how it would go before I ever got out of the car.

So on a mid-November day, Lila pulled up to the barn door, her blue pickup pulling a horse trailer. She hopped out of the truck cab, all smiles.

"Here they are. I'll need your help getting them into the barn. They're probably scared to death so they'll be a little skittish."

We managed to block the sides of the trailer ramp, so they had nowhere to go but into the open barn door. I watched them hesitantly take those first steps to freedom and knew just how they felt. Change was hard, no doubt about it.

Looking at the two Corriedale sheep, I suddenly felt stronger. They would be happy here, I'd make sure of it. I'd been told their lustrous white wool would be perfect for spinning and knitting.

"They're probably already bred so you may end up with a flock of four next spring," Lila said sheepishly "Our ram jumped the fence last week. He was supposed to wait a month, but obviously, he missed the memo.

"They might look a bit timid, but it won't take long before they get used to you. Especially if you start feeding them grain in the cold weather. I copied the recipe of the mixture I use. You can get it at the local feed mill.

"I'll teach you everything you need to know about their care," she promised.

I planned to hold her to it. We unloaded the hay she'd brought, and she helped inspect my pasture fence for any possible escape routes.

"You won't have to feed them grain until the winter gets cold. But if they are bred, extra grain will guarantee a better delivery and healthy lambs."

I stood in the barn, watching the sheep and wondering what would come next in this crazy life I'd chosen. The animals already seemed to belong, their soft baaing almost musical as they stuck inquisitive noses into the corners of the pen.

The sweet smell of the fresh hay permeated the air. Something about its scent and the pungent odor of the sheep seemed to belong here.

Maeve raced around the outside of the pen in ecstasy, back and forth like a mad woman. She'd found her purpose in life.

"Your pup is showing her natural instincts."

"What do you mean?"

"She wants to herd the sheep but doesn't quite know how to go about it. You should probably take her to herding school, and the two of you could learn together. She could be a big help."

"Herding school?" Oh, good Lord, *now* what had I gotten myself into? I was already worried about my own future in the business world. Her education would have to wait. "With two sheep, I really don't think it'll be necessary."

"Well, with any luck, you may have twins and

have six by spring. I started with two, and now I have twenty. They grow on you."

I turned to look at her, hoping she was joking but very much afraid she wasn't. She was in the truck before I could question her more.

"See you next week," she called back through the open window. "Just holler if you have any questions." She pulled out of the driveway so fast the gravel shot out in a spray behind her.

I was alone with the sheep. I looked at them, and they stared back at me. They looked as confused as I felt. Neither of us moved for a moment. That familiar panic began to rise in my throat as I realized once again I'd jumped feetfirst into unfamiliar territory. This was getting to be a bad habit.

The sheep depended on me now for their care. Did I really need this in my life? If they knew how clueless I really was, they'd jump the fence and follow Lila's truck down the driveway.

I coaxed them out the barn door and into their enclosed paddock where they finally seemed at ease. In a few minutes, they were running through the tall grass, stopping to munch periodically. I felt better.

My first thought then was to feed them some grain, even though Lila had said it wasn't necessary. But everyone felt better with a full stomach—even animals, I'd bet. Years of homemaking had taught me that. I had to make a trip to the feed mill before I could feed them, though. There was one not too far away. I'd seen it on my travels back and forth to town. I put my hand into my pocket and felt the folded paper with Lila's feed recipe. Relief washed over me.

I went inside to change, knowing that I smelled of sheep, hay, and other questionable odors. Not exactly the scent one wore to go shopping, even to the feed mill. At least, I didn't think so.

What would Robert say if he could see me now? I could visualize him shaking his head, wondering if I'd gone completely off the deep end without him to watch over me.

I can do this, Robert, I promise. You no longer have to worry about me. I should've been worrying about you, shouldn't I? How could I have been so blind to what was going on in Robert's life? Why couldn't he confide in me? What were those money problems he felt he had to deal with alone? It looked like I'd never learn the answer to those questions. Would I ever be able to push the guilt and fear out of my mind?

THIRTY MINUTES LATER, I PARKED IN FRONT OF THE feed mill, a gray corrugated steel building. It looked like it'd been there for a hundred years, and indeed, according to the date beneath the large red-and-white Purina Feed logo on the silo, it had.

It was late morning by now, and an unusually warm sun beat down on the sparse grass and stone of the parking area. Bulging white feed sacks lined the edge of the concrete porch, waiting to be loaded into a pickup. Some farmer with a lot more animals than me was doing business inside.

I climbed the worn and broken steps and opened the weathered wooden door to the office. Several farmers, wearing the requisite John Deere caps and denim coveralls, sat on stools at the counter, talking and joking. The conversation stopped, and they all turned and stared at me curiously. I had the feeling it wasn't too often strangers wandered in.

I clutched my feed recipe closer to my chest and tried to look confident.

"You lookin' for someone?" the owner asked in a friendly voice.

Okay, so I probably shouldn't be wearing black wool slacks and a camel-hair blazer over my white turtleneck sweater. Another habit that needed re-thinking.

"I came to—" Where did that falsetto sound come from? I cleared my throat and got my voice back. "—get some grain for my sheep."

"Sheep?" One of the farmers scoffed. "Why would a little gal like you want to waste your time and money on them dumb animals?"

The other men snickered.

Without thought, my protective instincts kicked in. How dare he insult my new babies? I put both hands on my hips and faced him directly.

"Dumb compared to what? A cow that stands in a pen all day chewing her cud?"

Where was this coming from? I didn't dislike cows. I'd never had any social interaction with a cow. For all I knew, they carried on intelligent conversations with their owner when no one was around to hear.

The men guffawed and slapped the speaker on the back. "She's got you there, Irwin."

He grinned back, his ruddy cheeks growing even brighter. I knew they were just teasing me when he lifted his cap in deference. It was taking me a while to learn to accept it as part of the culture in the area, but hey, I could enjoy a joke as much as anybody. I grinned back at them.

The owner looked at me with a bit more respect. "Is there a special mix you wanted?"

I handed him the copy of Lila's feed recipe, and he looked it over.

"Be ready in a few minutes." He went into the mill, calling for one of the workers.

The man named Irwin got up from his stool. "Have a seat," he offered. "You the woman who bought the place next to the Johnsons?"

"Yes, that's me." I looked at the fine film of grain dust covering everything. Wouldn't go well with my black slacks. "Thank you, but I don't mind standing."

The owner returned. "Jack's mixing it up. He'll put it in the back of your pickup."

Why tell him I drove a Toyota Camry? I had the feeling the jokes and laughter would really fly when I closed the door behind me as it was.

After preparing my bill, he said, "You want us to keep your mix on file? That way you can call in ahead, and we'll have it ready."

"Fine." I paid him and left after saying goodbye to my new colleagues. After all, I was one of them now, right? I chuckled, thinking of what their reaction would be to that statement.

I opened the trunk of my car and waited while the sacks were loaded in.

"Is someone gonna help you unload these?" the young man asked. That's when it hit me I'd no longer have to go to the Y to lift weights.

"I'll help John with his letters first, and then see if I can get Josie to tell me why she couldn't do her homework pages last night."

Ms. Brice gave me a grateful smile. She'd been working with reading groups again this afternoon, trying to keep the fast readers interested and helping the others to catch up while keeping an eye on the students still at their desks. It was a daunting task.

"And don't worry about the others. I'll make sure they stay focused on their workbook pages." I could see how exhausted she was. It had been one of those days filled with minor crises: lost shoes, missing crayons, you name it. I walked up and down between the desks, stopping to answer a question or ask one myself.

Winning over Ms. Brice had proved a challenge, but after these few weeks in the classroom, we were working together comfortably, probably because she could see that the children and I were bonding. It didn't take me long to realize she was overworked and challenged herself, trying to keep everyone in the class working at their particular level. Even so, these were her chicks, and she was very protective of them, especially those who needed extra attention. It was energizing for me to know I had gained her trust. The days flew by.

I'D CONTINUED WITH MY COURSES ON THE SPECIAL-needs child and gained a lot of helpful information. So I entered the classroom the Monday morning of our field trip with confidence, greeting each child by name.

It was a beautifully clear day, and we were going to a nature center farther up into the Door Peninsula. Perfect weather for our outing.

I'd assigned the children seat partners, one of the many techniques I'd learned in my class, making sure no one would feel left out. There was a bit of grumbling about not sitting with friends, but they got over it in their excitement to ride on the school bus.

I was especially concerned about Jake, knowing a change in routine could throw him off-kilter. I paired him with Daniel, a nice boy who seemed to have an empathetic soul. He'd come up to Jake several times on the playground and asked him to join in a game. Occasionally, Jake did, a big step forward for him since he couldn't throw a ball well or run as fast as the others and he was aware of it. Obviously, Jake felt comfortable with Daniel, and I teamed them together as much as possible.

The children were exiting the bus, excited and running toward the building.

"No running, please," Adele called out, but it was too late. They were like a school of lemmings, headed toward the door.

Jake was running behind Daniel, trying to keep up when I saw that same annoying boy who sat near him in the classroom stick out his foot and deliberately trip him. Jake fell down in the uneven gravel. I ran over and helped him up. His pants had a tear in the knee, and I could see he was trying desperately not to cry. I pulled up his trouser leg. He had a scrape but nothing major.

I looked around for the culprit, but he'd disappeared into the group. When I found him, I pulled him out and took him by the arm over to where Jake sat, cradling his knee.

"I saw what you did," I said between clenched jaws. "Apologize right now."

"He didn't do it. I tripped," Jake said.

I could see what he was trying to do. Wanting so desperately to be accepted, he wouldn't tattle, no matter what. Now, I was caught. I couldn't let the bully get away with it, even to save Jake's pride, could I?

"I saw him do it, Jake," I said softly.

"No, you didn't. No, you didn't." Jake was standing up now and shouting.

Okay, now this particular situation wasn't covered in my course. What should I do? If I didn't stand by my convictions and see the bully punished, I wasn't doing either boy a favor. But I knew my relationship with Jake would suffer if I pursued it.

I took the other boy by the arm again. "Come with me," I said, walking him over to Addy. I really had no choice.

The joy of the morning left after that episode, for me and for Jake as well. The rapport I'd worked so hard to develop between us was lost, and he steered clear of me the rest of the day. Rebuilding his trust would not be easy.

7

"But it's been over four months." I'd called the Chicago realtor again a few weeks after my visit to Chicago. "I can't believe we haven't had at least one offer." My voice rose with my frustration level.

"I can't control the housing market, Mrs. LeBeau, as much as I'd like to." Now I had put her on the defensive. But I was too scared to care.

"Have you been out to check on the house? We have to make sure there isn't any more vandalism." I sat at the kitchen table, leaning my head on my left palm in frustration as we talked. "Have the police been checking?"

"They've been out several times while I was there. I don't think you have to worry any more about that."

Little did she know. There'd been a small white envelope, no return address in the packet of mail

Brooke had forwarded that week. I tore it open with shaking fingers to find to find the cryptic note: I'LL FIND YOU WHEN I'M READY. BE PREPARED TO PAY UP, OR ELSE.

It seemed the police wouldn't be of any help.

"There has to be something we can do to sell this house quickly," I said, desperation in my voice.

"We can either lower the price or be patient," she said. "It's up to you."

I didn't want to do either, and after asking how much longer our contract was valid, I hung up. I knew darn well I'd just resigned a month ago but hoped to put some fire under her butt. She'd make a high commission on this sale. It was time she earned it.

I went over and poured myself a cup of coffee and snagged a cookie off the counter. Maeve trotted at my heels, wondering why she didn't get an evening treat if I had one, I suppose.

"You don't have to worry about your butt being thrown out onto the street, missy. You have me to take care of you." One look into her loving doggy eyes and I gave her a treat anyway. What the hell, we might as well go down happy.

The one bright spot at the moment was my job. It had been darn hard, but this past week, I'd finally seen some results in my struggle to regain Jake's trust.

We'd worked together on his classroom assignments, and he'd slowly eased up a bit on his need for perfection. I'd noticed a willingness to listen to my explanations without the constant erasing and rewriting. He was more relaxed and open to what else was going on in the classroom. I took that as a positive step.

It was Friday evening, and I looked forward to a quiet weekend spent working around the farm and then pondering my options about my former house and financial problems. I always thought more clearly after doing physical labor.

A car pulled into the driveway, and I got up from the table to see who was there. It was Carol, on her way home from school. As happy as I was to see her, I had mixed emotions about this visit.

"Any plans for tonight?" she asked after settling down with a cup of flavored coffee.

I knew what was coming. We'd been down this road several times. "There's a *Monk* marathon on cable. Thought I'd watch it."

She gave me a disgusted look and glanced down at the table. She turned her saucer in a circle and said in a wistful voice, "I was hoping you'd come out with me...go over to the pub and have a drink or two while my boys are busy. Could be some interesting men will show up." She raised her eyes in a hopeful look.

I couldn't contain the scoff. I'd never told her about my last foray into the pub. My ears still burned when I remembered that embarrassing episode at the bar.

"C'mon, Martha. You gonna sit here and stagnate the rest of your life? You have to get out and meet people, live a little. Who knows what handsome hunk is just waiting to find you?"

"In your dreams."

"I'm serious here. Look what's happened to me because I stayed home all those years while my husband went out alone. The world kept turning, and other people changed, leaving me behind like last night's leftovers."

I knew her self-esteem had been shattered by the divorce, and I wanted to help her, but I couldn't see how dragging me out with her would be of any benefit.

"C'mon, Carol, you know how I hate hanging out in crowds, especially when I don't know anyone. I'd just be a drag on your fun."

"How are you ever going to meet people if you never leave this farm?" She threw her hands up. "There's no logic there."

"Maybe some other time, when my life has settled more."

She gave a sigh of defeat. "Okay, I know there's no use trying to push you into it."

"Is something else going on?" I asked. "You look down in the dumps."

"The boys aren't handling the divorce well. Getting them to spend time with their father and his new wife is a major hassle. In fact, Nathan, my youngest, told me he hates his dad." She pressed both hands over her eyes. When she uncovered them, I noticed the weariness. "I don't know what to do about it. I'm at my wit's end. I have my own issues with the man and trying to put a positive spin on the situation is difficult. I know the boys are hurting, and it kills me."

"Won't he talk to them?"

"He tried at first, but now they've hurt his feelings. He's under the impression that they should just suck it up and deal with it. *Grow up and act like men*, he told them."

I'd never met the man, but I had the sudden urge to kick him in his manly parts. How could he be so unfeeling?

"Hey, I gotta go. The school bus will be dropping the boys off soon and I have to have a quick meal prepared. Believe it or not, they're off to a basketball game tonight with their father. It took a lot of pushing, but I finally managed to convince them to go." She put her jacket back on and opened the door. "I hope you're at least planning on coming to the Arts and Crafts Holiday Show tomorrow."

"Now that's more like it. What time does it start?"

"I'll pick you up late morning. Don't dress too fancy. We'll be in a barn."

Was that a clue that my past wardrobe had been inappropriate? Visions of my visit to the feed mill and the ensuing shower of grain dust danced through my head.

"Oh, by the way, you'll never guess what I found out today. My ex's young wife is expecting a baby. Can you beat that?"

The pain in her voice was enough to make me reconsider going out that night, but she was out the door before I had a chance. No wonder she'd wanted company. What kind of a friend did that make me?

I was ready and waiting at the door for Carol the next morning. I'd fed the sheep earlier and put Maeve in her kennel where she whined pitifully. But I knew better than to leave that madwoman loose in my house without supervision. The constant sight of my chewed-up couch leg confirmed my fears on that score.

"I'm really looking forward to this," I announced as I crawled into Carol's minivan. I'd had a niggling of excitement running through my body ever since awakening that morning as if something momentous was going to take place that day. Maybe I'd see something inspiring in the crafts or find some art treasure I couldn't live without.

"You'll have a good time, I guarantee it." Carol swung the car out the circular drive and onto the county road. She didn't seem annoyed with me for turning her down the previous night, but I was feeling guilty.

"Did you find someone to go out with last night?"

"Oh, yeah. Nancy was free."

Funny, I'd had the impression Carol didn't care much for Nancy. Guess she'd been pretty desperate for company.

"Unlike you, Nancy has no problem trolling for men." She winked conspiratorially and poked me in the arm. "Riley usually frequents the pub on Friday night for dinner. It's one of the few times you'll catch him out alone. I think she's set her hopes on catching him, but between you and me, her chances are pretty slim. His son is his number one priority. I can't see Nancy fitting into the scenario."

"I'm really sorry about the baby." That didn't come out right. "I mean—"

"I'll get over it. It's just that it struck me yesterday he was beginning a new life while mine was just plodding along in the same old groove." She waved her hand dismissively. "Life goes on, doesn't it?"

"Yeah, it does." I thought of those weeks and months after Robert's death, and the pain of being left behind to pick up the pieces. Giving up a past you'd invested your whole self in was very difficult. Even if that past was far from perfect.

We drove down the highway for about fifteen minutes and then pulled onto a side road. Cars were parked in an adjacent field across from a weathered gray clapboard and fieldstone barn. Kind of like mine, only on a much larger scale. We drove in and parked.

The day was cold and windy with a hint of snow in the air. Perfect for an early Christmas sale. After pulling our hand-knit caps over our ears, we hurried in.

The barn had been lovingly refurbished inside. It was a magnificent old building with huge hand-hewn timbers holding up the gabled roof. The floors were hardwood boards, varying in length and width and scarred from years of wear, but lovingly polished to a high sheen. The building had been divided into two sections, one for the sheep shearing and petting zoo and another for the craft and food sale.

We wandered through the craft section first.

It seemed Carol knew everyone, and everyone knew her. Before we'd covered half of the booths, I'd been introduced to at least a dozen people, vendors and customers, and even saw a few faces familiar to me.

Joan was there, manning a booth with her spinning wheel at her side. I was amazed at the progress she'd made with her physical therapy. She swore it was due to her determination not to give up on spinning and knitting.

"What's that you're spinning?" I asked.

A mound of mocha-colored fiber lay in her basket, and I reached down to touch it. It slid through my fingers like a buttery, soft web.

"It's a blend of alpaca and silk," she said. "I saw a knitting pattern for an open-weave summer sweater that I think will work up really well with this yarn."

"It's beautiful." Suddenly, I had the urge to get home and practice my spinning. I'd improved quite a bit in the past few weeks and didn't get nearly as frustrated. Saturday night wouldn't be lonely with a good movie to watch, a glass of wine to sip, and my spinning wheel. And, of course, Maeve would make sure I didn't get bored.

We wandered through several more booths, the air rich with the scent of herbal soaps and lotions—invigorating basil, relaxing lavender, and the overwhelming patchouli. I knew Suze and Lexie would appreciate the handmade soaps and lotions, so I purchased a few.

The mohair scarf and matching beret I decided on for Brooke were the same blue as the clear sky of an Indian summer day. Even she couldn't help but love it. It would bring out the blue color of her eyes.

Our next stop was at a spinning booth, and I immediately gravitated to a ball of red-orange mohair roving. It looked like a cloud at sunset, and I had to have it. I'd save it until my spinning improved enough to do it justice, but already I envisioned wearing the knit cardigan.

There were felt hats and purses, which Carol assured me I could easily produce, next to skeins of every color handspun yarn you could imagine. The idea that I could possibly create my own unique gifts by this time next year ran tantalizingly through my mind.

"All you need is time and the willingness to learn. We'll have a wool dying and felting day in the spring. It's a blast," Carol said.

"I'm hungry." The aroma of a rich chicken booyah, a local soup made famous by the early Belgian settlers, wafted through the room, mixed with the savory smell of frying hamburgers and brats. All the fragrances of food that bring comfort to the soul and fat to the hips.

Carol looked down at her watch. "It'll have to wait. Hurry, we'd better get to the shearing pen before all the good spots are gone. He's gonna start shearing in ten minutes."

I'd never seen Carol move so fast in the months I'd known her. The *he* she talked about had to be the notorious Riley, causer of palpitating hearts among women old enough to know better.

I laughed as she pulled me behind her like a recalcitrant child. I was a little embarrassed on her behalf. How could she act that silly over a good-looking man? I'd been immune for years.

Carol managed to get us close to the pen, even though she had to push her way through throngs of women and children to do it. The shearer had his back to us, so all I could see was a head of thick black hair streaked with gray and a slim figure. As I watched, strong, muscular arms caught a sheep and expertly flipped her onto her back before the creature even knew what happened. With a fluid motion, he picked up his electric shears and began shearing off her wool as she went into a trance.

It was like watching the horse whisperer. When he turned her back upright, the ewe stayed still until he finished and didn't even seem to want to move when she was free. He gave her a little slap on the rump, and she finally ran off. A woman swooped in then and removed the shorn fleece. I watched, fascinated, as he repeated the same procedure with a second sheep.

After he finished, he stood up and brushed the fiber from his well-worn jeans and shirt. He looked up, and our eyes met across the pen. Omigod. It was the man from the pub. The one who had reached for my fifty-dollar bill and then offered to pay for the spilled drinks. I'd been too upset to pay attention to names that night. Obviously, he was a man of many talents.

A crackling sensation shot between us; at least I felt it, like an electrical field gone haywire. He smiled, and his blue eyes crinkled at the corners in that most charming way, making my heart skip a beat. Did he remember me? I caught my breath, afraid to exhale in case he disappeared.

Be still my heart. I felt fifteen again and totally in lust. Those eyes. A person could drown in those eyes.

The moment shattered when he glanced down at the young boy tugging on his pants leg.

Jake.

His expression changed, a softness and unmistakable look of love changing him from virile man to loving father. He got down on his haunches to hear what the boy was saying. Of course. I knew somewhere in the back of my mind that *a* Riley was Jake's father, but not *the* Riley. The love between them was as obvious as if they each carried a neon sign on their backs, WE BELONG TO EACH OTHER.

This Riley wasn't at all what I'd expected. How could this man, the same one who drove mature women to act like hormone-overloaded teenagers, be so totally involved with his child? It made me wonder if he even had a clue as to what he did to the female population of this small town. I decided he was either oblivious or too smart to give a damn.

As for my own reaction, it was downright embarrassing. After months of secretly thinking I was above it all, I wasn't any more immune to his charming looks than the rest of them. How could I have had such a strong reaction when all he did was smile at me? Maybe Carol was right, and I'd been alone too long and needed to get out more. I decided right then to reconsider the next time she asked me to join her for drinks on the weekend. As long as our destination wasn't the pub.

I looked over at Jake, and my heart went out to the two of them. Riley had one more ewe to shear, but his concern for Jake obviously took precedence.

There was no look of impatience. No *don't bother me now* glance. So different from Robert.

I could see Jake was agitated. Most likely, the crowds and noise were causing circuit overload, and he couldn't handle it. Riley spoke softly in his ear and rubbed his back soothingly. Dare I step in and take Jake outside for a while? Or would Riley tell me to mind my own business? After all, I'd never even met the man. Why would he trust me? I hesitated.

Just then another boy came up to Jake with a kitten in his arms, and Jake broke into a wide grin. It was Daniel. He handed Jake the cat, and after talking together for a moment, Riley went back to shearing. Disaster averted.

"So, what did you think of Riley?" Carol asked after we started the drive home. "Didn't I tell you he was special?"

"He's handsome, all right." Even as I gave the bland reply, I knew it was more than his looks that had caught my imagination. I'd sensed a quality in the man I couldn't define. Something I'd seen in his eyes in those first few moments of contact. An understanding, a kindness, along with the instant attraction. It went deep into my psyche and touched my soul. His concern and handling of Jake only deepened my desire to know him and made him even sexier in my eyes.

"A few of us are going out tonight. Why don't you come along? Riley may show up," she added with a leer. "Don't think I didn't notice your reaction. He's close enough to your age to make things interesting."

"Not tonight. I want to get home and start spinning." And probably spend a good portion of my thoughts on the problems with my former home and husband. Okay, so I was already reneging on my new plans.

I needed to be alone to think about my strange reaction to Riley before I did anything stupid. Where had this outpouring of emotion come from? I didn't want it, I didn't need it.

Besides, why would a man who had only to crook a finger and have a dozen women of a certain age beating a path to his door be the least bit interested in someone like me?

"You're going to meet him sometime," Carol pronounced. "I'm going to make sure of it."

That should've upset me, but instead, I found the idea infinitely pleasing.

8

LATE ONE AFTERNOON, JUST AS THE SUN WAS SETTING, I went out to the barn to give the sheep their evening grain and hay, battling the wind all the way. Those gorgeous sunset colors, soft pink and orange and blue, reflected off the scattered clouds. I remembered my grandmother telling me that a colorful winter sky meant Mrs. Santa was baking Christmas cookies up in the North Pole. I'd squealed in delight.

The weather had turned unusually cold for mid-December, even for Wisconsin. At least, that's what everyone around here told me. I wasn't prepared for it. All those years in the city had thinned my blood, I swear. There was cold, and then there was freezing cold.

The air was clear and cold, but the weatherman predicted snow before morning. I could smell it in the air. Being close to Lake Michigan, we often got lake effect snow here, I was told. That same lake was supposed to have a warming effect, but I began to wonder if that was a joke played on unsuspecting newcomers.

I found the sheep huddled together in their pen, but they ran over as soon as I entered my little barn, eager for their evening snack. It hadn't taken them long to learn I was their new mama, the one who brought the food. I filled the bucket from the feed bin and walked into their pen. They nudged against me, pushing for the food in the grain bucket. The robust smell of molasses in the feed mix was rich and tempting.

"Hold on, girls, it's coming." The wind howled through the cracks in the old barn siding as I put the grain in the feed trough, and I shivered.

"Are you freezing in here?" I decided to give them extra since they'd be burning calories trying to keep warm.

I ran my hand over a wooly back, trying to convince myself that they were plenty warm. But this was an old barn with wide spaces between the boards in some places, and they didn't have a mother to cuddle with. Why hadn't I realized how cold it would get and hung canvas or plastic over the walls to cut the wind And why hadn't someone told me to do it?

I dithered around for several minutes, trying to decide what to do. Should I call my neighbor, Tony?

We'd become good friends, and he often came over to check on how I was managing with the animals. Of course, he did relish my stupid greenhorn questions.

No, I could handle this myself. I just had to think about it for a while. I'd come up with a practical solution on my own. I assured myself the barn must be adequate or someone would've told me. These were animals, not people, after all, and used to being outdoors in all kinds of weather.

But by this time, I had given the sheep names. Good, strong Irish names. Names that my Grandma Nellie Carey would be proud of. Bridget and Fiona.

I went into the house to make dinner. Hot soup was what I needed. I turned on TV news, banging around the pots and pans in frustration while listening to the weather report. It didn't sound good. The temperatures were supposed to fall to twenty below, an all-time low for this date, and the wind chill was too low to even fathom. What would happen to the ewes out there in that cold, drafty structure, away from the warmth of other animals? Maybe their wool hadn't grown thick enough yet to protect them? They could even be pregnant, for God's sake.

After another hour of listening to the wind howling around the house, I couldn't take it. I had to do something, or I wouldn't sleep all night.

As I fought my way to the barn to check on them again, I realized there was only one thing to do. I'd bring them into the unfinished basement of the house for the night. I wouldn't turn on the heat of course, but they'd be away from the howling wind down there and we would all get some sleep. Getting them down there would be a bit tricky, but I could do it.

Making a small pen in one corner of the basement shouldn't be too difficult, I reasoned. I could stack up a few bales of straw, just high enough so they couldn't jump over but low enough for me to be able to climb over. I set to work hauling the straw.

It took several trips to get enough down there. After placing newspapers on the floor, I opened a bale and spread it on top. It dawned on me then what a mess I'd have to clean up in the morning. A good night's sleep would be worth it.

When I had the pen set up, I coaxed the ewes down with a makeshift halter and a bucket of grain in hand. I gave them a pail of water and a small amount of hay, enough to last until morning, and then went up to take a shower, feeling quite proud of myself.

Checking on them later, I decided they looked cozy and content in their new home. This was a lot easier than trekking out to the barn every few hours. I went to bed and slept peacefully.

I MUST'VE WORKED HARDER THAN I THOUGHT

because I overslept the next morning. I hadn't even dressed when there was a banging on my door.

Looking out my bedroom window, I saw the world had been wrapped in a cocoon of white while I slept. I recognized Tony Johnson's truck in the driveway. Probably came to check how Maeve and I were faring in the cold. Personally, I think he had guilt feelings about pawning the dog off on me when I'd just moved in. As well he should. But I appreciated his concern and advice, most of the time anyway.

"Hi," I said, standing at the door. "What brings you around so early this morning?" A little voice told me it wouldn't be a good idea to let him know I'd brought the sheep inside.

I didn't open the door all the way, hoping when he saw me in flannel pajamas and robe, he'd take the hint and leave.

"Early? It's nine thirty for cryin' out loud. Where's the pup?"

I didn't care for his self-righteous smirk. What is it with people who get up at the crack of dawn and think everyone who doesn't is a slacker?

"You two getting along in this cold weather?" he asked.

"We're doing just fine."

I looked around for Maeve, opening the door wider for him, surprised myself that she hadn't started barking as soon as he knocked. They were great friends.

Tony stepped past me and set a plate of brownies on the kitchen table.

"I'm on my way to town, and Sue Ellen asked me to drop these off. She made them last night and thought you might like one with your lunch. She worries you're not going to bake anything just for yourself."

That's when I heard Maeve barking like crazy and the sheep bleating.

"What's she barking at?" Tony asked.

Damn. I must've left the basement door open a crack the last time I'd checked on the sheep. I hurried over to the top of the stairs, and I could see Maeve running back and forth past the makeshift pen, harassing the sheep as usual. She'd somehow managed to get through the door. She couldn't jump the straw bales either, so I quickly shut the basement door. I'd take care of that as soon as I got rid of Tony.

He sniffed the air and looked at me in wonder. "You don't have the sheep down there, do you?"

Okay, now I was embarrassed. I could tell by his incredulous expression that it wasn't something usually done. Last week, he'd noticed the shredded tissue and overturned wastebasket littering the kitchen floor and the teeth marks on my couch and hinted the dog belonged in the barn with the sheep.

Memories of Robert's reaction when Lexie spilled milk on the cushions of his prize sofa flashed before me. And that was something I could easily wipe up. What would Robert have to say about this latest fiasco? Not only did I have a teething dog in the living room, but I also had smelly sheep in the basement.

"Well, it was very cold last night," I said in my defense. "I knew I'd sleep better knowing they were warm."

His eyes widened, and he blinked rapidly. I could see he was having a difficult time keeping a straight face. "That's why they have wool, to keep them warm," he managed between gulps of air.

"Yes, but they're possibly pregnant and their wool isn't that long. They were just born last spring," I said, desperate now to explain my position.

"I gotta go," he said, practically running out the door. I could see him doubled over with laughter before he got in the truck.

Oh, great. Now I'd really made a fool of myself, and it would be all over the neighborhood before lunchtime. I needed help with this animal husbandry thing. I'd be darned if I'd call the neighbors every time I needed advice. I decided to get to the nearest library and find out all I could about raising sheep as soon as I ate breakfast, got dressed, and put things back in reasonable order.

THE LIBRARY WAS ONLY OPEN UNTIL 1 O'CLOCK ON Saturday, so I barely had time to comb my hair before leaving. Forget about makeup. As if anyone cared. I was able to park right in front of the building, confirming my belief that I wouldn't see anyone I knew there anyway. But just in case, I pulled my wool cap lower and slunk in quietly.

Entering the red brick building, I immediately got caught up in the familiar allure only shelves of unread books could bring. I took a deep breath, inhaling the familiar scent of books and newsprint. Where to begin? I immediately forgot all about my books and my mission and gravitated toward the stacks.

Stop.

I gave myself an imaginary slap on the side of the head. I was not here on a pleasure jaunt. I forced myself to head straight over to the computer terminal.

As I searched through the lists of animal husbandry books, the sound of a familiar child's voice caught my attention. I looked up to see Riley and Jake walking in my direction, toward the book checkout. They were each carrying several books and talking animatedly to each other. As a matter of fact, I had never seen Jake so animated.

Rats. Too late to make a run for the stacks without causing a scene. I pulled my wool cap lower on my forehead and ducked my head, staring intently at the computer screen, hoping I wouldn't be noticed. Only I couldn't resist a peek at Riley.

I must confess my heart picked up its pace a bit.

He was dressed in casual khaki pants, a pale blue oxford shirt, and a cobalt blue crew-neck sweater. The sweater looked hand-knit, in a pattern that looked familiar. Which of the local ladies had knit it for him?

I knew the moment Jake spotted me. He dropped his books on the floor and ran over.

"Hi, Ms. Martha. What're you doin' here?"

I smiled down at him, my own pleasure increasing at the look of adoration on his small face. "Getting books, just like you," I said before looking up at Riley.

When he looked back with a grin, I couldn't help but notice how the color of his sweater gave his eyes an iridescent glow.

"Hi," I said. We'd never been introduced, so I held my hand out. "I'm Martha LeBeau, a paraprofessional in Jake's classroom."

"I saw you at the Christmas sale...and one other time, if I remember right." That lethal grin turned up the corners of his mouth, and his eyes crinkled with laughter.

He would have to bring that up. I felt the heat in my face.

When he took my hand in his, a fizzle of excitement shot up my arm. "Nice to finally meet you. I think I've heard your name at least once a day for the past month." Looking down at his son, he smiled fondly, that same love I'd noticed at the craft sale splashed across his face. Looking back at me, he said, "It's nice to finally put a face to Ms. Martha."

Was I just dreaming in thinking his eyes told me he liked the face? Then I remembered my lack of makeup and came back down to earth. I was his son's teacher, that's all.

Jake smiled shyly and reached for my hand. The time we'd spent together in the classroom brought us closer these past weeks, and I surmised he felt more at ease with me than most people. A surge of elation warmed my heart. I'd finally regained his trust.

"C'mon, buddy, we've got to get back home. I have work to do in the shop." Riley tapped the books in his arms. I could see they were volumes on woodcarving and furniture making, and I remembered then that Carol had told me Riley had a business making custom furniture.

"I'll see you on Monday, Jake." I tried to pull my hand away, but he was having none of it.

"No, I want to stay with Ms. Martha." He clung to my hand, and I looked helplessly up at Riley, who was looking decidedly uncomfortable.

"C'mon, Jake. You know better." He gestured to the books Jake had dropped on the floor. "Pick up your books now so we can check them out."

"No, I'm not going. I want to stay with Ms. Martha, and you can't make me leave." By this time, his little face was beet red, and his voice had escalated to a screech. Everyone in the library turned to look our way, and I could see the disdain on their faces. Strangers who were quick to blame a parent for their child's behavior.

"Why don't we go for a little walk outside?" I turned to Riley. "That usually helps to calm him down."

The warm blue eyes had turned to ice chips. "I know how to handle my son, Ms. LeBeau. I really don't need your help." Resentment came off him in waves.

I stepped back, shocked at the change in his attitude. Did he think I, too, blamed him for Jake's behavior? I'd only wanted to help.

Jake was lying on the floor by this time, sobbing. Riley bent down and picked him up. "C'mon, son. Let's go home and take a nap. You'll feel better then."

"Goodbye, Jake," I called softly after them. "I'll see you Monday." I'd be darned if I'd say goodbye to the man carrying him.

I lost my pleasure in the library visit after that and hurriedly found a few books on raising sheep to check out.

Thoughts of Riley and Jake swam through my mind all the way home. Obviously, the man resented any interference. I'd worry about that except even when Jake was at his worst, his father never seemed to lose patience. A picture of Robert and my daughters crept into my mind. Why couldn't Robert have been like that instead of always wanting his girls to be perfect? The thought left me with regrets.

I decided then to make a determined effort to stay out of Riley's way. Obviously, I'd only imagined whatever rapport I'd felt between us. It would be best to only have contact with Jake at school.

I'd felt uncomfortable and out of my league that afternoon, not knowing what to say or do to make an awkward situation better. I was still shaking. Those familiar feelings of inadequacy swept through me like the aftermath of a bad hangover. Was that how Jake felt most of the time? I couldn't help but wonder if he had that same sense of not belonging I carried, only magnified.

He couldn't quite connect with the other students, just as I hadn't connected with the change in Robert during our marriage. The desire was there; I could see it in Jake's eyes. And yet, when the other students tried to include him, he couldn't respond in the expected way. We had that in common.

I don't know which of them touched me the most. The troubled child or the tight-lipped father who refused any advice.

I took my books into the house and tried to put the incident out of my mind. I planned to spend the rest of the weekend learning how to raise sheep.

Only one problem. It was impossible to forget.

9

"Ms. Martha, Santa's going to be in the parade on Saturday. Are you going to tell him what you want for Christmas?" The bright-eyed girl in front of me jumped up and down in excitement.

Oh, boy. Keeping the kids focused for the next few weeks would be a challenge. I'd tried reading them a Christmas story but that only raised their excitement level. It had been mounting since Thanksgiving, and even I succumbed.

I'd found myself dragging out Christmas decorations I hadn't even looked at last year. Boxes with the handmade ornaments I'd saved since the girls were in grade school, the silver garlands they'd always loved, and their favorite nutcracker. I'd spread them out in the spare bedroom, deciding what I needed to replace or add. I prayed my girls would join me for Christmas, determined to make this holiday better than the last one.

The weather had cooperated by moderating. Well, as much as it does in a Wisconsin winter. Carol and I took a drive up to Door County on the weekend, joining the Illinois tourists who filled the gaily decorated boutiques. We had lunch in a homey restaurant in Fish Creek, one frequented by locals. I had a wonderful butternut squash soup and Swedish pancakes. Best of all, the atmosphere was friendly and festive. Carol behaved like the upbeat woman I'd first met, never once mentioning her ex or the expected baby and I didn't pry. Sometimes, people needed time and space to grieve. Hadn't I learned that myself?

I purchased several ornaments to commemorate the first holiday in my new home, buying the same item for Lexie, Brooke, and myself. It was a figure of an Irish woman spinning wool at her cottage door. I hoped it would symbolize to the girls a return to our heritage, not of leaving theirs behind.

That evening the ladies in the Wool Gatherers were knitting and spinning up a storm, trying to finish up Christmas gifts for their families. I just kept up my spinning, determined to get enough yarn spun that would be suitable for knitting a sweater. Carol worked on the last of three scarves for her boys.

"Anything more complicated is beyond me this year," she moaned. "Just working out the details of who gets the boys for which holiday is enough to make me ready for a glass of wine and a lie-down."

I picked up the alpaca/silk yarn Joan had spun and ran it through my fingers. The rich mocha color of the fiber was perfect for her project. "This is so lovely. Have you spun enough to complete the sweater?"

"I wouldn't let myself start until I had," she confessed.

I watched with amazement as she furiously knit on the sweater for her daughter, picking up the dropped stitches awkwardly but with amazing patience. The back piece she'd completed was as soft as I'd imagined it would be, the open lace pattern perfect for a cool summer evening along the lake.

"Your daughter will love it."

"I hope so. There isn't much money for gifts this year, my husband is quick to tell me, what with all the medical bills."

"Isn't it too bad that we spend time worrying about paying for gifts at this time of year when we should be celebrating the gift of family and friends," Sue Ellen said. "You wouldn't believe the list my kids have made, dreamers that they are."

My feelings toward the group warmed even more these days, knowing we shared so many mutual feelings. I wondered if I'd ever be able to share my personal problems with them the way they shared with each other. I longed for someone to tell me that my problems with the other house and my fear of the threats would disappear eventually.

Nancy was hard at work on what looked to be a man's ski sweater and, I had to admit, doing a beautiful job. The complicated Fair Isle pattern looked so far beyond my reach that I couldn't imagine tackling it, and I had to give her a grudging respect.

"That sweater is gorgeous," I sighed. "Whoever is the recipient is very lucky."

"Thanks," she mumbled without saying who the lucky guy was.

Had she connected with Riley after all? The last time I'd seen Riley, he wore a hand-knit sweater. I knew I'd seen the pattern before. Nancy could've been working on it when I first joined the group. I wasn't about to ask.

In any case, she was welcome to him. After that last encounter in the library and the way he'd shut me out, I'd lost interest, no matter how gorgeous his smile. Whatever spiritual connection I'd imagined between us had been some sort of aberration on my part, a slip back into adolescence, if you will. It wouldn't be repeated.

I CALLED MY GIRLS AND INVITED THEM TO SPEND Christmas on the farm, and surprisingly, they both agreed. That kept me busy for the rest of the month, baking their favorite ginger and frosted sugar cookies and cleaning and even doing a little shopping. Not quite the same selection as Michigan Avenue, of course, but I found shopping in the small local shops to be a lot more fun. People recognized me and took the time to visit.

My family arrived together early Christmas Eve. Lexie and Donald had flown into Chicago the previous day and spent the night with Brooke.

"Wow, this place is beautiful. It'll be worth a lot of money when you sell," were the first words out of Donald's mouth. A Robert remark if I ever heard one. I looked over at Lexie in alarm.

They say daughters marry men just like their fathers. My hope was she wouldn't follow in my footsteps. Was she too docile to stand up to a man like her father? Brooke was a different story. Maybe I hadn't been the best role model for Lexie. The thought was enough to keep me awake that night.

I'd decorated the house with greens from the woods and put up a large Fraser Fir tree, with Tony's help, of course.

We gathered around the tree, open boxes of ornaments spread out around us.

"I made hot chocolate. Who wants a cup?" I asked.

"I do," they all answered."

"Don't forget the marshmallows," Lexie called out as I made my way to the kitchen.

"And some cookies would be nice," her sister called after me.

Walking back into the room, sounds of the Muppets Christmas album greeted me. It was part of the tradition.

"Oh, look. Remember this?" Brooke held up a wooden ornament she'd made in Girl Scouts one year and hung it carefully on the tree.

"Look at this," Lexie cried, holding out one of her favorites, a red glass ornament with the family portrait glued on the front. "I remember that year. It was the year I got Molly, my American Girl doll." She turned to me with shining eyes. "Remember, Mom? I'm saving her for my future daughter."

When we finished, I looked at the newly decorated tree with a heart filled with anticipation about my life and future. What a turnaround from last year when I barely managed to keep things together for the girls. But I wouldn't think about that empty house now and everything connected to it. This was a new start for all of us. But keeping secrets from my daughters was damn difficult.

Every time I remembered those threatening notes and blood-red graffiti on the bedroom walls, a wave of nausea roiled in my abdomen, threatening to spill the contents of my stomach. The words, I KNOW WHERE YOU ARE, popped into my mind at the most inopportune times. If he did know, what was he waiting for? Was he trying to drive me mad?

LATER, WE WENT TO THE EVENING MASS AT ST.

Anthony's, where Father John welcomed us warmly and people stopped to shake our hands in greeting.

Tony and Sue Ellen were there with their children, and they gave me a hug before shaking hands with the girls and Donald. They acted like we'd been friends for years, and of course, Tony had to bring up the story about the sheep in the basement. Only Lexie laughed. Brooke and Donald looked too shocked to speak.

Carol and her sons came in just in time for the service. The boys looked rather spiffy with their neatly combed hair, wearing dress shirts and pants. I don't think I'd ever seen them in anything but jeans and tee-shirts with obnoxious sayings, wearing bored expressions. Sadly, their expressions hadn't changed. They hurried Carol into a pew before we could talk, no doubt hoping the sooner the service started, the faster it'd be over.

My family was a little taken aback. They were used to the larger city parishes where they could blend in with the crowd in anonymity. Lexie's face flushed with pleasure, but the other two hung back in discomfort. Way too much touchy-feely for them to enjoy.

WHEN WE GOT HOME, WE SAT ON THE RED COUCH IN front of the stone fireplace, basking in the cheery firelight as we sipped a hot toddy and opened gifts. It was a real Hallmark moment. The handmade items were a hit, as I'd expected. Even Maeve seemed to enjoy her new doggy sweater. After I extracted it from her sharp little teeth and put it on her, that is.

"Mom, maybe next year you'll be the one knitting our gifts." Lexie took the words right out of my mouth.

"You can plan on it."

"Or maybe by that time, Mom will have recovered her senses and moved back to civilization," Brooke quipped, shattering my contented feelings.

Okay, we were back to the status quo.

"What's the matter with you? Can't you let Mom live her life the way she wants? Does everything have to be about you and what you want?" Lexie's face flushed in annoyance.

Brooke flinched. I don't ever remember my youngest daughter talking back to her sister that way. As much as it cheered a part of me to see it finally happen, Christmas wasn't the time for their first major battle—especially not on my behalf.

"Okay, what do you say we take a walk out to the barn to see if the animals really do speak at midnight on Christmas Eve?" The memory of the fable from their childhood popped into my head.

Brooke looked at me like I'd lost my mind, but Lexie's eyes lit with pleasure. She giggled like the happy child of my memories.

"Let's do it." She jumped up from the couch, eager to go.

"You've got to be kidding," Donald said. When he saw we were serious, he shook his head in disbelief. "I'll wait here," he said, rolling his eyes for Brooke's benefit. He was getting more like Robert with each passing day.

I looked at Lexie. Would she decide to stay in the warm house with him?

"Okay, suit yourself," she said.

"That's my girl," I whispered for my ears only.

The three of us put on our jackets and boots and tramped out to the barn with Maeve running ahead. Our breath hung in the air like frozen mist as we laughed and talked our way across the yard, even Brooke joining in the laughter at the collie's antics. I flicked on the overhead light, and the sheep raised their heads and trotted over to the gate, always up for a little extra handout.

"I don't hear anything," Brooke said dryly. "The dog hasn't said a word either."

I was happy to see Lexie reach over and pet their fuzzy heads. "Hi, guys, are you having a good life? I know you must be if my mom is taking care of you."

That pleased me more than it should have, but I needed encouragement and would take it whenever I could get it. Much as I loved Brooke, her constant sniping was wearing me down. I was in danger of losing all my self-confidence around her.

We only stayed a few minutes as the temperature had fallen again. Brooke ran ahead to the house, Maeve nipping at her heels in Border collie fashion.

"Mom, I'm sorry for biting off Brooke's head in there, but sometimes she really ticks me off. I think it's great, the way you're making a new life for yourself."

"Thanks, honey. It means a lot to have your support." I put my arm around her shoulders and gave her a squeeze.

"Don't let her get you down. You're gonna make it here. You've transformed yourself into a whole new person, and I'm so proud of you. It's made me realize I need to stand up and be my own person, too."

Looking at her earnest expression in the crisp night air, my spirits lifted. Any doubt she wouldn't do it disappeared.

It was two days later that I went out early to the barn, anxious to finish with the chores and get back in the kitchen to fix everyone a good breakfast before they left for Chicago. We'd had a wonderful Christmas day together, and I hated to see them leave, but it was time for us all to get back to our own lives.

In my haste, I slipped on a patch of ice in front of the barn door. As soon as I felt the twist to my right ankle, I knew it was bad. I went down with a whoosh, landing in the bank of snow along the path with a hard thump. You'd think it wouldn't have hurt so much with all my padding.

I tried to stand, but the minute I put weight on my foot, a stabbing pain shot up my ankle. I had to get to the house, no matter the pain. The other option was to lie in a snowbank and scream until someone heard me. Which was tempting, but not feasible with all the doors shut.

The pain was excruciating by the time I reached the porch, and I grasped the railing with relief. Getting up the stairs was a feat of endurance. I pushed open the door and fell into the entranceway. I could see Brooke in the kitchen.

"Brooke, I need your help."

She came around the corner, wearing a frown until she saw me. "What happened? You're white as a sheet."

"I slipped on the ice and twisted my ankle. It hurts like hell. Help me get my boot off."

She unlaced my boot and gently pulled it off. The ankle had already puffed up twice its usual size.

By this time, Lexie and Donald had come down the stairs. I was feeling bad, but when Lexie saw me, she looked worse.

"My god, Mom. It looks broken. We've got to get you to the emergency room right away." Her face crumpled with worry.

"It's probably just twisted. Don't get all excited. Let's put some ice on it."

"We'll put ice on it, but you're going to the emergency room whether you like it or not," Brooke said, her jaw in a determined line.

For once, I was happy with Brooke's take-charge personality and acquiesced. I didn't know if it was broken or twisted, but I knew I needed pain medication.

Lots of it.

Now.

Brooke muttered about being out in the sticks all the way to the hospital, but I managed to tune her out. Lexie and Donald insisted on coming along, and we made our way into the ER, looking like escapees from the L.L.Bean catalogue.

Except for me, of course. I hadn't taken the time to dress nicely, or even comb my hair for that matter, before rushing out to feed the sheep. Didn't want to waste any time. I had on my barn jacket and gloves and knew I gave off the faint odor of wet sheep. That's what I got for letting them rush me out to the car before I had a chance to think. I scanned the waiting room, hoping I wouldn't see a familiar face in the crowd.

SEVERAL HOURS LATER, WE WERE ON OUR WAY BACK to the farm, my pain level down due to the meds. Even Brooke was looking sweet and gentle to me at this point.

The ankle wasn't broken, but the ligaments had been badly twisted. Luckily, I didn't need a surgical repair. I'd have to wear a boot and stay off my feet for some time, however.

"How am I going to get out to the barn to feed the sheep?" It was my main concern, and I had voiced it several times. No one gave me an answer.

I asked again on the trip home.

"We'll worry about that later." Brooke gave her perfected sigh. "I suppose I can stay a few days."

I decided to let it go for the time being. Lexie and Donald ran up the stairs to get their luggage. They were leaving for Chicago in a rental car so as not to miss their flight back east.

"Mom, I don't want to leave you like this." Lexie threw a look in her sister's direction. "I could take a week off, let them find a substitute."

"That's not necessary. Your sister can handle things here." Donald waved her concerns aside. "There's no way we can get new reservations during the holidays."

Lexie stood at the door, coat in hand, still hesitating.

"Hurry or we'll miss our flight out of O'Hare." Donald picked up their bags and walked to the rental car.

"It'll be all right, kiddo. Brooke will stay a few days, and then I'll be back on my feet."

She bent down and whispered as she hugged me, "I love you, Mom. Don't let her boss you around too much."

"We'll get along just fine." I wished I could believe it. I caressed the bottle of pain pills in my pocket.

IT WAS THE NEXT MORNING WHILE SITTING IN THE living room with my ice-wrapped ankle propped on a footstool that I realized Brooke had to go out and feed and water the sheep. This did not bode well for the animals; they were used to a soothing voice and petting along with the food. And what about mucking out the pen? That was a whole other problem. Of course, I hadn't bothered to show her how things were done—like she'd have been interested. You couldn't plan for disasters like this, I guess. They just blew in on the whims of fate.

"You have to give them grain and hay, remember."

"Yes, Mother. I got it."

"And don't forget to give them clean water."

"This is so stupid. Why you would want to do this...at your age." She stamped toward the door, bringing back memories of the miserable teenager she'd been. "I just knew I'd get dragged into this *lifestyle* change of yours. I should be home in my condo, toasty and warm, celebrating the holidays with friends."

I stared at the door after she left. Wasn't it supposed to be the invalid who reverted to childish behavior?

The phone interrupted my foray into self-pity

land. "Hello." It was Carol. Luckily, Brooke had thought to put it within reach before going outside.

"Hi. How was your holiday?"

It was good to hear Carol's voice, a touch of normalcy in the midst of emotional turmoil.

"Fine. How was yours?" Okay, so I lied. It was a hard habit to break.

"Well, that didn't sound too enthusiastic. Is your family still there?"

"They've all left but Brooke—she's staying for a few more days."

Should I tell her about my ankle? I knew if I did, she'd be over in a flash, ready to help. But I was already beholden to her and didn't want to ask for more. I didn't like having to depend on the kindness of others. I wanted to do things for myself.

Yet here I was, in need of their help yet again. Someone had to show Brooke how to care for the sheep, no matter how much she protested. The dog I could handle. I bit back my pride and told Carol about my fall.

"Wow, I'll bet your daughter's not too thrilled." After meeting Brooke, it hadn't taken Carol long to figure out the girl's feelings on country living.

"That's an understatement. She just went out to the barn, muttering under her breath. I know she hasn't a clue as to what to do. I told her where to find the grain and how much hay to give them and to fill the water buckets, but still..."

"I'll come over and help her."

"Well, good luck with that," I said. "She doesn't take kindly to advice, especially from strangers."

"Give me a little credit. I learned something about headstrong kids from my years of teaching. I can handle her."

Carol pulled her van right up to the barn a few minutes later. It wasn't long before she and Brooke appeared in the doorway. Brooke had that tight smile that showed she was unhappy. Carol either didn't notice or ignored her.

"So, how's the ankle?" Carol looked at my boot and crutches. "Getting around on that will be a problem for a while, especially with this snowy weather."

"Yeah. But I'll manage," I said.

"Well, you won't be making trips to the barn for some time."

"The doctor said she had to take it easy for several weeks," Brooke piped up.

"How long will you be staying?" Carol asked her.

"I'm staying until the weekend." Brooke chewed her lower lip in that way she had since childhood. I could tell she was worried about me. "Tax time starts then, our busiest season."

"Don't worry about a thing. We live close enough that taking care of the animals until your mom is up and about is not a problem."

Instead of making Brooke feel better, I could see it annoyed her. "I was thinking she could come back to Chicago with me if someone could take care of things here."

"We could do that."

"No, that's not an option." That's all I needed, to be under her roof and total care. I could see myself regressing to that person I was last May.

"This is my home now, and I'm not leaving. It's not as if I am bedridden, for God's sake." I made a grab for my crutches, forgetting about the icepack, and had to sit back down again when it fell to the floor. "All I need is someone to feed the animals for a short time. Once I get walking, I can handle things in the barn."

They both looked at me with skepticism as Carol replaced the icepack. I stared right back without flinching. No one was ever again taking away my independence.

10

BROOKE PACED UP AND DOWN THE KITCHEN TWO DAYS later, about to drive me to the wine bottle and it was only II a.m.

"Why don't you go for a walk—burn off some of that energy," I suggested. If she was home, she would've already been at work for several hours.

"Walk to where? I don't see a Starbucks on the horizon."

"Drive into Green Bay then. Go to the mall. Whatever."

"And leave you out here in the boonies all alone? Don't think so."

"I can handle things, Brooke."

She looked at me, opened her mouth, and then closed it. Maybe it was my expression.

Honest to God, if she told me one more time how much easier it would've been for me to go to

Chicago, I swear I was either going to beat her with a crutch or just lie down and cry. Things were not looking too good for my drive toward independence at the moment.

FINALLY, THE DAY CAME FOR BROOKE TO LEAVE, AND we stood at the door saying our goodbyes.

"Now, Mom, you'll call me if you need help, right?" Her luggage in hand and wearing the hand-knit cap and scarf I'd given her for Christmas, she suddenly looked like the young girl I remembered. "Promise?"

"Yes, I promise." I would've agreed to anything at that point if it would remove the worried expression on her face. I hated this role-reversal game she was hell-bent on playing.

"Remember to keep your foot elevated while you're sitting and—"

"Brooke, I can handle it." I hobbled over and gave her a hug while she was still in the mood. "You'd better get going before the snow starts." The weatherman had predicted snow by late afternoon. I had my own worries about her driving to Chicago alone in this weather. "Is your cell charged?" At her nod, I continued. "And you'll call as soon as you get home?"

"Okay, Mom, now who's overdoing the worry bit?"

That brought us both a laugh. "We're quite a

pair, aren't we?" I gave her another quick squeeze, to hell with her personal space. I followed her out to the porch, my crutches tap-tapping across the hardwood floors, and lifted one crutch in a goodbye wave as she pulled away.

My heart weighed heavy, my emotions mixed. I hated to see her leave. She would always be my little girl, my firstborn. On the other hand, she drove me nuts if we were together for any length of time. Was she right about my move here? Had I made a disastrous mistake?

Back in the house, I tried to look at my new home with a stranger's eye. I hobbled over to the patio doors and watched the snow as it began falling gently on the fields and woods. So beautiful, so peaceful. My spirits lifted just looking at the scene. How could this possibly have been a mistake?

Okay, so it may have been a gigantic fiscal error, but I'd never regret it. I wouldn't give up the months spent here for anything. I had learned so much during this time, about myself and about life in general. I'd been forced to spread my wings and take chances.

Maeve whimpered in her kennel, and I opened the door. She vaulted out and streaked across the room, her little black-and-white body writhing with pent-up energy. After circling the kitchen table several times, she finally stopped long enough to catch her breath and get a drink of water.

"Brooke's gone now. We can get back to our normal living style." She cocked her head in that intent way she always did when I talked to her, and I swear she looked around and sighed in relief before promptly peeing on the kitchen floor. She'd spent a lot of time in her kennel while Brooke was in charge and apparently had her own issues with independence.

I lay back on the couch after cleaning up the mess and put my foot up on pillows as ordered. As if I wouldn't have anyway—after all, I was the one feeling the pain. Maeve immediately jumped up and plopped down in my lap, making a little nest for herself in the afghan I'd spread over my legs. I picked up one of the library books I was reading, entitled *Training Your Sheep Dog*. Now that I had so much time on my hands, I should be able to learn a lot about animal husbandry and do a lot of spinning.

Holy camolie. According to this book, I had better find ways to occupy the pup or be ready for disaster. She was a high-energy breed with a quick intelligence. I couldn't argue with that. The book made it sound like my answer to the problem would be keeping her busy with the sheep.

"You'd better rest up," I told her. "According to this book, we've got a lot of work ahead of us, young lady."

. . .

THE NEXT DAY, AS I DEBATED THE WISDOM OF TAKING down the Christmas decorations so early, my thoughts once again turned to Riley and Jake. I wondered what kind of Christmas they'd had.

I assumed Riley didn't have any relatives close by, but what about Jake's mother? I'd heard she was a local girl gone wild in her youth, but I hadn't heard anything about her whereabouts now. I was dying of curiosity but didn't feel right asking. Although I don't know if anyone here would consider it prying if I did. The locals didn't seem to have any trouble discussing my life among themselves.

I knew if Jake was gone for the holidays it would be rough on Riley. But then, for all I knew, Riley could've spent the time with Nancy or some other woman. Just because I hadn't heard anything about his private life didn't mean he didn't have one. Wait a minute. What was I thinking? *Private* life was a misnomer around here anyway. I'd learned more about my neighbors than I'd ever imagined, and all without asking. Everyone just seemed to take it for granted I'd be interested, as if we were all old friends.

Because of my injury, I'd miss the first week of school in January. I decided to call Riley so Jake would be forewarned. I'd learned a change in routine was one of the things that could be very upsetting to a child with his condition. He had to know about changes ahead of time to give him time to adjust.

I dithered around all day, trying to get up the nerve to call their home. Hopefully, Jake would answer and I could explain things to him.

But what if Riley answered? How would he react? After that episode in the library, I was gun-shy. Would he tell me to mind my own business again?

In the end, it didn't matter. I had to put on my big-girl pants and do what was best for Jake.

I picked up the phone, my gut tightening in rebellion. I dialed Riley's number. He answered after only a few rings.

"Hello."

The deep timbre of his voice sent an unwanted thrill through my body. I immediately pictured his handsome face and compelling eyes. My throat locked.

"Hello," he repeated, a twinge of annoyance in his voice.

"Mr. O'Connor?" I hated that darned hesitancy in my voice again and cleared my throat, determined to do better. This was ridiculous. "This is Martha LeBeau calling, the paraprofessional from Jake's class."

"What can I do for you, Ms. LeBeau?" he asked in a guarded tone.

"Would you please give Jake a message for me? Tell him I won't be in school all next week. I thought he should be prepared."

"Is something wrong?"

"Nothing serious. I had a minor accident, and

I'm temporarily incapacitated." Sheesh, why didn't I just tell the man I slipped and fell on my butt and twisted my ankle? No, I needed to keep a wall of formality between us.

Silence for a moment. "Is there anything Jake and I can do for you?"

That shocked me.

"No, I'll be fine and back to school the following week. I just thought Jake should be told. I know how important it is that he's prepared for any change in routine." I wish I could've bit off that last part. Nothing like a little unwanted advice. "Thank you for offering though," I said hurriedly and hung up the phone before he could make a snarky reply.

How had we gotten off to such a bad start when all I wanted to do was help him and his son?

Joan came over the afternoon of New Year's Eve for a private spinning lesson. I don't know how her husband felt about driving her back and forth, but it didn't seem to be a problem with Joan. The other Wool Gatherers were busy with family doings that week between Christmas and New Year's. Just as well since I wasn't up to trudging out in the snow in my boot or having the group here, as much as I missed their company.

I was surprised to see her using a cane instead of the walker.

"Oh, yeah. I got rid of that thing a few days ago.

We're working on driving a car in therapy now." She dragged her left foot a bit as she crossed the room to the chair I'd set next to my spinning wheel. Her gait was still off, but it was remarkably improved from when we'd first met.

"I can't believe how well you've done."

"So they say. But it won't mean a thing until I get my independence back."

"I hear ya." I could've bitten my tongue as soon as the words were out. As if my little accident was any comparison to what she'd been through.

"I'm sick and tired of asking my husband to drive me everywhere...not used to it and never will be. He gets that martyred look on his face and I just want to smack him."

After several days with Brooke, I had an inkling of what she'd been going through for months. It must've been especially bad today. I'd never heard her complain before.

"Take my advice," she continued. "Never let anyone tell you they want to take care of you. It's a trap. It might be made of silken threads, but it's just as confining nonetheless." She sat down heavily and rested her cane on the back of the chair. "Enough of my jabbering. Let's get to work. Do you have the bobbins ready?"

At my nod, she continued. "Today you're going to learn how to ply two or three strands of yarn together."

"Ooo-kay." She had a lot more faith in my abilities than I did.

"You could use the single ply you've already spun onto the bobbins for knitting, but in most cases, a two-ply yarn is best." She grabbed a strand of yarn from each filled bobbin and threaded them through the orifice of the wheel, tying them onto the empty bobbin on the wheel. "Plying strengthens the yarn, and also makes it more even. When you ply them together, if you're lucky, the thick places on one strand will match with all the thin places on the other strand. It works especially well with the lumpy, bumpy yarn of a beginner."

She showed me how the yarn from the two bobbins was twisted together in an anti-clockwise direction—the opposite direction in which the singles were spun. This made the plied yarn softer and bulkier than the singles.

"This is fun," I commented, liking the speed of the process. It went a lot quicker than the spinning and I soon had a full bobbin. We worked and talked for an hour or more before I remembered that this was probably tiring for her.

"How about a cup of tea or coffee?"

She looked at her watch. "Carl will be here any minute." She grimaced. "He doesn't like waiting."

The two of us made our way slowly toward the door so we could watch for his car.

"Aren't we a pair?" she quipped. "Me with a bum

arm and leg and you with a bum ankle. But we got a lot done today. Just goes to show what a couple of stubborn dames can do if they're determined enough."

I flushed with pride at the comparison. If only I had half of this woman's determination. I could learn so much from her. And spinning was the least of it. I hated to see her leave.

"It's just us again, missy. How should we ring in the New Year?" I sat on the couch later, Maeve stretched out beside me, trying unsuccessfully to get thoughts of Riley and how he'd be celebrating out of my head. Why I even cared was a mystery best left unsolved. The dog cocked her adorable black-and-white face, listening intently to her morose owner and searching for her favorite word—cookie—in my words. She gave a sharp bark.

"Yes, I know. No more pity parties. You've told me that before."

She jumped to the floor and ran to the kitchen. Why did our conversations always end with her getting a treat?

I hobbled along behind her, deciding to put her out one more time before bed. I looked out into the dark night. The air smelled crisp and fresh, and a full moon reflected off the snow, lighting up the winter night. I could see my neighbors' lights twinkling in the distance, and I didn't feel so alone. I wondered how my sheep were doing. I hadn't been to the barn for almost a week, and I missed them. I hated leaving their care to others. It was that nurturing instinct I just couldn't suppress coming out again.

Maeve didn't stay out long, too cold to dawdle.

"Let's make fudge," I said. "We'll have our own party." She didn't look too enthused; instead, she padded over to her dish to see if it had magically filled up while she was out. "Just because you can't eat chocolate, don't give me attitude, young lady," I said.

We curled up on the couch at midnight, watching the ball lower in Time's Square. Well, the dog curled up anyway. My leg was sticking out in front of me on the ottoman.

I bit off a piece of fudge and washed it down with merlot, trying to dispel the image of Riley and Nancy celebrating together. "Happy New Year, Maeve," I said and kissed her wet, black nose.

SUZE SHOWED UP AT MY DOOR A FEW DAYS LATER, carrying a thermal bag and a stack of magazines. The shocked look on my face when I answered the door had her ducking her head with embarrassment.

"I know, I know. I should've called. But when the bad weather finally broke, I just grabbed the opportunity to get up here. I was afraid your damn newfound independence would rear its ugly head and you'd tell me not to come." She set her things down and gave me a hug.

"Brooke stopped on her way through and said the neighbors were taking good care of you." She gave me one of her penetrating looks. "And how is that going?"

I looked away, not willing to admit, even to her, what an ungrateful slug I was.

I'd been alone in the house for several days except for the short afternoon visits with Carol and the one from Joan. I blamed my bad behavior on a severe case of cabin fever.

"It's going okay, considering I've been shut in here with mostly my own company for days."

"Well, I have something that will perk you up a bit. You'll never believe what I found in the attic while putting away Christmas decorations." She plopped a stack of knitting books in my lap. "I don't know what ever possessed me to keep these old patterns of Gram's. Maybe I had some wild dream of trying to knit at some point in my life."

"Suze, you really should try it. You won't believe how relaxing it is. When nothing else in your life is going right, just knowing that if you keep putting those stitches on the needle, you'll create something beautiful—or at least useful—is comforting."

"Relaxing is not a word that fits into my lifestyle at the moment," she muttered.

So, she hadn't made the trip up here just to drop

off knitting books. Things were making more sense. "What happened?"

She bent down to pet the dog, avoiding my glance.

"I'm probably just making a major problem where there isn't one. Ignore me."

"Wait a minute. You can't just drop a statement on me like that and then walk away from it."

She lifted angst-filled eyes. "It's Nora. She and Dave are having problems." There was a catch to her voice. "I've never seen her so miserable."

"Oh, Suze, I'm so sorry." Nora was Suze's oldest child and had been living with her boyfriend, Dave, for years. He'd already been accepted as part of their family. It seemed like forever that we'd been waiting for a wedding announcement. "What happened? Can you talk about it?"

"I would if I knew what the hell was going on between those two. Nora came home the other night, crying her heart out. She wouldn't say much, other than they were having *problems*, and asked if she could stay."

"That doesn't sound so unusual. They'll work things out. Every couple has their ups and downs, you know that." Why is it that those familiar bromides just fall off your lips when faced with someone's troubles? Do they comfort the one repeating them because deep down we so desperately want it to be true?

"How I wish I could believe that. I have this

awful premonition the problem goes much deeper than she's letting on."

We made our way into the kitchen, and I pulled out the coffee pot.

"Thanks for listening, anyway. I didn't come up here to unload my problem on you."

"Hey, that's what sisters are for, right?"

"Let's not talk about it anymore. I can't fix it anyway." She opened the large thermal bag she'd brought and took out the familiar grease-stained bags from our favorite hamburger joint. "Let's eat while these are still warm."

I wasn't about to argue with her and sat at the table while she got things organized.

I didn't mind having my big sister wait on me. I'd learned a lot of my nurturing skills from her after all. Mom was too busy working minimum-wage jobs to help support the family. Only, Suze had managed to learn where to draw the line on that nurturing thing, something I was still working on.

Suze left late that afternoon, not wanting to tempt fate and the weather. We'd talked more about Nora and Dave, but there really wasn't much I could say to help her. She assured me again she felt better after talking to me though. This was a switch in our relationship. I'd always been the one going to her with my troubles.

That evening, I thumbed through the knitting books for hours trying to decide on a pattern I liked.

A lot of them were outlandish sixties patterns with garish colors and bold stitching. But some were classics with colors that would never go out of style. Finally, I found the one I wanted.

The pattern came from a book of authentic Irish knits. It said in the introduction that every stitch originated long ago in the cottages of Ireland's Galway coast and the Aran Islands. They told Irish tales in their stitches, symbols of life, faith, family, and work; symbols of the sea, the rocks, and the hills. I chose a pattern with an interlocked maze of cables in the wide center panels. I felt it told a story of many kinfolk and many marriages joined together in this ongoing story of life with all its joys and tragedies.

How would Robert and I have fit into this pattern? Would the cable of our intertwining marriage show a break or continue on? I wanted it to go on and the pattern to continue through the lives of our children and grandchildren, adding more cables as people entered our lives.

If I knit this sweater of my handspun yarn from my own sheep, it would connect me to my grandmother and my ancestors before her. I would be one of them. Her long-ago faith in me would not go unrewarded. I would never be rich or famous, but I could do this one little thing to preserve our family heritage.

It was a tradition I could pass down to my daughters, or granddaughters if I ever had any, connecting us all together with our family history. My new goal in life was to get enough yarn spun for the project.

THE NEIGHBORS HAD KEPT TO A SCHEDULE TO TAKE care of the sheep for me all that week. Early that Thursday morning, I watched Tony's truck pull into the driveway and go straight to the barn. School had started that Monday but I wasn't there. I missed the kids, especially Jake. We'd formed a bond, and I was anxious to see how he would do after the long vacation.

Carol came after school, or, if she was busy, one of her sons showed up. She usually stopped in for a short visit and called frequently to see if I needed anything from the store. I knew any offer of payment would be taken as an insult and quickly rebuffed. It left me feeling frustrated instead of simply grateful as I should've been.

They held the spinning group at my home that week, now that I was more mobile. My emotions were in a constant state of flux. Grateful one moment for these wonderful friends, afraid of being obligated to them the next.

How would I repay these new people who'd entered my life? They brushed aside all my thanks, saying that's what neighbors did around here. It left me with guilt feelings when I should've been feeling relief.

I finally cast aside the boot and was able to walk without the crutches. I'd be back in school next week as planned. I still had a slight limp because of the pain and stiffness, but I knew if I continued my exercises and used a little caution I'd be as good as new. The one bright spot in my weeks of incapacitation was that I got a lot of spinning done. Thankfully, I only needed one foot to peddle my spinning wheel. I now had enough yarn to start on a sweater.

SEVERAL WEEKS LATER, MS. BRICE AND I WERE preparing the class for parent/teacher conferences.

"I'd like you to sit in on the conferences for the children you've been helping."

"Are you sure, Addy? I haven't been here that long." I still didn't feel qualified to judge the children's progress, and my anxiety level started to sky-rocket. Especially when I realized it meant I'd have to talk to Riley.

"Anything you can tell the parents that will help them deal with their child better on a daily basis will be so helpful. I know you've learned a lot in your classes because I've seen the results in the classroom. Don't worry, I'll be here to guide things."

Her attitude toward me had softened considerably since my time off with the injured ankle, and we had progressed to a first-name basis. I guess she'd decided I was worth having around.

I really wanted to help with the conferences,

and her words gave me the confidence I needed. After dealing with the kids all day, I had a lot of empathy for the parents. The methods I'd been taught were so simple, yet immensely helpful, and I was eager to share.

The first two interviews went well, and the parents were very receptive to my ideas. My nerves stretched to the breaking point, though, when it was time to meet with Riley on a face-to-face basis. Our last interlude had left me feeling anything but confident. I hadn't seen him since, but I'd heard his name bandied about plenty, especially by Nancy. She was out to get his attention, no doubt in that corner.

When he came into the classroom, looking ridiculously out of place among the small desks and chairs, my heart did that familiar flip-flop. I flashed him a friendly smile. It was hard to believe a man his age was still dealing with a second grader. He had to be, at the very least, in his late forties. That could be in Jake's favor, though. More than likely, he had more patience and understanding than a twenty-eight-year-old father would've had.

"Ms. LeBeau will tell you about Jake's social progress. She's taken some special classes in that area and has proven to be very helpful to the students." We were seated around Adele's desk, sitting on student chairs like two giants in Lilliputian Land. "Jake hasn't had any problems in the academic area as long as Ms. LeBeau is here to see that things are going well for him in the classroom."

Just then another teacher poked her head in the door and said, "Adele, you're wanted in the office."

"Excuse me," Adele said. "I'll be back as soon as I can."

I started to explain the methods I'd learned in my classes that Adele and I were using to lower Jake's frustration level and how he was beginning to relate better socially to the other kids.

"What activities is Jake involved in? Being with other kids in fun activities would give him more practice with his social skills."

"I do the best I can to keep him involved but it isn't easy." His nostrils flared, and he straightened up abruptly.

"I'm sure you do, Mr. O'Connor. Jake is a lovely boy."

His expression said he was taking all of this as a personal affront on his care of Jake.

"What I want to suggest is that he might benefit from a form of group therapy called Cognitive Behavior Therapy that I learned about in my classes— to help him get along better with his peers." Where was Adele? I didn't seem to be handling this well.

He looked skeptical.

"You've probably noticed he doesn't 'read' other people well but takes things too literally. In this therapy, he and the other children learn to interact with each other, guided by the therapist."

"Yeah, I've noticed it." He straightened in the chair. I'd piqued his interest. "Where do we have to go for these sessions?"

"I'll get some information and send it home with Jake. You check his backpack every night, right?"

His mouth twisted in a form of grin. "Yes, teacher. I check it every night, just like you told us at the beginning of the school year."

Now, I was embarrassed. I had gone into that condescending but authoritative teacher's voice I'd always detested.

"He seems to connect well with Daniel Baker." I'd recognized what good friends they'd become when he handed Jake the kitten at the Christmas Festival. "I've been fostering a relationship between them, pairing them as a team whenever I can."

"Dan's a great kid." He relaxed back into the small chair, clearly at ease now.

"Is it possible for you to invite him over to your home occasionally?" I asked. "So they get some time together out of the class room?"

"I'll try." His glance swept noncommittally over my face. "Anything else?"

"I'm sure you're already aware of how important it was to help Jake with organization." But his closed expression didn't give me a clue as to his thoughts about that.

"I've also learned some things which you probably are well aware of but I'll mention them anyway.

For instance, it's very important when he has a meltdown, like in the library, to take note of what occurred beforehand. Was it an unexpected change in routine, for example, or was he unusually tired? I've had a couple of incidences in the classroom that could've been avoided if I'd been paying closer attention, I'm afraid." I gave him a rueful smile. "Once you know the signs, it's easier to distract him before things get out of control. But then, I'm sure you know that already."

Leaning forward in his chair and looking intently into my face, he said in a controlled voice, "What you're saying is all well and good, but how does it relate to his life when I can't be there to help him?"

I had a flashback to Robert and the way he'd looked at me when I tried to give my opinion on financial matters. Those old feelings rose up, and I wanted to back down. I looked around for Addy, but she still hadn't returned.

I turned back to him, angry with myself now for almost wimping out. He might know and love his son, but that could be more of a hindrance than a help in this case. I thought of sweet little Jake and made up my mind. We were going to talk this through. I could tell he was too polite to just get up and leave. I owed it to both of them to persist.

"That's why I suggested the group therapy. It could be really helpful to both you and Jake. There's one more thing I want to mention that you probably have already figured out. Don't try to answer his questions if he keeps repeating them. Change the subject so he can refocus. It took me awhile to get used to that. I kept trying to explain things, and we were getting nowhere."

"You're right. I figured that out for myself."

He slouched back in the chair, jean-clad legs stretched out in front of him like a bored kid, looking everywhere but at me. I began to wonder if he hadn't had his own problems in school as a youngster. He seemed to be reverting back to childish behavior.

"I think it's important that you try these things at home," I said softly. "You may know Jake a lot better than I do, but I've worked with him a lot these past months and I can see he's made substantial progress."

"Okay, sorry." He sat up again. "If you think the therapy will help, I'm all for it. I'll do anything to help my son."

He stood up, gave me an abrupt nod and a curt thank-you, and left. It was hard to tell what he was thinking at that point.

"How'd it go?" Addy asked me later.

"Not too well. He didn't seem too impressed."

"Don't let it get you down. Judging from the few times I've talked to him, Mr. O'Connor is a very concerned parent who wants only the best for his son. He probably just has to adjust to the fact that others might have different ideas about what that is. It's a shame that Jake's mother left them the way she did. It hasn't been easy for him raising the child alone."

I sure hoped she was right because I wanted to see their life get easier wherever possible, even if Riley O'Connor was the most exasperating man I'd ever met.

11

JOAN AND CAROL WERE EXPLAINING THE QUALITIES OF wool from various sheep breeds to me at our Friday night gathering. I was surprised to learn each breed has its own type of fleece.

"Merino produces a soft white yarn you can use for baby sweaters and caps and a nice fluffy shawl," Carol said, holding up a skein. "At the other end of the spectrum is Lincoln, which would make a great rug for your hardwood floors."

Who knew? I'd assumed wool was wool, period.

"I really like a merino/alpaca blend like the sweater I knit for my daughter. You can't beat it for softness and lightweight warmth." Joan's satisfied smile made my own heart swell with pride for her accomplishments. If only she could bottle that determination and sell it.

I'd felt a special connection to Joan since the afternoon she'd spent at my home. When I paid her for the private lesson, her face had flushed and her head lowered. She'd always taught beginners for free. She'd told me then she planned to get her job at the local paper back soon. Her therapy was going well, and she was determined to regain full use of her arm.

"Carl doesn't want me to go back to work," she'd muttered. "He thinks I should stay home and rest. Not gonna happen, I told him."

I pulled my mind back to the present conversation. "How do you know if a fleece is good for spinning?" It all seemed so confusing.

"It's pretty simple, really," Sue Ellen explained. "You look at a lock of the shorn wool called a staple. The crimping, that's the wave pattern in the lock, and the length of the lock will tell you what you need to know. The crimp is what gives the wool elasticity, and you'll want a good length for spinning. The shorter locks are good for felting. You have to decide what it is you want to do with your wool."

"Your Corriedale should be the best fleece for you," she added. "It's a fine/medium grade with a staple length of four to six inches and a close crimp spacing. Very suitable for a beginning spinner. You can knit lovely sweaters with it, and it felts well, too. A Merino fleece may produce a softer yarn, but it would be too difficult for you to handle at this point."

"That's why I settled on the breed," Lila said.

That made a lot of sense. These women were informed and practical. No wonder I admired them so much.

"It's time to get your sheep sheared," Carol said unexpectedly.

"What?" It was February and well below freezing most nights. I knew she'd heard about the episode of the sheep in my basement. Was there anyone in the county who hadn't? I thought at first she was teasing, but her business-like expression told me otherwise.

"Isn't it too cold for a shave?" I had visions of Bridget and Fiona shivering in the barn all night, their skin bare of warm, wooly coats.

"It's better to shear them before they go into labor and much easier for lambs to nurse without all that dirty wool in the way," she explained.

"You can give them extra grain. That'll raise their body heat up," Lila said. She'd been more sympathetic than my milk-producing neighbors about the whole basement fiasco.

Then I remembered her telling me about the extra grain when she first brought the lambs over. Another new fact to process. Oh, lordy, I had so much to learn.

How had this gotten so involved? It had all

seemed so simple when I started out. You get a couple of sheep, you feed them, shear off their wool in the spring, spin yarn, and knit sweaters. Only now, I found there were a lot more steps to the process.

"Who can I get to shear?"

"Riley, of course." Carol looked at me like I was slipping into dementia.

"Anyone *but* Riley." The less I saw of that man, the happier I'd be. He may be good at shearing sheep, but he was lousy at personal relationships.

"Are you crazy? He's the best there is," Lila said.

"We didn't hit it off too well the few times we've met."

All activity stopped. You would've thought I'd said I had a fight with the Pope.

"I never heard of anyone not getting along with Riley," Lila murmured.

"You didn't tell me that." Carol's face lit with interest. "Tell us about it."

"I can't go into it, it's private." It wouldn't be professional to tell tales out of school. "Let's just say I didn't impress him with my teaching credentials." Or with anything else for that matter. The man had made me feel like a worm.

"Your problem is you're too sensitive," Carol said. "Men don't always let on when they're impressed. They have to think about things for a while."

I couldn't hold back a loud laugh. She hadn't seen the annoyed look on his face when I last saw him.

"Regardless, I don't want to call him. I'd rather shear them myself with barber scissors."

"Oh, don't be such a wuss. He's very professional about his work. And I know he likes small jobs because he can take Jake with him. And don't forget to have a good dinner prepared." She laughed at my shocked expression.

"What? What does that have to do with shearing sheep?"

"It's tradition. The host farmer always feeds the shearer if he's there near mealtime." Joan gave me a sympathetic glance.

"Yeah, and if Riley was traveling any distance to the area, you'd have to put him up for the night."

I couldn't believe the dreamy expressions on their faces at the thought.

"It might be worth moving to another city just for that experience alone," Carol said.

"Oh, for crying out loud," I muttered. "You people are unbelievable."

They sure had a different opinion of the man than I did. He might be eye candy to them, but after that awkward thirty-minute session in the classroom, I could easily put my first impression of those dreamy blue eyes down to an aberration of my people-reading skills. When I talked about his son's problems, those eyes had turned downright glacial.

"Now I really don't want to call him." Things were going downhill fast.

"I'll come help," Carol said. Her eager expression was a dead giveaway.

"It'll be fine," Lila assured me. "Maybe they won't even stay for dinner or lunch. Anyway, Jake will be with him, and the two of you get along, right? You can talk to him if being around Riley bothers you so much."

She made it sound so simple. Why didn't I believe her?

THE NEXT MORNING FOUND ME STARING AT THE phone, trying to get up the courage to talk to Riley again.

I kept telling myself I was doing it for my sheep. I wanted the best for them and to get the best spinning fleece possible. Lila had assured me that with Riley I wouldn't get any second cuts, those little short fibers caused by the shearer going over the area twice, and the fleece would come off in one piece—very important for a hand-spinning fleece.

I had to grudgingly admit a part of me wanted to see him again. That was the part that scared me.

Then again, it was possible if we met under these different circumstances that I could smooth things out between us. Common sense told me it was just a misunderstanding. We both only wanted the best for Jake.

But would he even want to come and shear at my place? That was the question of the moment.

I dialed his number, all prepared for a refusal. I just hoped Lila was right, and he'd be professional about it.

"O'Connors."

"Mr. O'Connor, this is Martha LeBeau."

"What can I do for you now, Ms. LeBeau?"

I broke out in a sweat at his guarded tone and rushed to get out the reason for my call.

"I was wondering if you could come out and shear my sheep. I have two ewes that need shearing."

"I could do that."

I heard the relief in his voice. He didn't want to discuss Jake's progress with me any more than I wanted to talk to him about it.

"When did you want them sheared?"

"Whenever it's convenient for you. I'm not in a rush."

"It won't take long to shear two sheep." He paused. "I have to deliver a piece of furniture to Milwaukee on Saturday morning. By the time I get back and get my shearing equipment set up, it'll be late afternoon. Will that work for you?"

"That'll be fine." Even as I said it, I realized it meant I'd have to provide dinner. Why hadn't I spoken up and said it wouldn't work for me?

Because I really was a wuss, that's why.

. . .

WHEN RILEY PULLED UP TO THE BARN LATE SATURDAY afternoon, my nerves were as tight as the elastic in new underwear. I quickly gulped down my coffee and set the cup on the counter. I gave the stew simmering on the stove a quick stir and plugged in the bread machine.

I'd worked all afternoon, preparing for him as the sheep watched with concerned eyes from their pen. They sensed something was going on and looked as uneasy as I felt. Hopefully, they'd settled down after I left.

I had already set up a table in the barn for sorting the wool, put garbage bags out for the dirty stuff, and tried to remember if there was anything else my friends had told me to do.

I was halfway to the barn when another car pulled up. Nancy and Carol climbed out.

"Has he started yet?" Nancy's eyes gleamed with anticipation.

"He just got here," I said, clenching my fists briefly. Was I making it easier for Nancy to spend time with him?

"We came to help," Carol said, hanging back a bit.

I gave her a smirk. Even I wasn't gullible enough to fall for that.

We walked into the barn and saw Riley setting up his equipment. Jake stood by the pen, talking softly to the sheep.

"Hi, Jake," I called out after greeting Riley. "Did you come along to help your dad?"

He gave me a shy smile and nodded.

"I know someone who will be very glad to see you. Come with me." I put out my hand, but he looked toward his father before taking it. After Riley's nod, he grabbed my hand and walked with me out of the barn and toward the house. I found it much easier to deal with Jake than the grown-ups in the barn. I'd leave them to their own devices as long as I dared.

We got Maeve out of her crate where'd I put her for safekeeping while I was busy that afternoon. I didn't think Riley would appreciate her running between his legs while he worked.

The three of us walked to the back pasture, and Jake and Maeve started a game of fetch, running back and forth. It was good to see Jake run with such abandon, something he didn't do on the playground. I knew they'd be safe there, close to the barn and fenced in.

"You can go into the house to warm up if you get cold, Jake."

"Okay," he yelled back, too busy throwing a stick to pay much attention.

I couldn't put it off any longer. I had to go back into the barn.

Riley was doing his stretching exercises in the open area of the barn where he'd do the shearing when I walked in. I noticed he'd put two sheets of plywood down. Easier to keep the wool clean, I assumed. The two women were standing by the table I'd set up, watching him and trying to be discreet. *Give me a break.*

Okay. I had to admit it. It was a sight worth staring at. For a man his age, his body remained lean and toned, and he moved with an easy grace as he stretched his bare arms over his head and then down to the floor, stretching out his back muscles. He'd cut the arms out of his sweatshirt, and the sight of those rippling muscles was rather impressive, even to me, who'd usually equated the largeness of a man's muscles to the smallness of his brain.

"Jake all right?"

I blinked, thrown abruptly out of my fantasy world.

"Yes, he and the dog are playing in the pasture. They'll be safe there. I told him to go in the house if he gets too cold."

Riley finished his stretch and walked over to pull Fiona out of the pen, muscles bulging as he dragged the animal over to the plywood and his shearing machine. With one expert flip, he had the sheep on her back and her loud baaing stopped. She lay as limp as a boiled noodle, mesmerized by the soft hum of the electric clippers and the words he murmured that only she could hear.

He'd managed to get the fleece off her in one

piece except for the soiled belly wool, which I planned to discard.

"Do you want me to trim her hoofs?"

"Oh, could you?" This was an unexpected bonus. I'd been worrying about that for weeks and wondering whom I could ask to teach me how to do it. He had hoof trimmers with him and was done in a flash.

By this time, I'd forgotten all my animosity toward the man and just wanted to give him a big hug.

When he finished, he let Fiona, looking ridiculously naked and embarrassed, out in the paddock. Before Bridget could get too close to the open pen door and follow her sister, Riley had his arms around her, and she was out the pen door in his grasp.

I went over to the table where Carol waited. She showed me how to throw the fleece, cut side down, onto the table and trim a strip about three inches wide from the edges. This removed the belly wool, neck wool, leg wool, and any manure tags, leaving the clean wool for spinning.

The wool was still warm and rich with the feel of lanolin. We measured the length of a lock, and I was really happy to see a staple length of five inches and a close crimp. It would be a good fleece for spinning.

While we were working on the wool, Nancy swept up the plywood and carried on a low conversation with Riley. Try as I might, I couldn't hear what they were saying and still listen to Carol. I shouldn't be the least bit interested, but sue me, I couldn't help it.

Carol and Nancy left soon after we'd finished with Bridget's fleece. While Riley gathered his equipment, I went out into the paddock to get the newly shorn sheep. I wanted them in their pen with extra grain where they'd be warmer.

They weren't anywhere in sight. It took me a moment to notice the gate to the big field had been opened. Uh-oh. Jake must've gone through and forgotten to close it behind him. I eyeballed the area but didn't see my sheep anywhere. Of course, they were a lot smaller now that they'd lost their thick coats of wool.

I walked to the top of the hill in the center of the field and looked over. Empty. A feeling of impending disaster made my heart pick up a beat. They couldn't just disappear. And where were Jake and Maeve? I loped back toward the barn and their paddock. Maybe I'd missed them hiding in a corner or something. By this time, the sun was low in the sky, and I was feeling the cold through my light jacket. I hoped Jake and the dog had gone into the house to warm up.

That's when I saw the gate that led out of the field and toward the house was also wide open. I always kept it locked, even though the sheep would stay in their paddock until later in spring.

I ran through the gate in time to see two naked

sheep wandering along the drive between house and barn. We'd only had snow showers the last few weeks so they searched for sprigs of anything green between the old snowdrifts. As I watched, Jake and Maeve came out of the house. The pup took one look at the sheep, and her herding instincts kicked in. She took off after them like a bat out of hell, and they high-tailed it toward the driveway, no doubt memories of the indignity they'd just endured fresh in their minds.

Fear, stark and vivid, welled up my throat. I picked up my speed, yelling to Jake to get his dad as I ran, and then screamed for Maeve to stop. She, of course, ignored me, intent on doing her job. If they reached the driveway and ran onto the highway be-fore I could reach them, I'd be eating a lot of lamb for the next year or two.

As I got closer, still calling for Maeve to stop at the top of my lungs, a dark streak passed me by.

"Go get a bucket of grain," Riley yelled, his long legs eating up the distance between him and the sheep. "I'll circle around and get in front of them."

By the time I got back with a bucket of grain, the sheep were walking down the road but turned and started back toward me. Riley, with Maeve in his arms, and Jake beside him, formed a barrier behind them, driving them toward my driveway. I rattled the bucket, and they picked up their pace, running toward the familiar sound. Nothing like food to en-tice a pregnant female.

I walked backward, holding the bucket out in front of me. Of course, my neighbor Tony would pick that moment to drive by, stopping as the sheep neared his truck. He waved as I passed and opened his window.

"Trouble?" he asked with a big grin. The neighbors were in for another tale of my greenhorn antics. Oh, well. The sheep were safe, and that was all that mattered.

The animals followed me into the barn, and I locked the pen behind them. Leaning over the gate, I gulped several deep breaths while the adrenaline pumping through my system receded.

"That added a little excitement to the afternoon, didn't it?"

I straightened up and turned to Riley, my chest still heaving. He looked like he hadn't even broken a sweat. "I could do without that kind of excitement, thank you," I managed to choke out.

"How did the sheep get loose?" Riley looked at Jake, and I surmised he'd figured out that answer himself. "Jake?"

Jake stared down at the ground, his chin dipped toward his chest. I felt so sorry for him, I was tempted to cover up the truth, but I knew in my heart that wasn't the answer.

"Jake?" Riley asked again when the boy failed to answer.

"I musta left the gate open when we went in the

house." He swiped at the tears now rolling down his cheeks.

"You've been around animals enough to know better, son." Riley put his hand on the boy's shoulder. "This is a pretty serious matter. What do you say to Ms. LeBeau?"

"I'm sorry, Ms. Martha."

I knelt down in front of him. "I'm sure you'll remember to shut the gate next time, right?"

"I sure will." He nodded emphatically.

"Let's go eat then." I took his hand, and the three of us made our way to the house.

"Is there a place we can wash?"

"Right in here," I said, directing them to the guest bathroom off the kitchen.

Riley had taken off his coveralls, sweatshirt, and work boots in the barn and was looking handsome and relaxed in jeans and a denim work shirt. He could've been my neighbor in suburbia. He didn't fit the pattern I'd formed in my mind of a local farmer. There was no air of bashfulness or self-deprecating humor about him. He gave the impression of a self-confident man, assured of his place in the universe.

I set out our places and put the crock of Irish stew in the center of the table. Lamb had always been a delicacy in our family, but now I was beginning to lose my appetite for it, seeing as how I had a few right in my own barn and become so protective of them. Too late, I wondered how he and Jake felt about it.

Setting the loaf of warm bread on the table, I asked. "I hope you don't have a problem with eating lamb."

He halted, the serving spoon held in midair. "Why would I have a problem with that?"

Now, I really felt stupid. Why had I brought it up? Only city people like me would question such things. I'd learned country people mostly had a different perspective on the cycle of life.

"How did you get into the business of shearing sheep?" I asked, doing a quick change of subject.

"It was one of those serendipitous things. After graduating, it struck me I wasn't the least bit interested in using the business degree I'd just earned. I'd been stupid enough to take the advice of others instead of following my own instincts and going with a fine arts degree.

"To make a long story short, I packed a knapsack and headed abroad for a few years. I found myself in Australia and after finding a job on a sheep station, discovered I had a knack for shearing and handling sheep. Been at it off and on ever since." He refilled his dish while he talked. "It doesn't pay enough to support us, especially in this dairy farm area, but it's a nice diversion from my other work and helps keep me physically fit."

"Those must have been some interesting years," I said with envy.

"Oh, yeah. I saw and learned a lot. Not all of it good, either."

"Whatever made you settle here?" I'd learned a bit of his background previously from Carol. Knowing I wasn't the only one around who wasn't local gave us a connection, and I was curious.

From the guarded look he directed toward Jake, I realized I was getting into personal matters. "Well, that's a different story."

"Whatever. I'm just glad you did," I said, directing my glance at Jake, who'd been listening to our conversation with great interest I now realized. "Otherwise, I wouldn't have met this young man, would I?"

Jake grinned at me. He'd recovered from the disgrace of letting my sheep loose, I was happy to see.

"Did you know your sheep are about ready to deliver?" Riley said with raised eyebrows. "I'd say within the next week or two."

Excitement surged through me at the prospect, but the sensible part of me froze in panic.

"How will I know when to call the vet? And what vet do I call? I don't have a name."

"The vet won't come out for the delivery unless there's a problem. He wouldn't have the time for that. Besides, most large-animal vets around here only deal with horses and cattle. I'm afraid you're on your own."

"What?" I felt the blood drain from my face.

He laughed. "Don't look so scared. The animals handle things by themselves ninety-nine percent of the time. You'll know if one of them is in trouble and have time to call a vet. Although, once in a while, you get a young ewe who doesn't know what to do with the lamb, and you'll have to help her clean it up and put it to nurse until instinct kicks in."

"Oh, boy, that's enough to keep *me* awake at night. I've never seen a sheep being born, or any animal for that matter." I took a deep breath, wondering how I would handle such a catastrophe. "I barely remember the birth of my own children."

"I could come out. If you'd like," he said with a smile.

I felt faint with relief. There'd be no hesitation on my part in calling him this time.

"I would really appreciate it and gladly pay whatever you think fair."

He looked affronted at the suggestion of pay. "Consider it a payback for helping Jake."

Maeve began circling the table in her usual madcap way, trying to get Jake's attention. She knew a soft heart when she saw one. He reached down and handed her a piece of meat.

"Jake, you know better," Riley said.

Jake flushed at the rebuke and looked at me in consternation.

"Eat your dinner," Riley continued.

I didn't know what to do. I wanted Jake to feel at ease, but after that last encounter at school, I was afraid to stick my neck out. After all, this was an entirely different setting, and it was not my place to interfere.

"I'll put her in her crate until we finish eating. Then, you can play with her."

Relief shone in his eyes. He began eating again, and his dad smiled. Had I actually done something right in Riley's presence this time? It was hard to imagine how swiftly this Jake could change into a tantrum-throwing, out-of-control child.

As much as I wanted to forget it, a part of me was still upset at Riley's attitude at the parent/teacher conference. I couldn't help but make the comparison to Robert. I just wished when Riley gazed at his son he didn't look so damned vulnerable. It made me want to give him a hug and tell him all would be well. Like that could ever happen.

I knew he only wanted the best for Jake. Why was he so stubborn, just like most of the men I'd known? And why did I find him so attractive? It wasn't his looks. I'd met handsomer men over the years and never given them a second glance. But when he looked up at me with gratitude in those midnight blue eyes, my heart did a little happy dance. Was it my imagination, or did his eyes show a connection, too?

After Jake finished his dinner and was excused from the table, Riley said casually, "By the way, I've tried your methods of handling Jake, and they're working well." He ducked his head and took a spoonful of stew, hiding his expression now.

"I'd appreciate any other suggestions you could give me. I'm waiting to hear about the group therapy."

I think my mouth hung open in shock. Was that grudging admiration or an apology? I'd assumed he was one of those men who found it difficult to accept advice from a woman, and I couldn't speak for a moment from the shock of it. Finally, I recovered my voice.

"I'd be glad to share anything new I learn."

Had I been wrong in comparing him to Robert?

It struck me then that he was exactly the kind of person I was striving to become. He depended on no one. He and Jake lived alone; he had his own business and, from what I'd heard, socialized only when it suited him. And yet, he was willing to take advice if it would help his son. How could I not admire that?

"Sorry if I cut you off earlier when you asked how I ended up here. No big secret. I met Jake's mother. She was from this area so when we found out she was pregnant, she wanted to come home. Turned out *home* wasn't where she wanted to be after all."

"I'm sorry. I didn't mean to pry." Oh, God, I wished I could crawl in a hole.

"As I said, no big secret." He shrugged. "As a matter of fact, I hate secrets. They only cause trouble."

I didn't have a reply to that. My own secrets lay

heavily on my conscience, but it wasn't something I could share.

Riley and Jake left soon after that. I went back out to the barn and looked with pride at the bags of newly shorn wool. Everything was good.

Why did Riley have to mention secrets and spoil it?

12

I MADE MY NIGHTLY TRIP OUT TO THE BARN BEFORE bed the following week. It had become a ritual now that labor was imminent. Bridget stood alone in the shadows, stamping her foot on the hard-packed earth in agitation. This was a sign Riley had told me to watch for. Animals didn't moan or scream in pain for relief like some of us humans.

I slipped across the pen, hoping to get a better view in the dim light without upsetting her. Sure enough, I could see a bit of a bulge protruding from her rear, just as I'd been told. Panic mode kicked in. I froze in place, my heart pumping madly, half in anticipation and half in dread.

Sympathy pains started. I wanted to lie down in the straw next to her and cuddle her and tell her it would soon be over. But since that wasn't going to be of much help, I pulled myself together.

What should I do first? Call Riley—of course. I hated leaving Bridget alone, but that weaker part of me hoped it would all be over by the time I returned.

I ran to the house, my mind filled with questions. What if Riley couldn't come? Jake would be in bed. It was a school night. Why hadn't I brought my cell phone with me? Aughhh!

I made it to the kitchen in record time and frantically grabbed for the phone book. I remembered Brooke snickering at it when she was here. She'd never know how I appreciated the small size right now. Riley answered on the fifth ring after making me wait just long enough to raise my stress level to epic proportions.

"I'll be there in fifteen. I have to get the neighbor girl to stay with Jake. He's sleeping."

Back in the barn, I tried to soothe Bridget with soft words and petting. She rolled her eyes in a wild way that told me she wanted to be left alone. I remembered the feeling only too well, so I moved out of the pen after busying myself laying clean straw on the floor.

I've never known fifteen minutes to pass so slowly, except during my own labor. At last, Riley's truck pulled up outside the barn, and he walked in, looking his usual cool and calm self.

Okay, as annoying as that was, I must confess it made me feel better. By this time, Bridget's labor was in full force, and I was glued to the pen as tight as wallpaper, ready to spring over the rail at the first sign of trouble. I could barely tear my eyes away to greet him.

"Isn't there anything I can do to help?" The pain of my own labors was back in full force. Whoever said you forgot it all the moment your baby was born was full of baloney. You might know immediately that the beautiful creature you held was worth every moment of pain, but you never forgot.

Riley put his hand on my shoulder and whispered, "Just let her be. She'll take care of things."

It was only a few minutes before the protruding sac was expelled, and the squirming, kicking lamb lay on the clean straw. Bridget immediately began licking and cleaning her newborn, nudging with her head for the baby to stand up. After only a few minutes, the lamb stood, and Bridget stopped her cleaning and turned away.

"Oh, no, is she rejecting the lamb?"

"I think there may be another one coming. Now there's something you can do. Did you bring in the old towels?"

"Yes, they're right here." I went over and got the cardboard box I'd been storing the cloths in for weeks.

"Okay, you can dry off the lamb while she's busy giving birth to the other one."

Darned if he wasn't right. A few minutes later, another skinny lamb stood next to the mother, and between us, with Bridget's help, we managed to wipe both clean.

"Make sure she has plenty of water and food. She's going to need extra to provide enough milk for both lambs."

"I have some molasses to add to her water. One of the books I read suggested that."

Later, we stood at the pen gate, watching both lambs nurse. It was a beautiful moment. I felt like I'd been given a special gift to witness it all. Riley looked as pleased as I felt. We had shared something unique, at least to me.

"I'd say our work here is done." He gave me that devastating grin I hadn't seen for a while, and my insides turned to mush. As if I wasn't feeling emotional enough.

"Come into the house and have a hot drink before you leave."

We sat at the kitchen table a few minutes later, sharing an Irish coffee. I did us both a favor and used decaf. As my grandmother was fond of saying, "Who needs a wide-awake drunk?"

"Now, do you think you can handle the next birth by yourself?"

"I guess so." Was he serious?

Oh, yeah. He was serious, and I couldn't blame him. He'd been called out on a cold night to help the greenhorn farmer. I really had been dependent on the goodness of others again.

I straightened my spine. Of course, I could

handle it. *But what if something goes wrong?* My confidence wavered.

"You can call me, you know. I was teasing." He leaned back in his chair, a rakish gleam in his eyes I hadn't seen before.

"No, seriously. I think I can handle it now that I know what to expect," I said. "But I'll keep your number handy, just in case."

"You know, not to change the subject, but I really meant it when I said I appreciated your help with Jake." He took a swallow of the hot brew. "For the first time, he seems happy to go off to school. You had a lot to do with that."

There was more than gratitude in the look he sent my way, and my heart went into the little happy dance again.

"Thank you," I said. "Jake has become very important to me."

He flexed his shoulders, and I suspected he'd had a full day of work before coming here. I felt a little guilty.

"I'll admit, it's been tough putting him in the hands of others. It's been just the two of us these past years." His hands wrapped around the mug, and he stared into it as if searching for his words. "It kills me to see him scared or hurting."

"Raising children is tough in the best of circumstances." I ran my finger around the rim of my own cup. "I understand a bit how you feel. When my girls were young, it was really hard to leave them at the school door those first days. And they didn't have the challenges Jake faces."

"Maybe if I was younger, I wouldn't be so aware of the trauma others inflict, even without meaning to." He put down his cup and really looked at me. "It hasn't been easy having my first child at forty-two. The learning curve has been pretty steep."

"Do you mind my asking where Jake's mother is?"

"She left when he turned three," he said, a bitterness in his voice I hadn't heard before. "Her pregnancy was a shock, not something she'd planned. When Jake started with the tantrums, it was more than she could handle. She was young and looking for a storybook marriage and happily ever after. Jake and I couldn't give her either."

I fumbled for words. The pain in his voice touched me deeply. Hadn't I experienced those same feelings of failure?

"Look, Jake is making wonderful progress. There's no reason why, with continued therapy, he won't grow into a productive, happy member of society. It may not be the storybook life his mother wanted, but few of us ever have that, right? I know my life didn't exactly turn out the way my family expected."

"Oh?" He raised his brows. "I would've guessed your life followed a well-planned track to success."

His eyes met mine with such candor; I had to be honest, no matter how painful. After all, he'd let me in on his personal pain. The least I could do was be honest in return.

"I was the first one in my family to go to college. They all expected wonderful things from me—I was so full of dreams." The pang of regret that I hadn't done more with my education still lay heavy on my heart some days. "Instead, I fell in love and married my college sweetheart."

"So, what did that have to do with your not achieving success in life?"

"Robert didn't want me to work. He thought I should stay home and take care of the children."

"Is that how your family measured your success —by what you achieved in the business world? Isn't raising children the most important job there is?"

"Yes, but they assumed I'd first do things never open to them, along with having a family. At least, that's the feeling I always got from them. They never said anything. I don't know, I guess I felt I was supposed to help make the world a better place."

"Couldn't you have gone back to work when the children started school if that's what you wanted?"

"By that time, Robert was pretty successful and we didn't need the money, so he didn't see the point. Looking back though, I think he really wanted me always there for him, even if he didn't know it." Too late, I realized this had turned into a discussion about me and my problems. I picked up our empty mugs and put them in the sink.

"Too bad. I have a feeling you would've been

very successful at whatever you tried. It's obvious you're a damn good teacher."

Thankfully, he couldn't see my face flush with pleasure. Why a compliment from this man would mean so much, I couldn't imagine. Maybe it was because I sensed he didn't give them lightly.

"I'd better get going," he said, rising from the table. "The babysitter has school tomorrow."

"Well, thanks again for coming. I guess you know how much I needed you."

"Not as much as I need your help with Jake. Glad we could work this arrangement out." He put on his leather jacket. As he reached for the doorknob, he turned back with his usual casual stance. "Would you come out and have dinner with us on Saturday night? I'd like to show you some of my work."

Oh, boy. A little warning voice inside shouted, *NOT A GOOD IDEA*. Being with Riley was getting way too comfortable and a little bit dangerous. The thoughts I'd been having about him lately were anything but platonic. I didn't need more complications in my life. Worrying about my unsold house and other major problems, along with pregnant sheep, already kept me up at night. I searched my addled brain for an excuse to refuse.

"I'd like that." Where did that come from? *Have you lost your mind?* I scrambled to placate my inner common sense. Maybe seeing Jake in his home environment would give me a better indication of what help he needed. Yeah, that sounded plausible. I'd take it.

"Don't expect anything fancy. The cooking I've picked up along the way is mostly of the meat-and-potatoes variety. Or a steak or burger on the grill."

"Hey, I've discovered I like anything if I don't have to cook it." I wasn't being nice, but honest, with those words.

A cold, light rain had begun to fall while we'd sat in the kitchen. As soon as Riley drove away, I went back out to the barn to check on the lambs and Bridget.

Riley had shown me how to set up a heat lamp we found in the garage, but I still had to make sure they were warm enough if I wanted to get any sleep myself.

The lambs were cuddled up together under the light, their mother standing nearby, chomping on hay. She looked very pleased with herself. I was pretty proud myself, as if I'd played a major role in bringing new life into the world.

I ran back to the house, still on an adrenaline high, and called Suze to give her the news. She was as thrilled as I was as I relayed the saga of the births.

"Who is this Riley guy? I think I'd like to meet him. From the way your voice perks up whenever you mention his name, I'm thinking there could be something interesting going on up there."

"Sorry to disillusion you, sis, but he's the father of one of my students, who happens to shear sheep on the side. All he's interested in is making a life for his son, and all I care about is making a life for myself."

"Are you sure about that? Having a male friend could be very good for you."

"Oh, please, don't even go there." All I needed was my family adding their two cents to the mix. "How are things with Nora and Dave?" That should get Suze off my case.

"Nothing has changed." She sighed heavily. "I just don't get it."

"She'll talk about it one of these days. Be patient."

I called my daughters next, deliberately playing down Riley's part in the whole thing. Their response was pretty much what I'd expected. Lexie could hardly wait to visit again and see the lambs. Brooke of course, had a different response.

"That's nice, Mother. I'm glad you didn't have any problems. But it isn't as if your first grandchild was just born."

Leave it to Brooke to suck the joy out of the experience. Would she ever accept this new life of mine? It was looking more and more doubtful.

I NEVER MENTIONED MY UPCOMING DINNER INVITATION when I went to Wool Gatherers that Friday. Don't ask me why, but it just seemed too private to share, even with these women who were becoming so important in my life. Also, Nancy wouldn't be too happy to hear about it. I didn't want to throw fuel on the fire of her dislike. We were finally getting to the point of tolerating each other. She'd stopped the snide remarks at my expense, and I'd actually found myself occasionally laughing at her caustic humor.

Instead, I told them all about the birth of my lambs. Carol, of course, had already heard a play-by-play description. I'd called her early the following morning before she left for school. As I retold the story, she beamed like a proud mother.

"So, when is the other one due?" someone asked.

"I guess it'll be pretty soon. Fiona already has all the early signs of labor so it won't be long, according to Riley."

"Maybe you should've stayed home tonight," Nancy said, suddenly busy with her knitting. "There could be trouble."

At my stricken look, Carol said, "She's teasing. You can't be there all day and night for weeks."

Carol's words made sense, but I still left earlier than usual. I got home around ten and went immediately to check on things in the barn. I laughed when I remembered how terrified I'd been of the sounds in the barn that first night I'd spent on the farm.

The ewes were eating hay, and the lambs were asleep under the heat lamp. I sighed in relief. Just as I turned to leave, I realized I'd caught something unusual out of the corner of my eye, and I turned back to check. Next to Fiona stood her own two little lambs, nursing happily. I opened the pen with shaking hands.

"Oh, Fiona, you took care of everything yourself." I patted her gently on the head and reached down to touch the babies. They were already dry. They must've been born soon after I left. "I guess your sister was a good teacher."

I quickly put out extra grain and added molasses to the drinking water again. I was reminded once more of how nature handled things long before we humans got in the way. I moved the new babies under the heat lamp as soon as they stopped nursing, anyway. Fiona gave me that look again. I knew if she could talk she'd say, *Stop fussing, woman.*

This time, I didn't bother calling anyone but Carol. We laughed together at how I'd worried for nothing.

I had a peaceful night's sleep for the first time in weeks.

WHEN I ARRIVED AT RILEY'S THAT SATURDAY NIGHT, there was still light in the sky. I could smell spring in the air, even if there were still pockets of snow visible against the metal sides of his shop.

Jake answered the doorbell, hopping from one foot to the other in excitement. It was probably a great event for him to have his teacher come to his home for dinner. Hopefully, it wouldn't be enough to send him into a frenzy of hyper-activity.

"Hi, Jake."

Riley came up behind him and opened the door wider.

"Come in, come in." We all moved into the living room, where Riley proceeded to take my coat.

"Jake was just about to set the table, weren't you?" he said to his son with raised eyebrows.

Jake hesitated for a moment and then ran into the kitchen. I glanced around the room while Riley hung my coat in the tiny guest closet.

The place was small and rather sparsely furnished—a leather loveseat, recliner, and wooden rocker were the only seats. The clean, elegant lines of the cherry end tables were decidedly out of place. If they were an example of his woodworking skills, I was impressed.

"Can I get you a soda or a glass of wine?"

"A glass of wine would be great," I answered, relieved I'd soon have something to hold. Hopefully, it would keep me from wringing my hands with nervousness.

"Let me just check on dinner first."

"What are we having?" I asked, disgusted with myself again for being such a wuss.

I wandered into the kitchen while Riley checked on the meat grilling outside. Jake was still setting the table.

"Can I help?"

"No, I can do it myself."

I noticed how he straightened each plate so that the floral pattern was exactly centered and the cutlery precisely aligned alongside. He kept going back and forth between the settings, rearranging each piece to perfection.

"It looks lovely, Jake," I said in my soft teacher's voice. "Your dad will be very pleased."

He looked up, doubt in his expression. Looking down again, he straightened the fork in front of him.

"You don't need to change anything, honey."

"Jake, it looks great. Why don't you get the napkins?" Riley had come up behind me, and I jumped.

"Sorry," Riley said, handing me a glass of red wine and looking distracted. "Is merlot okay?"

"Merlot is my favorite."

"This is what I don't seem to get." He shrugged in exasperation. "Is it good to give him tasks that he agonizes over, or should I just not give him any responsibilities?"

"It's better if he learns responsibility along with his routine. When he gets too involved with perfectionism, try distracting him with a calm voice, just as you did now. You're doing a great job with him."

After dinner, we took a tour of Riley's workshop. I'd grown more comfortable as the three of us talked throughout the meal, surprised at how easily the conversation flowed between us. I sensed Riley's pride as he showed me several pieces he was con-structing.

"This block-front chest is in the Chippendale style. It'll have solid brass hardware."

"Wow, I'm impressed. I didn't think pieces like this were made by hand anymore."

My enthusiasm seemed to energize him, and he walked over to another piece in the beginning stage of construction.

"This is a walnut sideboard I'm just beginning. It doesn't look like much now, but the lines will be beautiful when it's finished."

"Is it difficult to find a market for such one-of-a-kind things?"

"I'm finally breaking into the larger city market. One of my best pieces is in Milwaukee in a high-end furniture store right now. They seemed confident it would lead to more orders. Of course, they take quite a commission, but that's the way it goes in any business. I know they have to cover their overhead."

The air in the shop was ripe with the clean smell of fresh sawdust and varnish. He patted a large object wrapped in quilts as we walked past it.

"This piece is finished and ready for delivery to a home in Door County."

Jake had wandered from our side and picked up a power tool lying on a bench.

"Put it down, buddy. You know better than that."

"No." He ignored Riley's admonition and lifted

the tool to eye level. Riley was there in a second, prying the tool out of his hand.

"I want to play with it. Give it back," Jake screamed before he picked up wood scraps from the floor and began throwing them with abandon.

"Jake, stop it." Riley frowned as he put the tool in its case. "I don't often let him in the shop—you can see why. Too many dangerous tools lying around, and I can't leave him out of my sight for a second." He started back across the room after Jake.

I could see the boy was over-stimulated and embarrassed now by his behavior in front of me. I searched my mind for a way for him to save face.

"Hey, Jake," I called over to him. "What do you say we go back to the house while your dad cleans things up here? I'm a little tired. Maybe we could read a book together."

It was something we did during lunch period if he was too upset to go out on the playground with the other kids. He nodded, looking relieved.

A tearful Jake followed close behind as I made my way back to the house, rubbing his eyes and stumbling a little as he went. He wouldn't allow me to take his hand. Not only had my visit caused over-stimulation, we'd interrupted his nightly routine. It was too much for him to handle without blowing off steam.

"Why don't we go up to your room and get you ready for bed?" I hoped the bedtime routine would help him calm down. "You can show me how you do things every night."

He took a few sniveling breaths before answering, "Okay," and leading the way up the stairs.

A framed picture of a beautiful young woman on his dresser caught my eye, and my curiosity got the better of me.

"Who's that?" I asked as nonchalantly as I could.

"That's my mommy," he said matter-of-factly.

"She's very beautiful." He made no reply and continued his bedtime routine.

My head filled with questions I longed to ask but couldn't.

When Riley came into the house later, he looked frustrated, torn between his son and his duties as host. His expression changed to surprise when he saw Jake in his pajamas, sitting next to me on the loveseat. I knew he wasn't used to letting anyone else take over the handling of Jake, and the mixed emotions of relief and anxiety flitted across his face in rapid succession.

"Could you stay until I get Jake settled in his bed?"

"Sure." I watched him take his son upstairs with mixed emotions of my own. Should I have left? I'd felt his resentment when I tried to work with Jake on other occasions. Why did he want me around tonight?

"Thanks for staying." He looked tired when he came back downstairs, and my heart softened for this man who tried so hard. He joined me on the loveseat, surprising me. "Can I apologize for my son's behavior?"

"Of course not. There's nothing to apologize for. We interrupted his usual schedule, and he was over-stimulated by having his teacher over for dinner. That's bound to cause trouble for him. We should've thought about it ahead of time."

"I was hoping it wouldn't affect him that much since he sees you at school several times a week and talks about you constantly." He flashed his crooked grin for the first time that evening. "I thought you'd be old hat by now."

I hit him in the shoulder playfully. "Thanks a lot."

"Seriously though, he thinks the world of you." He picked up my hand and began tracing the lines on my palm with his calloused finger. "And so do I." Lethal warmth had crept into his blue eyes, the same warmth I'd seen directed at Jake.

Suddenly, my mouth went dry, and I licked my lips. I couldn't tear my glance away from his face even as he leaned in closer. I felt my eyes widen as his lips touched my lower lip first, then the upper one. Just a little friendly kiss, I told my fluttering heart. Nothing sexual about it.

He drew back, looking as surprised as I felt. Without thinking, my hands reached out for the lapels of his shirt, drawing him close again. Instead of resisting, he gave a soft sigh a moment before our lips locked together in a kiss much more passionate than it should've been. I closed my eyes in ecstasy. What had I been missing these past years?

When I finally pulled back and looked at his shocked face, reality hit. This was moving too fast in a direction I never expected. It was scary. I hadn't been with a man other than Robert for many years and hadn't a clue how to act. Besides, Robert hadn't even been dead two years. It was too soon to move on. What would my children think? I was swamped with guilt for losing control of my emotions so easily and enjoying his kisses so much.

"I think I'd better go. It's getting late." I scrambled off the loveseat and reached for my purse, which I'd set near the door. Riley retrieved my coat from the hall closet, looking as stunned as I felt. "Tell Jake I said goodbye, will you?" I managed to blurt before running out the door.

Glory be to God, what had just happened in there? I got into my car and could see him watching from the front porch. My heart continued to pound erratically. I was too old for this nonsense, for God's sake.

When I looked at the speedometer a few minutes later, I realized I was way over the speed limit and slowed down. How would I explain to a cop that I was running from the devil in sheep shearer's clothing?

I should've known better than to have dinner alone with Riley—even if I did think having Jake there as a buffer would protect me from myself. What was I thinking?

The only excuse I could come up with was I never expected to feel that way about a man again. Oh, God. What must he be thinking? I'd practically grabbed him for that second kiss. My face flamed in embarrassment.

13

I woke up a few days later, the blankets wrapped tight around my waist and my prized afghan tossed on the floor. Another night battling with a thousand regrets and wishes had left me exhausted. My wonderful new bed was no longer the haven of comfort I'd envisioned. That had changed with one evening in Riley's company. I'd gone to sleep replaying a mental tape of those kisses over and over in my head until they'd grown into an act of momentous consequence.

Had Riley felt the same high-voltage sexual attraction? It'd been like electric shock therapy to me —awakening all sorts of sexual stirrings I'd thought left behind long ago.

And then my mind began playing the game of *what if*...?

What if he expected to pick up where we left off

the next time we met? What if he thought I was some sex-starved widow anxious for an affair? What if he wanted an affair? Why was I even wasting my time thinking about such things? Argh!

Ridiculous. I punched my pillow into a better position. He wasn't interested in a relationship with a woman like me, not when he had women like Nancy throwing themselves at his feet. And if we ever did get intimate, he'd take one look at this over-the-hill body and run for cover.

Which was fine by me. I wasn't interested in a relationship anyway. I had enough on my plate right now. The thought of Brooke's reaction was enough to bring a smile to my lips. Good thing it would never happen.

I decided to stay in bed a little longer, try to catch up on the hours of sleep I'd lost. It was Wednesday, the day the kids had several extracurricular activities and parent volunteers came to help so I didn't need to be there. Wednesdays were my day off unless there was a problem with the volunteers.

After fifteen minutes of tossing and turning, I gave extra sleep up as a lost cause and dragged myself out of bed, vowing to stay away from Riley O'-Connor. Who needed this stress? He'd probably run in the opposite direction the next time we met anyway. I threw on some clothes, slurped down a cup of hot coffee, and went out to do the morning chores.

Maeve swooped in and out of my legs as I

walked back into the house, still exuberant from her time spent with the sheep. The herding book said to put her in with them for short periods while she was a puppy so they'd get used to each other. She'd been trying to herd them into a circle while I was busy getting their grain out. Finally, Bridget got ticked and gave her a non-too-gentle head butt. But to Maeve, it was only a minor setback and she was up and running after a short whimper. Ah, the resilience of youth.

The phone rang just as I was walking up the porch steps. I shut the door behind me and whipped off my work boots before running across the room. Phone calls were few and far between these days, and I had a need to connect to another human this morning.

Especially this morning.

"Hello," I said before even checking caller ID, my breath coming in short gasps.

"Hi." The masculine voice was immediately recognizable once my heart started jumping in my chest "I didn't see you when I dropped Jake off this morning—was afraid my cooking the other night might've done you in."

"I have the day off." Could he hear the breathlessness in my voice and think it was because of him? I hoped not. Just to be sure, I wasn't saying another word until I knew what he really wanted.

"In that case, are you busy this morning? That customer of mine with the place in Door County is in from Chicago and would like his piece delivered. I could use some company on the drive if you're up for it."

"Sure, sounds good." Who was that idiotic person putting words in my mouth again before I had a chance to remember I didn't want to get into a car with him? Especially without Jake as a buffer. Although, that little ploy hadn't worked so well anyway.

But it would give me a chance to play down the way we'd parted Saturday night before things became terminally awkward between us. The idea soothed the sensible part of me.

A few minutes later, I found myself in front of the bathroom mirror, putting on makeup and fussing with my hair in anticipation of seeing him again, all the while telling myself I was a fool who'd lost all common sense. This wasn't a date, for heaven's sake. Thinking that way could only lead to trouble, and it had to be stopped.

Right now.

I barely finished putting myself together when Riley's truck pulled into my drive. I hurried out and scrambled into the vehicle before he had time to help me, scrambled being the operative word. I didn't want his hands touching me, not when I still remembered their warmth and energy. The memory of his touch wasn't exactly calming to my scattered nerves.

"You're in a hurry this morning," he said,

sending a fleeting glance up and down my body. "I would've helped you get up there, you know."

"Sheesh, I didn't know I'd need a ladder to get into this thing," I said, smoothing down the legs of my jeans.

"I'll bring Jake's stepstool next time," he said, a smile in his voice.

I buckled up and turned to face him, anxious to get these first awkward moments of conversation behind us.

"Anyway, I didn't want to keep you waiting," I said. "I know you'll need to get back before Jake gets home from school."

"It's only a thirty-minute drive."

But it would be a long thirty minutes if I didn't get my mind on other things. "Tell me about the piece you're delivering. Is it one you had covered and ready to go?"

"Yeah, it's a curio cabinet. I didn't get the chance to show it to you the other night after Jake's little episode. The guy ordered it as a birthday gift for his wife. They're Chicago people who summer up here. Their place is new, and they're still furnishing it."

"I'll bet it's lovely." I looked out the back cab window and could see the piece, wrapped in quilted blankets, lying in the bed of the truck.

He was right about the timing. It only took thirty minutes to arrive in Fish Creek. As we began the descent down the hill into town, I was struck by the difference since my last visit.

There were fewer cars and people than I was used to seeing along the main streets of town. But then, I'd always been here at the height of tourist season. It was too early in the season for most tourists to be visiting the many boutique and gift shops lining the highway. I had a view of the bay in the distance, and it looked cobalt blue and cold.

We drove through town and turned into a side road leading to a secluded area along the shore. Exclusive summer homes lined the road, some with high privacy fencing, others open to view. These were not "cottages" by any stretch of the imagination.

When we arrived at his customer's home, the owner came out and greeted us and helped Riley carry the piece into the house. The home was gorgeous, with sunlight pouring in and warming every surface, even if the décor was more modern than my taste.

The back of the house faced the bay waters with a wall of windows. The view was breathtaking, and I could only imagine what it would be like on a summer evening. It was situated on a small bluff with a large deck with wooden steps leading down to the water and a dock extending far out into the bay. We stepped outside to the deck for a better view.

Spring had been slow in arriving this year, so there were still pockets of snow among the shrubbery and ice piles along the edges of the shore. The wind was cold and biting, even though we were situated on the bay side of the peninsula, more sheltered from the fierce lake storms than the Lake Michigan side.

I followed the two men back inside and stood watching as Riley unwrapped the cabinet. It had the same clean, elegant lines of the cherrywood end tables in his living room.

It truly was the work of an artisan. I could tell by the customer's face how pleased he was with the piece. I envied his wife, both for the beauty and the thoughtfulness of the gift. He asked for several of Riley's cards so he could pass them on to his Chicago friends.

When we got back in the truck, Riley said, "Do you have time for lunch?"

"Sure," I said. Why not? So far, things were going well. There hadn't been any awkwardness about the way Saturday night ended, and I assumed, like me, he'd just as soon forget it.

"We have to talk."

My breath caught in my throat for a moment. Rats. Couldn't he just let me bury my head in the sand, pretending those kisses never happened?

I sat back against the vinyl upholstery in his macho truck, trying to look unconcerned and as though personal conversations of this nature meant little to a sophisticated woman like me. Not an easy achievement when your feet didn't quite reach the floor.

Maybe he wants to talk about Jake. A little voice of hope reared its head, only to be immediately squashed by Riley's look of determination.

He drove to a small white inn located in the midst of the many tourist shops that lined the village street.

"They serve a great lunch here," Riley said as he parked the truck.

The older building was lovingly cared for, from the gleaming hardwood floors to the cheery glow of the fire burning in the stone fireplace that dominated one wall of the dining room. I could smell the fresh bakery and a savory soup as soon as we entered.

We sat in worn captains' chairs and placed our order, my stomach dancing to the tune of a rumba. I made up all kinds of excuses in my head for what had happened between us. Even I didn't find one of them plausible.

The problem, as I now saw it, was the more I knew of this man, the more I liked and respected him. Far from being the Lothario I had expected, he'd become a man I could really admire. I only hoped my behavior of the previous Saturday wouldn't ruin what could become a great friendship.

"Listen, about the way we ended things Saturday..." He looked as uncomfortable as I felt. "I want to apologize for my behavior."

His behavior?

"What do you mean, exactly?" I managed. This time I would not stick my size sevens in my mouth until I heard what he had to say.

"About the way the evening ended..." His dark eyes searched my face, and I had the crazy notion he could see into my soul. "I had a great time and so did Jake. I don't quite know what happened there at the end, but it was just dumb on my part. Can we just forget it and pretend it never happened?"

I sat in stunned silence for a moment. Looking across the table into those dark, earnest eyes, I realized I didn't want to forget and I couldn't pretend. I wanted to keep the memory of those kisses in my heart forever. How crazy was that?

He'd kissed me, and I'd returned the kiss. Okay, so maybe it was the other way around, but regardless, he'd enjoyed it. I wasn't so old I couldn't feel mutual sexual attraction when it grabbed me.

He was fooling himself just as I had until a moment ago. I realized I wasn't sorry at all, and I'd do it again if I got the chance.

What made it so dumb anyway? Why were we supposed to deny the physical attraction between us? I could feel my hackles rising and made myself take a deep, calming breath. The man was saying exactly what I'd been thinking for days. Only, now it annoyed the hell out of me.

The need to save face took over. "I agree totally. Let's forget about it, and keep our relationship friendly but impersonal."

His smile of relief irked me on various levels. When he reached across the table and covered my hands with his, I had the urge to snatch them away.

"I knew you'd understand. I have to admit, sometimes I get damn lonely—wondered if maybe you do, too? It would be great to have a friend to share dinner or an occasional movie—no strings. As long as we both know the score, it should work out well for both of us."

"Sure," I said. "When are you going to bring Jake over to see the lambs?"

"Just let us know when it's convenient," he answered, looking as relieved as I felt at the change of subject.

After a quick sandwich and cup of soup, we were back in the truck and on our way home.

"It's great we were able to clear things up. I'd hate to ruin a friendship because of one stupid slip-up on my part," he said, giving me a sidelong glance as he drove.

"Of course." My mouth said the words, but my gut reacted in a totally different way.

The more time I spent with this guy, the more I cared for him. It hurt that he could push aside those kisses so easily. He must've had some inkling about how I felt. But then again, he had women throwing themselves at his feet constantly.

By the time we got out onto the highway, common sense hit me in the side of the head like a brick. Of course, Riley was right. It was really only my pride that hurt.

If there was one thing I didn't want or need at this time in my life, it was a commitment to a relationship. I'd just begun to get my act together as an independent person, and there was no way I'd again give it up.

Yet, when sitting so close to him, every cell of my body cried out for his touch.

I had to stay away from Riley, no matter what I'd just agreed to. The only way we could be together was with Jake as a safeguard between us. And next time, I would make sure it worked. Getting out of the truck later, I was both relieved and depressed.

I looked forward to the Wool Gatherers the next week, anxious to share my news about my first project. I tucked my completed skeins of spun yarn lovingly into my knitting bag with excitement.

After we'd shared potluck and settled into Joan's living room with our various projects, I broke the news.

"Ladies, you won't believe it, but I think I've got enough yarn spun and plied to knit my sweater." I proudly pulled the skeins from my bag.

"It's beautiful, Martha." Joan ran her hand over a soft skein.

Lila nodded in agreement. "I can't believe how fast you picked up the skill."

"Having a little one-on-one with Joan was a major help. Along with being shut in the house for several weeks with nothing else to do. Actually, it was the spinning that helped keep my sanity."

"You've been a great pupil." Joan inspected the skeins closely. "You've got a good twist, and your plying is pretty even. I'm proud of you." She'd never know how much those words meant to me.

"Not as even as yours, of course. But I think it'll do nicely for the pattern I have in mind." I couldn't keep the excitement out of my voice.

Nancy got up to take a look. "It's pretty good—for a beginner."

Faint praise but I'd take it.

"You don't want it perfect. That you can buy in any yarn store. Did you bring the pattern with you?" Joan asked.

"Yes. It's from an old book of my grandmother's. A book of Irish knits—lots of cable and knot patterns."

"Could I see it?" she asked.

I handed her the book with the page open to my chosen pattern.

"Oh, yes, this is perfect for the weight of yarn you've spun." Her eyes gleamed with the fanaticism of the true knitter. "This is a pretty complicated pattern."

"I know, but I think I can do it."

"Of course, you can," Carol assured me. "I'll help you decide what size needle fits the gauge, and you'll be all set to start." She pulled a stack of knitting needles from her bag. "Let's start with #8. You'll probably have to try a few practice pieces to see what works for the pattern."

I was so engrossed in my knitting that I didn't listen to the conversation around me until I heard Riley's name mentioned. My ears picked up like ant antennae. There could only be one Riley discussed in this group.

"Someone said they saw him with a woman in Fish Creek the other day having lunch at the Black Kettle."

"You're kidding," Nancy said. "Oh, well, it was inevitable—some rich summer resident, no doubt." She spit out the words with contempt. "I guess my hand-knit sweater wasn't that impressive."

I bent down over my knitting, trying to look engrossed in casting on stitches. Could they see my ears burning?

"I just hope whoever she is, she doesn't get her hopes too high. Riley has never been known to date a woman more than twice since Brandi left," Sue Ellen said, concern flitting across her face. "He's just obsessed with that boy of his, and he'll always come first, as far as I can see."

I was surprised to hear her comment. She usually kept her thoughts pretty much to herself.

"It's just a shame the way Brandi took off on the two of them." Lila talked above the soft clacking of her knitting needles. "Even after all this time, I can't believe it. I always thought she'd come back."

"When she first returned to town with that handsome man, no one ever thought it'd last. Such an age difference. But I sure didn't think he'd be the one to give up his wandering ways for the boy. Just goes to show, one shouldn't judge," one of the younger women said.

I kept casting on, dropping stitches and starting over and then over again. This conversation was upsetting. What would my friends say if they knew I was the woman with Riley? And how long before they found out?

"The boy won't need his dad 24/7 forever, though," Carol said.

"The kid's got problems from what I hear. And Riley isn't getting any younger, either. If he plans on settling down with another woman, he better do it soon before he loses his charm." Nancy jabbed her knitting needle into her yarn with a fierceness that was anything but relaxing.

"Riley's the kind of man who'll charm the ladies when he's in a nursing home." Carol grinned mischievously.

Finally, Joan noticed how intently I worked. "Are you having problems?"

"No, just trying to keep all the stitches even."

She gave me a penetrating look. "You're only doing practice swatches. Something else is bothering you."

I looked up at her, knowing guilt was spread across my face.

"Ahhh," she whispered.

She knew. I could see it in her eyes, but thankfully, she kept her silence. Leaning over, she patted my shoulder. "Sometimes, you have to listen to your heart and not your head. Remember how we talked about choices?"

The rest of the evening passed in a blur.

A FEW WEEKS LATER, RILEY AND JAKE STOPPED OVER early in the evening. Jake had asked several times if he could come over and play with Maeve. I was a little tired of playing "fetch" and "tug-of-war" myself and always looked forward to the break. The dog needed a child to play with, so they'd been coming by on a fairly regular basis. But each time they came, remaining emotionally detached got more difficult.

The early May air was still quite cool, but the sky was light after dinner. We went out on the deck where dog and boy ran around. He still hung back at school, never joining in the roughhousing on the playground with the other boys. He was already, at the young age of eight, known as a loner among the kids.

Life was going to be tough for him if he didn't learn to interact with others. I hoped his therapy would help him handle the rough give-and-take of young boys and keep his self-esteem intact. His father wasn't doing him any favors by protecting him.

"How is the group therapy going?" I asked.

"He's only had a few sessions, but he seems to enjoy it."

I'd done my best to integrate him into the games on the playground, but he really needed a one-on-one friendship with another child.

"Have you invited any of his classmates over to play?"

"It's not as easy as it sounds. Everyone is so busy these days. And let's face it. Jake isn't exactly popular among his classmates. The few times I've asked, the parents have come up with an excuse."

After about thirty minutes of their racing around, I could see Jake was getting wound up and over-stimulated.

"Hey, how about we go in and have a cup of hot chocolate?"

"No, I want to stay out here." His little cheeks were red, and he hopped from foot to foot in excitement. Riley stepped forward but before he could correct him, I intervened.

"Well, you might like it, but I can tell Maeve needs a drink of water and a bit of a rest."

He looked down at the dog lying on the deck, her tongue hanging out as she panted. "Okay, I guess so."

I sighed in relief. One temper tantrum avoided. Riley sent me a grateful look.

A few minutes later, Jake was lying on the living room floor, his tummy full of hot chocolate and cookies, Maeve curled up beside him in a blanket as they watched PBS KIDS. Riley and I were still at the table, holding our coffee mugs in hand. He watched his son and the dog, a winsome expression on his handsome face.

"It's amazing how well you handle him. I could get used to having you around 24/7 real quick." He reached over and covered my hand with his, giving it a gentle squeeze.

Warning signals flashed through my head. Oh, boy. This was not what I wanted to hear. Hadn't I spent the last thirty years being needed by others? This was dangerous territory for me, and if I wasn't careful, I'd slip right back into those old habits. This was my chance to break that pattern, friendship or not.

But, if I was completely honest with myself, I realized I'd thrived on it.

I cared way too much for Jake and Riley, and it scared me because, at times, those feelings went well beyond friendship. But any relationship we developed had to be based on my remaining independent. As much as I liked helping Jake, I couldn't make him the focus of my life. I had to find the real Martha before I could even think about sharing her with anyone else.

"I appreciate the kind words, but there's something you have to understand about me before we go any further in this friendship or whatever you call it." I took a deep breath and finally spit it out. "Look, I really like you and Jake—maybe a little too much, actually—but at this point in my life, I have to stay with our no-attachment relationship."

"Hey, wait a minute." A frown clouded his face. "You're reading more into my words than I meant. I really appreciate all you've done for us, but the main focus of my life right now is Jake. I wouldn't want to get involved with anyone either—especially because of Jake. He normally doesn't get emotionally attached to people, and if he does, it's very difficult for him to let go. I won't do anything that'll cause him emotional upheaval."

"Well, I'm glad we got that cleared up," I mumbled.

"Me, too." He picked up my hand and whispered, "I have to admit, though, it's not always easy." The look in his eye was anything but teasing.

14

IT WAS A SATURDAY MORNING IN MAY WHEN I STOOD on my deck taking in the beauty surrounding me. Waving grasses and shoots of alfalfa had replaced the dreary brown of the fields and rolling hills. White windflower, delicate trillium, and the purple lushness of violets dotted the woodland floor. I'd survived my first Wisconsin winter, and although it was a tough one, things looked pretty good right now.

I reluctantly pulled myself inside when I heard the ringing phone. It was Carol, with a tightness in her voice I'd never heard before.

"Do you have a few minutes to talk?"

"Of course. What's up? Something new in your life?"

Uh-oh. It was Saturday afternoon. She was going to ask me to go out for drinks. I hated turning her down again. Why couldn't she take the hint? I mentally prepared a list of excuses.

"That's one way of putting it," she said in that same distant tone.

I could feel bad vibes across the phone line. Something was seriously wrong. I immediately thought of her boys and had a sudden flicker of dread.

"What happened? Did someone get hurt?"

"In a way..."

"Carol, spit it out." My gut tightened as each second passed without an answer. "I'm dying here."

"You're not the only one." She took a deep breath. "I just found out I have breast cancer."

Okay, I've said a lot of stupid things in my day but talk about bad choice of words. "Oh, God, I don't know what to say," I blurted.

"Me either. I keep hoping if I don't talk about it, it'll go away."

I sat in silence for a moment. What could I possibly say to make her feel better? Nothing came to mind. My mind blanked out. We were too close for platitudes. I wanted to ask if there could possibly be a mistake, but we'd both know this was way beyond wishful thinking.

"Tell me exactly what happened," I finally managed.

"I went in for my annual mammogram, and they found a suspicious thickening. The doctor recommended I have a biopsy. We both assumed it was a cyst, but he said we couldn't take a chance." Her voice carried her fear, loud and clear. "The results came back last night. I guess if there's a bright spot in all of this, it's that we caught it early."

"I'm coming over right now." I could at least offer my company.

I grabbed a bottle of her favorite wine off the pantry shelf and a couple of brownies from the pan in the fridge. So what if it was the middle of the afternoon. I'd almost reached the door when I turned back. What the heck—I'd take the whole pan. Maybe the boys would be home. They'd be as frightened as Carol. Nothing strikes fear in one's heart like the word cancer.

I found her sitting on the couch, staring into space. She attempted a smile when she saw me, but the tears glistened on her lashes, no matter how hard she blinked.

I sat beside her and pulled her close. "It's going to be all right. You said yourself; you caught it early. You're a fighter, and you'll win."

"We're talking surgery, chemo, and radiation," she said. "It scares the hell out of me."

"Of course, it does. It'd scare anyone with a working brain." We sat quietly for a moment. "Have you told the boys?"

"No. They're spending the weekend with their dad, after a lot of protesting. At least that worked in my favor." She wiped her eyes with a wadded-up tissue. "I can't face them like this. I have to pull myself together first. Seeing me cry will scare them to death."

"They may be a lot stronger than you give them credit for."

"We'll soon see, won't we?" she whispered.

I poured us each a glass of wine. "To your recovery," I said with conviction and lifted my glass.

We each took a sip and set our glasses down. The seriousness of the moment weighed heavily on both our minds, making casual conversation impossible.

"When I first got the news, I was totally numb. It all seemed surreal." She picked up a brownie, looking at it thoughtfully. "I wish I could've stayed that way."

"No, you're going to face this head-on like you always do, as soon as you get over the shock."

"You know what's really sad? I've been thinking about my ex since I got the news...how his new life is just beginning with a new baby and all...and mine might be ending."

"Oh, Carol, don't go there."

"I know. I'm wallowing in self-pity." She lifted red-rimmed eyes. "Truth is, I miss having his support now. Even if he did turn out to be a major bastard."

"Forget him. You have to focus on yourself for the next few months."

"Guess I won't be fussing with hair spray and gel much longer." She ran a hand through her blond hair. "Maybe I'll end up with curls. I've heard that happens sometimes." She gave me a watery smile. "At least I won't be bugging you to go out on Saturday nights." She took a deep breath and straightened her shoulders.

How would I have reacted to receiving her news? Not nearly as brave, I suspected.

"It's the not knowing what lies ahead that's driving me crazy. I don't meet with the surgeon and oncologist until next week."

"Once they give you a complete diagnosis, you'll have a plan. Then, you can start to fight."

We began to name the people we knew who'd waged this battle and come out successfully on the other side. Surprisingly, we came up with quite a list between us. Amazing, how we always dwell on those who lose the battle, rather than on those who win. Already a spark of her fighting spirit was returning.

"Enough of this pity party. Let's talk about something else."

Carol's mom came in then like a whirlwind, determined to spend the night, carrying a large pot of chicken soup and a no-nonsense attitude. It was clear where Carol got her fighting spirit. I could see she would be in good hands.

I left Carol's, very much aware of my own vulnerability. How quickly life could change. Hadn't I witnessed that firsthand with Robert's heart attack? And now it had been brought home to me yet again how futile it could be to plan out one's future.

What could I do to give support to my friend? She'd been there for me ever since my arrival on the farm—a friend when I needed one and yet never interfering in my personal life.

What kind of a friend had I been to her in return? She must've been lonely all those weekend nights when her sons were busy with friends or her ex. Would it have killed me to go out for drinks with her occasionally?

I'd been too wrapped up in myself and my quest for independence these past months, afraid I'd slip back into my former lifestyle. All my life, I'd been a giver of my time and energies to my family and others, and then I tried to do a total turnaround. I'd taken the friendship and help she'd offered, but what had I given in return until today? Had I crossed that fine line between a giver and a taker, and completely missed the middle ground I'd been striving for?

I called the other Wool Gatherers, and they immediately swung into action. Before the week was up, meals were prepared and delivered along with warm scarves and caps knit for her soon-to-be bald head.

Everyone's spirits lifted the next week when Carol learned for sure she was one of the lucky ones. She'd caught the disease early, and her prognosis was excellent.

We'd set up a schedule for driving her back and forth to the hospital for treatment. It was on one of those trips, a few weeks later, she voiced the question that had been haunting me for weeks.

"Whatever happened to that woman who moved here from Chicago?"

I gave her a blank look.

"You know, the one who was going to be totally independent and answer only to herself. It seems there are a lot of people depending on you these days. Myself included."

I didn't answer immediately because the answer still eluded me. Was she right? Did I have people depending on me again? And if so, was it a bad thing? I thought about my life and the twists and turns it had taken these past months.

Arriving here alone, eager to be on my own for the first time in many years, I had planned a different lifestyle. But, as usual, reality got in the way.

First I had Maeve and then the sheep. They were certainly dependent on me for their care. But the amazing thing was, I liked it. Caring for them was a joy. Most of the time anyway. It made me feel useful and gave me a sense of purpose, a reason for getting up in the morning, no matter how down I'd been feeling the night before. The animals couldn't voice their thanks but showed their gratitude just the same with their eagerness to be close to me.

And of course, there were the Wool Gatherers, the first real friends I'd made in years. The memory of that first night—when I'd met them and decided they were too nosey and pulled back from their personal questions—haunted me. In those days, there was such a disconnect in what my heart wanted and my head demanded. Now, I realized they were only being open and friendly.

I'd become close to them in ways I hadn't been with other women since my marriage, maybe because of the silent understanding that permeated our meetings—we'd be there for each other. I knew I could depend on the Wool Gatherers for help, just like we were all helping Carol in her time of need, the same way they'd been there for me when I'd injured my ankle. That knowledge gave me great comfort.

And then there were my students, Jake, in particular. They depended on me to teach them ways to adjust to society and to run interference for them when necessary. It was a job, and yet so much more. I knew I'd do it for free if I had to.

I thought long and hard before giving Carol an answer.

"I guess I've realized something this past month. Being independent doesn't mean you can't be a good friend or that you have to go it alone all the time. I like to think I can do both."

I looked over at my friend, pale and bald but putting up a valiant fight, and I felt so imperfect. Carol was going to make it, I knew that as well as I knew my own name. But seeing her like this made me come to terms with my own mortality. I'd thought I wanted to spend the last third of my life alone and without the worry and heartache that came with caring too much, afraid to get emotionally involved again.

I could see now how wrong I'd been.

What I needed was to find the balance between giving and accepting. I'd never been good at accepting help, even when I lost Robert. It'd been my only grasp at independence and a poor choice, I saw now. I'd always done the giving. That could've played a big role in the way I interacted with my former Chicago neighbors. I'd kept myself aloof in times of trouble, not allowing them to help. Everyone wanted to give as well as take, I realized too late.

My thoughts turned to Riley. Where did he fit into the complicated twists and turns of this pattern that was my life?

Was Riley right in his own quest to remain emotionally unattached? Or was he making the same mistake I almost had? And where would that leave me? I was beginning to see my life would have a big void without him and Jake. Should I let Riley know how my feelings had changed? Or would he repeat my earlier words—*no strings attached, please.*

"Does this not going it alone have something to do with your feelings for Riley?" Carol broke the silence between us.

I drew in my breath. "How did Riley get into this discussion?"

"C'mon, we all know you two have been seeing each other for weeks. You should know by now that you can't keep such things a secret around here."

Busted. I gripped the steering wheel and put all my concentration on watching the road ahead. She was right. I should've known it was only a matter of time.

"Hey, it's only been a few casual dinners and a movie. Most of our time together has been spent entertaining Jake," I said.

"We're worried about you." She said it so quietly that I had a hard time hearing her at first.

"For heaven's sake, why would you worry about me?" I think I already knew the answer but put off having to face it.

"Because of Riley."

"What about him?"

"You could get hurt. He's not looking for a long-term relationship. And you're vulnerable right now."

"Me? Vulnerable? C'mon, I can take care of myself, thank you very much."

"Think about it. A woman who's as sensitive and caring as you, coming out of a thirty-year relationship and facing life alone for the first time. You're not the love 'em and leave 'em type."

"Not true. I want to be alone. No strings attached."

"Is that your head or your heart talking?"

We'd reached the hospital by this time, and I took my seat in the waiting room while Carol went in for her treatment. I'd brought my knitting as it would be some time before she was clear to leave. It left me plenty of time to delve through my thoughts as I knit and purled my way through the intricate cables.

Were my friends right to worry? Had I been too emotionally involved to face the truth? Should I just chalk my time with Riley up to a good experience and move on with my life of independence?

It was too late for that. I'd already fallen for him. Hard.

Not only for Riley, but for Jake as well. They'd become part of the weft and warp of my newly woven life, along with the farm, the animals, and my friends, and I would simply enjoy being with them as long as it worked. I was putting myself in danger of once again becoming dependent on others to give my life meaning. The idea shook me to the core. No, not going to happen. As long as I kept remembering our time together was temporary, it would be okay. I knew Riley was affected, too. At first, it showed in the sudden withdrawal of his hand and apologetic glances.

Never mind those occasions when our hands had accidently touched, and I'd felt the heat travel up my arm, right to my core. Even his hand resting on the small of my back as he'd directed me into the theatre was enough to send an electric current up my spine.

Our goodnight kisses had escalated from a friendly peck on the cheek to a gentle brush across the lips. That last night, the kiss was deeper, with a hungrier intimacy. When Riley had lifted his lips, he leaned his forehead against mine and whispered, "This friends-only agreement isn't as easy as it sounds, is it?"

What was I supposed to do? Give up being with them in case I got hurt? Not going to happen. I dropped a stitch...and then kept on knitting.

It was my turn to host the Wool Gatherers, and we were in the midst of a great discussion about the local political scene when the kitchen door opened with such force it slammed against the wall. Brooke stood in the doorway, her eyes red with passion, back rigid with righteousness. She looked tired and overwrought on top of it.

"My God, Brooke, why didn't you tell me you were coming?" I ran over and pulled the overnight bag out of her clenched fist.

"What happened?" I searched her face. "Is it your sister?"

I was scared. It must be something bad. Thoughts of accidents and illness flashed through my mind. I felt unusually vulnerable to the vagaries of the human condition these days after what had happened to Carol.

"Lexie is fine, as far as I know. I had to see for myself just what you're up to now, Mother."

This was just too weird, but now wasn't the time to deal with it. "Come in and meet my friends."

The smile she gave us was so rigid you'd swear she'd had a bad facelift. Talk about throwing a wet blanket on the party. Immediately after the introductions were made, the women got ready to leave, offering all kinds of excuses. Who could blame them? Brooke's demeanor was enough to scare anyone off. Even Nancy gave me a sympathetic look. I watched with mixed feelings.

"Please, you don't have to leave on Brooke's account. She can get settled in the guest room while we finish."

Brooke nodded and walked toward the stairs. Now what had I done to incur her wrath? Or maybe I would be lucky, and this would be all about problems with her job. She did tend to be totally focused on her career when she wasn't minding my life.

Who was I kidding? I knew that look she'd given me as soon as she came in. This had nothing to do with her, and everything to do with me.

Carol and I exchanged glances. I'd told her of Brooke's feelings about my moving in a moment of commiserating about her sons' teen behavior.

"I need an early night," she said, waggling her

hairless eyebrows and smiling mischievously. "These treatments wear me out."

I was left standing alone at the door, muttering to myself about rats deserting a sinking ship and dreading the upcoming scene with my daughter.

Brooke was not a person who liked surprises. Her life was always neatly laid out weeks in advance. That damn weekly planner was like an extension of her arm. So I knew this was not a pleasure call.

"Are they gone?" she called down from the top of the steps.

"Yes, they've left. Now, would you mind telling me what this is all about?"

"I had a long talk with Aunt Suze this morning."

Uh-oh. A bad feeling washed over me. I could think of only one thing that Suze could've said to incur this anger.

It'd been a long time since I'd talked to Suze about Riley. I should've warned her to keep her mouth shut about it. She probably thought she'd be soothing my daughter's worries by telling her I'd made a male friend.

"Mother, how could you?"

It had become her favorite new line and gave me the answer to my question. I decided to play dumb again, hoping for time to gather my talking points. One had to be quick when dealing with Brooke.

"How could I what?"

"A sheep shearer? Where did you manage to

find such a man? I thought they lived in the Australian outback?"

"Good lord. Is that what's got you in this state? His name is Riley, and we're only friends. And in answer to your question, he only does shearing as a side business. He happens to be a furniture craftsman with a young son."

"Is that supposed to make me feel better?" She raised her hands in the air and rolled her eyes. "Are you one of those women who can't survive without a man?"

That was over the top, even for Brooke. Time I got over this need to explain my actions to her. She was my daughter. She should be more understanding and be happy for me, no matter what. Anger flowed hot and heavy.

"What is your problem? Can't you stand to see your own mother happy for the first time in years?"

Her face turned white, and I realized I'd gone too far. I couldn't let her know how I felt about the wasted years in my life. Or the state her father had left me in with his secrets and betrayal. It would break her heart and ruin all her childhood memories. Besides, it wasn't as if I'd never been happy; I'd just felt empty.

"Listen, this arguing isn't getting us anywhere. Let's sit down and discuss this like two adults."

"What is there to discuss? Am I supposed to stand idly by while you throw your future away with some gigolo? What does he want from you? Are you going to put all Dad's savings into a business for him?"

I tried to interrupt her, but she was beyond listening. Was this the time to tell her there were no savings and her father had only left debts? One look at her face told me I couldn't. She had worshiped her father. Her loss was still too raw for her to understand that he was just a mortal man, like the rest of us, who made mistakes.

Since his death, she'd made him into a saint, conveniently forgetting the knock-down, drag-out fights they'd had when she was a teen. In hindsight, his judgment was perfect. No wonder they say only the good die young.

"And what about that need for independence, which we've heard about ad nauseum for months? Are you just going to throw that idea away to spend your life babysitting some other woman's child? I thought you wanted away from all that Isn't that why you left us?"

Ah, so that was the crux of the situation. The pain in her words forced me to look at my actions through her eyes. My daughter felt abandoned. How could I explain my actions without belittling the life I'd lived with her father?

"I haven't left you. I could never do that. You and your sister are my life." I searched for the right words. "Please, try to understand. I had to leave. I was suffocating in that place, and it had nothing to do with you."

"It had everything to do with me, Mother. You left our home and all our memories. I'm beginning to think you never even loved Dad."

I felt the color drain from my face. "How can you say such a thing? I devoted thirty years of my life to him."

"And he devoted his to taking care of us—trying to provide for you even when he was gone. But now the house he invested so much in is sitting empty. And the way the market looks, it will be for a long time. What are you going to do then? How will you pay for this house with no income? Your little nest egg will disappear before you know what hit you and your future is tied to an itinerate sheep shearer and his son. Is this how you plan to honor Dad's memory?"

She'd gone too far. I clenched and unclenched my fists in frustration. She had no right to drag Riley's name into our family problems. I'd tried to be understanding, but she made it impossible. The desire to tell her exactly what her father had left us almost overcame my compassion.

"That's quite enough." I would hold my tongue. "I appreciate your interest in my life, but it really isn't your affair. I'm not in my dotage yet, even if you're hell-bent on sending me there with your constant interference."

"Someone has to try to talk sense into you. It sure didn't take you long to pick up with another man, did it? What was it you used to say? 'There's one perfect mate out there for each of us.' Obviously, Dad didn't fill the bill, did he?"

"That was uncalled for."

The bitterness in her voice cut to the quick. We hadn't had arguments like this since she was a teenager trying to set her own rules. Arguing with her wore me out, just as it had then.

"I don't want to argue any more. I'm going to bed. We'll talk in the morning." I started turning out the lights, telling myself it was her pain and fear of loss talking.

Her body stiffened with contempt as she stamped off to the guestroom without saying good night.

I followed behind. Was my daughter right? Had I become one of those women who couldn't live without a man in their life? Maybe there was a glimmer of truth in her slam.

Sitting on the edge of my bed, I thought about how my life had changed in the past year.

I remembered the day, almost a year ago now, when I'd finally woken up from the depths of depression and faced the truth of my past. If she had accused me of this the day before I went out and bought my beloved red couch, she would've been right. I had behaved like a woman who couldn't live on her own.

But that was then. Hopefully, the old Martha, the one from my youth, was back. I didn't need anyone to take care of me, not even Brooke, as much as she'd tried. I'd proven that to myself this past year.

Wanting to be with Riley and Jake had nothing to do with depending on them for my happiness. I'd already found new friends and established a full life, all on my own.

I no longer needed to prove my independence to myself or to anyone else. And that meant I could chose to be in a committed relationship if that was what I wanted, didn't it? But this was all a tempest in a teapot. There wasn't any commitment between Riley and me, and it was very unlikely there ever would be.

BROOKE'S ATTITUDE HADN'T CHANGED BY MORNING. She was wound up like a corkscrew, and the bags under her eyes were proof of a sleepless night. I felt pretty much the same. Would this nightmare ever end? She pulled out a chair and sat at the table.

I walked over and put my hand on her shoulder, hoping to bring her some comfort. "For your information, I have had weekly contact with my realtor and she assures me that the market will pick up very soon. There's been an increase in traffic through the house, though she did say that selling a home empty of furniture was more of a challenge. But she sounded pretty upbeat."

That didn't change her mood so I decided to

take the chance and ask the question I needed to know.

"Did anyone contact you—about your dad's business?" I asked.

"No." Her forehead furrowed. "Why would they?"

"I just wondered since I moved and the house is for sale. There are a few loose ends I'm waiting to tie up."

"What kind of loose ends?"

"Nothing important." I turned away. "Would you like some blueberry pancakes?" They'd always been her favorite.

"Toast and coffee will do. I'm not very hungry."

The hurt and anger still radiating off her were beyond reaching with logic. The silence between us grew unbearably thick as I poured her coffee and buttered her toast.

"Maybe if you met Riley, you'd feel better."

The look she gave me would've turned a lesser woman to stone. But I was used to it.

"I don't think so," she said in that supercilious tone that never failed to irk.

Nevertheless, I gave it one more shot.

"Listen, Brooke. I love you very much, just as I love your sister and loved your father. But now I have to live my own life, just as you and Lexie are living yours. If that includes dating, that's the way it's going to be. You're going to have to adjust. I didn't die with your father, even if you'd like to think so."

A spasm of guilt washed over her face at that, and I hoped for a moment we'd get the chance to put this discussion behind us once and for all.

"And as far as that old saw about there being only one perfect partner in life, maybe I was wrong." I could eat crow when I had to. "Remember the boy with all the piercings you were so crazy about in high school? The one whose ambition was to be a tattoo artist? You were sure he was the one for you."

"Whatever."

She got up from the breakfast table and went upstairs. I picked up the dishes with a heavy heart. As annoying as this child of mine was, I still loved her like hell, and it weighed heavy on my heart that she was so unhappy.

She came down the stairs a few minutes later carrying her suitcase.

"Where are you going?"

"Back to Chicago. I have a lot of work to catch up on." She put her bag in the car and came back to where I stood on the porch. Surprisingly, she kissed my cheek and gave me a quick hug. "Goodbye, Mom."

"Call me when you get home," I called after her, and she nodded. Had I cracked her shell of self-righteousness a little? Oh, God, please have it be true.

15

It was late Monday afternoon, and I waited for a call from the realtor, hoping she'd have something positive to report after the weekend. I'd been on pins and needles all day, hardly able to focus at school, knowing I had to do something about selling the house. I couldn't wait much longer—a month or two at the most before I had to apply for another loan to make my payments.

Who would lend money to someone like me? There was already a second mortgage on the suburban home. I didn't have a history of good credit. Robert had had everything in his name. It would have to be a personal loan. The bank was out. They weren't even loaning money to well-qualified buyers at this point. Who did I know that could possibly loan me enough cash to tide me over a few more months?

That would be Brooke, of course; she owned her condo and earned a great salary. It would also mean I'd have to tell her about her father's financial status when he died. What questions would that lead to? Could I do it? Did I have a choice?

When the phone rang just before dinner, I picked it up with an equal mixture of hope and dread.

"Hi, Mrs. LeBeau. How are you doing on this beautiful evening?" That perky realtor voice was like a nail pounded in my skull.

"Hello, Jennifer. Any news?"

"You'll be glad to hear we've had some activity on the house again. Several couples went through this weekend."

"Really?" I perked up myself. "Did anyone seem interested?"

"They asked a lot of questions, always a good sign. And two of the couples asked for my card and took the printed sheets with all the info. One couple returned today for a second look."

Relief washed over me in waves. There was hope after all.

"I told you things would pick up soon," she said. "Families want to be settled in a new home before school starts. Summer is a great time for home sales."

"I sure hope you're right."

"Oh, and by the way, the police were here today when I was showing the house—wanted your phone number. I explained you had moved to Wisconsin and had changed your number to a local area code. A Chicago Police detective was with them. Luckily, the buyers had just left because they walked through the house. I hope it was all right—the place is open for buyers after all."

"Did they say what they wanted?"

"No, I just assumed it had to do with that broken lock and graffiti. Have you heard any more about it?"

"No, no one called. The police had told me there wasn't anything more to do but keep an eye on the place. They didn't seem that concerned." I drew in a deep breath and released it slowly. I would not worry about this until I had to.

"I haven't heard of any trouble in the area. But then, the police aren't always forthcoming with information. "

Was it possible something else happened in the neighborhood? My hands shook slightly as I disconnected the call. Could their visit somehow be connected to Robert and the notes? An unnatural premonition of disaster made the saliva in my mouth dry up and my heart beat rise. *Get a grip. I have no reason to be afraid. I haven't done anything wrong.*

There was a knock on the door while I sat on the couch staring into space, assuring myself the police visit meant nothing. But my insides screamed something different. This had to be bad. I could feel it in my bones.

"Who's there?" For the first time in many months, I hesitated before opening the door.

"Mrs. Martha LeBeau?"

"Yes?"

"This is Detective George Brady from the Chicago Police Department," a stranger's gruff voice answered. "I'd like to ask you a few questions. May I come in?"

"Yes, of course." Maeve barked so loud by this time I could hardly hear him, and she scrambled for the door as soon as I opened it a crack. This time, I didn't hold her back. Keeping her between the stranger and me gave me a little more control. "Could I see your identification?"

He reached into his breast pocket and pulled out his badge. It looked authentic. As I opened the door wider, I saw a county police car parked in the drive and gave him a questioning look.

"They said it'd be quicker than trying to find the place on my own," the detective explained.

"What is this about?"

"We understand that you and your late husband own a home in Cook County?"

"Yes. I do now. It's been for sale since last fall."

"Yes, and that home was broken into and graffiti painted on the walls?"

"Yes..." Now, I was confused. What did this have to do with a Chicago detective?

"Also, there was a threatening note left in the mailbox?"

"Yes, but what does that have to do with the Chicago Police Department?" I asked.

"There's been an incident involving a Chicago citizen which may be connected. I'd like to ask you a few questions."

"Of course, ask away, but I doubt I'll have any useful information."

"This involves a murder case, ma'am. We think you may be able to help us."

"A murder?"

"Yes, ma'am."

By this time, he'd come into the house, and I'd offered him a seat. When he reached down to pet Maeve, her barking stopped, and she sat at his feet. My nerves settled a bit.

"Okay, what in the world does a murder in Chicago have to do with me?"

"The murder actually took place in Indiana, outside of a well-known casino. Since it was a Chicago citizen, we're helping with the investigation." I could feel him studying my reaction.

"This is ridiculous. I've never even been to a casino."

"Maybe not. But your late husband has."

"What? Robert? No, I don't believe you." Even as I uttered the words, the credit card printout flashed in front of my eyes with the multiple cash withdrawals. So, it wasn't another woman. But gambling? A weird sense of relief washed over me. Robert had been faithful.

"The person found murdered was named Cash Devlin—a well-known loan shark in the Chicago area. He had a black book in his pocket listing all his clients. Your husband's name was listed as owing $300,000."

I felt my eyes widen in shock. Everything was falling into place—the notes, the graffiti.

"Yes, Mrs. LeBeau." He'd been watching me closely. "What can you tell me about your husband's relationship with this man?"

"I've never heard of him or met him." I put my hand over my mouth for a moment and then dropped it into my lap. "My husband was in charge of all our finances—he kept secrets." I was babbling now and couldn't stop. "I don't know what happened to all our money—I only know when he died I was left only with debts."

He pulled a photograph from his breast pocket. "Have you ever seen this man?"

I blinked back the tears of shock. "Yes, he's the man who showed up at Robert's wake and said he wanted what was owed to him. I had no idea what he was talking about."

All the while we talked, he'd been taking notes. "Well, it seems you got your answer." He closed his notepad with a bang. "Thank you for your cooperation. We'll be in touch."

"Surely, I'm not a suspect?" I gasped.

"Let's say...a person of interest."

The police car had barely left when my phone rang.

"What's going on over there? Do you need any help?" Carol's frantic voice brought me back to my everyday life. All who passed would have noticed the appearance of a police car in my driveway.

"No, nothing bad happened. Just some information about that break-in at my old house." The humiliation of Robert's duplicity and my own ignorance was too fresh to share. "I really can't talk now. Catch you later." I hung up before she had a chance to ask more questions.

I ran to my desk and took out all the financial information I'd stored. The credit card bills for the months preceding and immediately after Robert's death were on top. I would have to check the location of the ATMs he'd used.

It didn't take long to check the addresses against the list of casinos on the Indiana and Illinois websites. The detective was right. I had my answer. Now, what was I supposed to do about it? I sat on my red couch, once again in shock.

FOLLOWING A DEER PATH THROUGH THE WOODS ON A warm June afternoon, I found relief from the hot sun in the shade of the old hardwoods and pine trees. Maeve ran beside me, veering off and on the path, smelling each and every branch and leaf along her way.

Wow. It seemed we'd moved into the warmth of summer in the blink of an eye. The first hay cutting filled the air with the sweet scent of alfalfa, and I breathed it in, my head filled with thoughts of the summer ahead. How I longed to share these warm days and nights with Riley and Jake. The days apart were hollow. Stopping short on the path, I closed my eyes for a moment, overwhelmed with the intensity of my yearning.

I should be happy, really happy. Life was looking sweeter at the moment. Carol was handling her treatments well. A young couple was interested in the Chicago house and working on financing. The question of what Robert had done with our money was finally answered and I'd come to terms with it. He wasn't the perfect person I'd thought him to be, but I'd found peace there, too. Even Brooke's attitude had mellowed a bit. I could almost believe she was beginning to accept I had a life of my own to live.

She hadn't met Riley and wouldn't ever meet him if she had her way. But that was okay. As long as Riley and I could remain only friends, what did it matter? My goal was to keep the status quo, no matter my growing feelings for Riley.

I walked in the house to hear the phone ringing. Before I even could say hello, the voice of my realtor shrieked in my ear. "Your house is sold!"

Weak with relief, I called Riley without a second thought. What did that say about my state of mind?

"This calls for a celebration. How about I get a sitter, and we have a celebratory dinner?" he asked.

"Sounds wonderful," I said. What could be better than sharing my happiness with Riley?

But it wasn't only Riley I cared about. I had fallen in love with Jake.

I had become overprotective, more like a mom than a teacher. He'd made wonderful progress but still had a long way to go to fit into society with comfort. I realized I wanted to be there all the way to his maturity—replacing the mom who'd left him. Those were dangerous thoughts, and I knew it. It was a blessing that he'd moved up a grade and would now be spending time with a new teacher.

It was easy to accept the word love to describe my feelings for Jake but not for Riley. You could love a child that wasn't yours. Affection was the word I needed to use to describe my feelings for Riley. That fit the status quo very nicely.

Dear God. I closed my eyes. It would be so easy to backslide into old habits.

When Riley pulled up an hour later, happiness rose from a spot deep within, pushing all thoughts of an impersonal relationship aside. I'd worry about that later. Now, I had a celebration to attend.

We'd decided on Chinese takeout, as neither one of us wanted to cook. The tourist season was at its peak, meaning all the nice restaurants would be noisy and full to capacity. He carried dinner in those small white cartons familiar to all and a bottle of wine.

I grabbed a couple of the cartons. "It looks like you got one of everything," I teased.

He took my other hand in his as we walked toward the house, the grip of his calloused palm warm and steady. How could such a simple gesture become so intimate? I'd felt myself growing as close to him as to my own children in many ways. Actually closer, now that they were grown and had their own lives away from me.

The conversation I'd had with Brooke on her last visit had played over and over in my mind. The talk about only one perfect mate for each of us. She'd never understand the connection I felt with this man. She would think it meant I didn't love her father, and that wasn't true.

Robert had come into my life when I was subconsciously looking for a Prince Charming, someone who would make me his Princess and provide for me the rest of my life. Why, I don't know. Maybe it was part of the culture at that time, or maybe I was afraid of failing on my own. I didn't know, and it didn't matter anymore. The problem was that when Robert did *take care* of me, it made me feel useless and resentful.

"That looks like a pretty good bottle of wine," I commented to hide my sudden awkwardness. It struck me that being alone with Riley all evening in this light mood would test my fortitude.

After my earlier thoughts, I was having a real problem dealing with the no-strings thing. If he knew what was going on in my head, how would he react? By hot-footing it out the door?

"Is something wrong?" He looked at me with eyes that saw more than I wanted to share. "You're kinda quiet for a woman who just received such great news."

"I'm still digesting it," I lied. "Let's eat. I'm starving."

After dinner, I put on a CD, one I thought would be particularly relaxing after an eventful day. As it turned out, it was incredibly romantic as well. After several glasses of wine, being alone with Riley didn't scare me at all.

"Dance?" he asked.

"Sure," I answered, inordinately pleased. It'd been years since I'd danced with a man. Robert never liked dancing. Soon, we were swaying to the music and moving slowly across the hardwood floor. I clasped my hands loosely behind his neck while he placed both arms around my back, clasped at my waist. Slow dancing, we'd called it in my youth.

I smiled up at him, now a bit shy because my thoughts were anything but platonic. Desire shot through me like a flaming arrow when I recognized the seductive glitter reflected in his dark blue eyes. I pulled back in alarm.

Ignoring my hesitancy, he pulled me close to the heat of his body, so close I felt his breath warm against my ear and the beat of his heart against my chest.

"Martha, you make me crazy." His whispered words fell against my ear in a sensuous rhythm, mirroring my own longing. Did this mean that sex wasn't over—even for someone like me? Could a man like Riley find me desirable? In the physical sense, that is?

Next thing I knew, we were clinging to each other, sharing hot kisses that made my knees weak and my breathing labored. We were like teenagers in the throes of first lust.

Sex had been one of the good things in my marriage, and obviously, I'd missed it more than I'd admitted. For once in my life, I just lived in the moment. To hell with the consequences.

I don't remember who said or did what after that, things moved so fast. I never had time to be embarrassed or worried about my aging body and lack of experience, like I'd imagined I would if such an occasion ever rose. But then, I never believed it would.

And what about all that sexy underwear I should've been wearing? Champagne-colored with lace in all the right places. Cotton briefs from Target weren't supposed to be a turn-on, but Riley didn't seem to notice. Or if he did, he sure didn't show it.

We were in my beautiful brass bed with my hand-knit afghan wrapping the two of us in a cocoon of warmth before I ever took the time to dwell on the pros and cons of making love to this man. By then, it was too late for second thoughts.

Making love with Riley had been perfect. Even better than I'd imagined in all those lonely hours I'd spent in this very spot.

I'd felt beautiful wherever he touched me with his warm and clever hands, no time to worry about flabby body parts—greedy sexual need made short work of those inhibitions. And I'm sure he felt the desire and tenderness in my own touch as well.

As I lay in Riley's arms feeling well loved and satisfied, I knew things had changed between us forever. There would be no turning back.

"Are you feeling even as remotely satisfied as I am right now?" he asked with a sheepish grin.

I think he read the answer in the answering grin splashed across my face. But even then, I felt a need to explain.

"As you've probably guessed—this isn't normal behavior for me. I might as well admit it. You're the only man, other than Robert, I've ever been with."

"I figured that out."

"Was I that bad?" I wanted to crawl under the sheets and die. But that would be too easy. Instead, I had to face him and my actions. Had I really thought eagerness and passion could make up for lack of experience and youth?

"Don't talk stupid." He pulled me closer, running his hand down the length of my back in a sensual caress. I wrapped my arms around his waist. "What we just shared was great, and you know it."

I pulled back and searched his eyes for the truth, and I think I found it there. I sighed in relief.

"I never thought I'd meet an open, honest woman like you. A woman without secrets. Someone I can trust and love." He held my face gently in his palms. "I've been attracted to you since our first meeting, and I hope the feeling is mutual. Unless I'm way off here?" He looked a little unsure himself, and I loved him for it.

I tightened my grip around his waist. "You couldn't be more right, but I was afraid to admit it." I rested my head against his chest, feeling the strong beat of his heart.

"It seems to me we have the perfect arrangement. Togetherness and none of the hassle, just like you wanted, right?"

Yeah, it was what I wanted, wasn't it?

It was after he left that the loneliness hit me. He was going home to Jake and their life together while my life was here. Alone. I squelched the feeling.

He was right, of course. We had the best of both worlds. Why, then, did I feel rejected? Why did I want him to declare his undying love for me? We were a pair of middle-aged losers with years of baggage trailing us. Even though we'd admitted our feelings, there could be no commitment. And of course, there was that honesty thing now. But those secrets about Robert didn't have anything to do with my relationship with Riley anyway.

I was filled with conflicting emotions. There was a part of me that wanted him to be mine and mine alone. This non-commitment thing was a double-edged sword.

16

WAKING UP THE NEXT MORNING, I HAD TO FACE THE fall-out over my actions. Was I prepared for the consequences to my emotions?

Riley talked like our relationship had been taken to a new level. Call me old-fashioned, but in my book, that meant commitment, and he was kidding himself if he didn't think so. As much as I loved him and Jake, I wasn't ready for it. It would mean a step back into my former life.

I wasn't sorry about what happened. It would be a lie to deny how much I'd enjoyed being with him. But I couldn't give my body to Riley without giving my heart. This friends-with-privileges relationship couldn't work for me. It would be an emotional disaster. Better if I just stepped back now—put some distance between us and tried to get back to the casual friendship stage. I did an emotional backstroke away from him and my heart's desire. Riley would have to find someone else to fill that need. That wouldn't be a problem for him.

I pulled myself out of bed, no time to lie around and stew over my predicament. In a moment of recklessness, I'd agreed to take a gentle yoga class with Carol. It would be good for her, and it wouldn't hurt me. At least, that's what I'd thought at the time.

An hour into the class, I changed my mind. Memories of the group I'd joined years before in the Chicago suburbs came back to haunt me as I viewed the other women in the class. Most of them were young mothers in their early thirties, determined to keep their shape and sanity after giving birth. They were dressed in sleek yoga outfits, their brightly painted toenails peeping out from under the black pants.

The instructor had said to wear something comfortable. I looked down at my baggy sweats—no bleach stains this time—and over-sized blue tee-shirt left over from the Reagan Administration with JUST DO IT printed across the front. It didn't take long to remember why that slogan never registered with a lot of us.

Carol talked animatedly to one of the other ladies, the usual sunny smile splashed across her face. Some of my own tension fled in response. It was good to see her involved again. The last time I'd talked to her, she mentioned her ex and the new baby for the first time in a long while and the hint of sadness in her voice cut. If my going to this class with her helped at all, it was worth a little pain. I put aside my petty worries and threw myself into the class.

That's when I remembered I was as flexible as an ironing board. "The next position is called the plank," the instructor said in that annoyingly cheery voice they all adopted.

I am the plank, I realized.

Forty minutes later, my body crying out for relief, we left the gym. The class had one thing going for it. It hadn't left me any time to cry over Riley; I was too busy feeling sorry for myself.

"Wasn't that great?" Carol asked as we walked to our car.

"Oh, yeah. I can hardly wait to come back," I whispered, my voice breathy with exhaustion.

"Oh, come on, it wasn't that bad." Carol poked my shoulder, grinning broadly. "Besides, you were supposed to modify the positions like I did if they were too hard. That's your problem. You're always trying to prove something to the world."

Is that what I was doing? Trying to prove to the world that I could do anything—and by myself?

Riley and Jake stood on my porch when I got home.

"Jake misses you...and so do I," Riley said. His eyes said so much more, and my heart felt so full of love at the moment I thought it would explode. I stood aside as they entered.

"You're just in time for lunch," I said.

"We already ate, but a cup of coffee would be good."

"I think I have a few chocolate chip cookies— how does that sound, Jake?"

"Okay," he said, so busy looking around for Maeve he barely answered.

"She's out in the barn pestering the sheep, I imagine." With that, he ran out the door, cookies forgotten. "I guess he wasn't hungry," I said with a smile and grabbed a mug off the shelf. I had just poured a cup from the thermos when the phone rang. Handing the mug to Riley, I picked up my phone with my other hand after checking caller ID. "Excuse me," I managed to get out. This could be important."

"Yes, this is Martha LeBeau. Good afternoon, Detective." My heart dropped to my feet at the sound of that gravelly voice.

"We have a confession in the murder of Mr. Cash Devlin."

"That means I'm no longer a murder suspect, right?"

"That's correct."

Relief soared through my body at his answer. "Oh, thank God. And what about the IOU?"

"We don't have anything to do with that ma'am. His loans were all personal and probably illegal."

"Oh my God! Thank you so much for calling."

I hung up the phone and squealed with relief,

jumping up and down. "Yes, yes," I said, pumping a fist in victory as I smiled at Riley. It took a moment to see the thundercloud of his expression, and I stopped dead in my tracks.

"What was that all about?" Riley asked. "I couldn't help but overhear."

"It's a long story...a mix-up back in Chicago."

"Did I hear you right? You were suspected of murder?" To say he looked incredulous was an understatement.

In my state of utter relief, I kept blathering on. "Well, not really. More a person of interest in the investigation. It's over now—nothing important," and I waved my arm in dismissal.

"Sounds pretty important to me."

"It's a family matter. I can't discuss it because of my daughters."

"Ahhh, I see. *Secrets*." The emotion in his voice when he uttered the word brought back his earlier thoughts regarding secrets. His face fell with a look of defeat, and he stepped away from me physically and emotionally.

"No. It's not like that. I would tell you if I could." I'd walked into a trap of my own setting.

"I'm sure you would." Was that sarcasm?

While I was still weighing the pros and cons of the situation, he got up and strode toward the door.

"It's time I get back to work anyway."

"Wait a minute. We have to talk about this."

"Some other time." He was down the steps and

corralling Jake before I could say another word.

A few minutes later, they were gone, leaving me to sort through all kinds of emotions. *What the hell?* He couldn't even stay long enough for me to explain? Fury brought relief from the pain. I didn't need this in my life. I didn't need him in my life. It was over.

Staying away from Riley wasn't as easy as I'd hoped. He'd called several times, but lucky for me, caller ID gave me a heads-up. I couldn't talk to him yet. I was angry about the whole situation. Granted, finding out I'd been a murder suspect was a shock —but hadn't I explained as best I could at the moment? He was the one who'd left.

Instead, I walked around the kitchen, my hands clasping and unclasping as I listened to his messages. The last one was especially difficult to ignore.

"I'm sorry I acted like such an ass. I have my own issues with secrets. If you're ever ready to talk about it, give me a call. I'd hate to lose our friendship."

That sounded like the ball was in my court, so I was surprised when my phone rang late on a Saturday evening and his name showed on the caller ID again.

"Martha, please pick up." A pause and a sigh followed. "I need to talk to you. It's important." His voice had an unfamiliar roughness.

I immediately picked up the phone. "What's up?"

"I need some advice. Can I come over?"

Alarm bells went off. Riley and I alone in this house? The same house where I'd almost declared my undying love for him? The same house where I now crushed my pillow to my head each night, hoping to get him out of my mind and heart?

"It's late. Can it wait until tomorrow? Jake must be ready for bed."

"I can get the neighbor to sit with Jake."

I still hesitated. I didn't want to have this conversation yet. Especially not on the phone. I needed more time to explain my position logically—to him and to me.

"I really need to talk to you. It's about Jake."

"Did something happen?" Visions of an injured Jake flashed through my mind. "Is he all right?"

"He's fine."

"What is it then?"

"I'll explain when I get there. He's here, listening."

RILEY'S TRUCK PULLED INTO THE YARD A SHORT TIME later, and I soon heard heavy footsteps on the porch. I opened the door before he could ring the bell and set Maeve off into her usual welcome of barking frenzy.

"What happened?" I asked, finally letting go of

my held breath. It had to be something momentous for Riley to ask my advice.

"Jake's mother called." His desperate expression confirmed it.

I waited, but he wasn't any more forthcoming. Honestly, sometimes getting this man to open up was like chasing a rainbow. Pointless. Was I supposed to know something here?

"So, what does that mean?"

"She hasn't called in a very long time. I discourage it." He slid me a sidelong glance, expecting derision, I suppose. "Gets Jake all worked up and confused, and I have to deal with questions for weeks afterward."

My heart went out to him when I saw the pain in his eyes.

"Here's the deal. She got married a year ago and has a new baby. Must've woken her maternal instincts because now she's all hot about seeing Jake and introducing him to her family. They're staying at a resort in Door County for a week."

"Uh, huh." I remained noncommittal. After all, the man and I had no permanent future together. "Not to seem callous, but what help could I possibly be?"

"Brandi—Jake's mother—asked about him, and when I said he was doing just fine, she got all excited and started making plans to visit. I only said it because I hoped she'd leave things alone."

"So, what happened?"

"She's bringing her family over tomorrow afternoon." A long pause before he said, "What I'm asking is for you to be there with us. I don't know how Jake will react when he sees her." He needed a hug, but I didn't dare touch him. "He has no idea why his mother left. He's stopped asking, and I don't offer any explanation. She's not like you, Martha."

"You mean like the woman who keeps secrets to protect her children?"

"Yes, I was wrong, and I apologize for that." Frustration and pain rolled off him in waves.

I couldn't remain indifferent. This was a setup for disaster. How could I refuse? The child would need all available support. This would be a day Jake would always remember. I wanted it to be a good memory. It could be the beginning of a normal relationship between mother and child and a real step forward in his development.

"I guess I could do that."

"I'll never be able to thank you enough...I had no right to ask."

"It's okay." I put my hand on his arm. Big mistake. The heat in his glance told me we'd forged a bond between us, whether I liked it or not. I knew I'd caused some of the pain that glittered in his dark eyes.

Riley left then. He wasn't in a state of mind for small talk, and frankly, our personal problems seemed pretty unimportant after this bombshell.

Jake was the one who mattered now. All we could do was wait for the visit and see what happened.

JAKE WAS ON HIS BEST BEHAVIOR WHEN I ARRIVED THE next day. His mother, her new husband and baby, were seated in the living room. The room looked even sparser with these "pretty" people in it.

I knew Jake wanted desperately for his mother to love him and to have a family like the rest of his classmates. He'd mentioned it several times. Riley was kidding himself, thinking Jake didn't wonder why she left. The look on his face when she held that baby and told him it was his little sister spoke volumes. You could almost visualize the questions forming in his mind.

She looked the same as the picture at his bedside, a beautiful woman but young for her years, in voice and actions. She was everything a young boy could want in a mother though. Pretty, vivacious, and eager to please. But even in the short time we visited, I could sense she didn't understand Jake and his problems at all. She kept questioning him, pushing for answers he couldn't give.

They stayed for an hour, and before they left, Jake had even got up the nerve to sit next to his mother on the couch. I could see the interaction was making Riley nervous. What was he so afraid of? Surely, he didn't think Jake would want to leave him and live with her?

Before she left, Brandi sprung a loaded question in front of Jake.

"We're staying at a very nice resort. Can Jake come and spend a few days with us?" She wrapped her arms around the boy and looked lovingly into his face. "We really would like to get to know you. I've missed my little boy."

Riley sat speechless for a moment. "I don't know if that's a good idea."

Brandi's husband, who'd mostly sat quietly watching the proceedings, chimed in. "We'd take very good care of him." It was clear the man would do or say anything to please his wife.

"Please, Daddy? I'll be good, I promise," Jake whined, an almost feverish expression on his little face. I could see he was getting worked up, and his impulsive nature was about to gain control.

"I'll have to think about it." Riley sent a murderous look in Brandi's direction, but she didn't even flinch. In fact, if I wasn't mistaken, her spine straightened up a bit, and she looked back at Riley with a very determined expression.

"We'll be back tomorrow," she promised as they left.

"I want to go with my mommy." Jake stamped his foot and screamed as their car pulled away. There'd be no reasoning with the boy right now.

"Go to your room and play with your toys for a while, buddy."

Jake stamped his way out of the room, but not

before he threw several pillows on the floor and made a move toward a dish on the table.

"That's enough." I was surprised at the sternness in Riley's voice since he usually talked softly to his son.

"Don't you want Jake to have a relationship with his mother?" I asked when he was out of hearing range.

Riley had never seemed the type of father to deny his son anything that would benefit him. I couldn't imagine him taking his own feelings toward the woman out on Jake. The pain-filled expression in his eyes told me I was right.

"It'd be great if I thought it could work, but I know Brandi." He sighed. "I suppose she does love him, but unless she's changed a lot, she'll never be able to handle the tantrums."

"She seemed very eager to connect with him. Maybe she has changed."

"Look, Brandi and I had a few good years, but in the end, it was a disaster. I think I know her better than she knows herself. Her attitude with Jake only made it worse." He stoically cracked his knuckles in the silence of the room.

"Do you still have feelings for her?" A little voice whispered this could be the real reason he wouldn't commit to a permanent relationship.

"The only feeling I have about the whole affair is regret. It never should've happened. But then I wouldn't have Jake, would I?" he said with a wavering smile. "And he's the best thing that ever happened to me, no matter what."

"Can you tell me why she left?"

"She wanted marriage, and I couldn't give her that—not the way things were between us at the time. The only thing holding us together was Jake, and when his unusual behavior became more noticeable, things between us went south fast. We were fighting constantly, and it wasn't good for him. In the end, she just wanted out—of the relationship and parenting."

"Why did you want me here?" I was confused. "I'd like to help, but I don't see what I can possibly do." I could see the fear etched in his brow, and the feeling of helplessness was killing me. "It's really none of my business." The hurt in his eyes at those words would stay with me forever. "I mean, it's not like we're related or anything." Oh, lordy. I should just duct tape my mouth shut.

"You're right," he said tonelessly, shoulders sagging. "I had no business dragging you into this."

"It isn't that I don't care, you know that." I put a hand on his shoulder.

"The truth is, I can't believe Brandi has changed as much as she'd like to believe. I don't mean to bad-mouth her. Lord knows, I failed the kid enough myself."

"Are you afraid he'd get hurt, that they wouldn't watch him?"

"No, it's not that. She'd never intentionally hurt

him. But mostly her life has been about Brandi and what makes her happy. There were a lot of things in her past I never knew about. She's got this bug about Jake now and won't give it up until something else comes along to grab her attention. Let's just say she sometimes talks first and thinks later."

"But surely, if she loves him, she'll be careful how she handles him."

"I've been with Jake all his life and can still say or do the wrong thing on a daily basis. She refused to believe the doctor when he said Jake might have a neurobiological disorder. That was too scary to accept. Instead, she was determined he'd outgrow it. I have to confess it was easier to go along with that. It's just recently that I've come to grips with the reality of his condition. How can I believe she's changed now? What's she going to do when he throws a tantrum, and she can't control him?"

"She is his mother and has some rights."

"It seems to me she gave up those rights when she left us." He shoved his hands in his pockets and looked away.

"Be that as it may, she has legal rights, I presume?"

"She signed over his custodial care to me so I could get him into school and medical services." He turned to look at me, his expression grim. "At the time, she was out looking for a new life and didn't want to be saddled with a kid. Especially one with problems."

"So, what's your plan?"

"I don't have one. That's the problem. If I put up a fight, Jake will probably never forgive me. He wants a mom like the other kids. I can actually see that. I'm really not blind." The tortured look in his eyes squeezed my heart. "I'm just afraid she'll crush his self-esteem if she rejects him again. And by god, he can't stand to lose the little he has. I need your professional opinion before I make any decision. That's why I wanted you here to see their interaction."

"Tell me honestly. Why did Brandi leave?" I sensed there was something about their relationship he wasn't telling me.

"I told you. I couldn't give her total commitment." He averted his glance.

There was more to it than he was letting on. I wasn't going to let him off the hook this time though.

"C'mon, Riley. I need to know the truth."

He lifted those pain-filled eyes. "You're not going to let this rest, are you?"

I shook my head but didn't speak.

"All right. You want to know why she left? She was having an affair with a younger man—keeping secrets like so many women—my own mother is a great example. She had no problem leaving my father and me either. But at least she never came back to screw me up even further."

"Oh, Riley. That doesn't mean Brandi doesn't

love Jake. She was young but seems to have matured. Every woman loves her own son, your mother included. She most likely thought she was doing what was best for you."

"Just let it go, okay? What I need now is for you to give me some insight into how to handle this mess."

My heart bled for him, but I only had one answer. "I think you have to take the chance of letting Jake spend some time with his mother. You really don't have a choice."

He flinched, but I could see the answer wasn't totally unexpected.

"What if she decides to challenge me for custody? They're the traditional nuclear family—father, mother, son, and daughter. He's a successful lawyer. They have the money to bring a lawsuit and prove they have the finances for any future care Jake needs. How can I fight that?"

"You can fight it by showing you've taken care of Jake all his life. You didn't leave when times got tough. You've changed your entire lifestyle to care for him. Any judge would give that more weight."

"You'd think so, but I've heard horror stories."

"Listen, if Brandi is as shallow as you think she is, she won't fight you for custody. And if she has changed and is genuinely committed to Jake, then you may have to share him. But in the end, that could be a good thing for Jake." I hated voicing those thoughts, but it was the truth and he had to hear it. The stricken look on his face told me he had never come to terms with that hidden fear.

"I was hoping you wouldn't say that."

I realized again, with a sudden pang, how different this man was from Robert. He not only asked my opinion, he valued it, even when it wasn't what he wanted to hear. It made me love him even more, if that were possible.

I was torn between my desire to help Riley and my fear of losing myself again. His personality was so strong. As strong as Robert's.

But I'd do anything to keep Jake with the one person who loved him most, and without much thought, I put my future and my pride on the chopping block.

"Would it help if you were married?" I'm sure he heard the hesitancy in my voice. My mouth had spit the words out before my brain had a chance to process them.

"Let me guess. You feel so sorry for the poor bastard who could lose his child you'd put your own needs aside and marry him." The bitterness surprised me. I'd expected him to be grateful at the very least. "Forget it. We don't need rescuing."

He walked toward the door, my clue to leave. "I'll call you later, after I've had some time to think."

I left quietly, my feelings once again conflicted. I had offered to marry him and been rejected. How painful was that? And then there was that part of me that was relieved.

17

WHEN SUZE SHOWED UP ON MY DOORSTEP THAT evening, I was still playing "What if." What if something bad happened to Jake because of my advice? What if Riley never forgave me? What if Brandi left town with Jake? And on and on.

"What are you doing here?" Two unexpected visits from my sister? What was with her anyway? It wasn't as if she was just riding across town, for crying out loud. "Have you ever heard of the telephone?"

I didn't mean to be rude, but I was already in my pajamas and in no mood to entertain. I looked a little closer. This time she wasn't bearing gifts or wearing a smile.

She stepped into the house, looking teary-eyed and shaky—not the self-confident woman I'd grown used to.

"Martha, I've been a terrible mother and role model, and I don't know how to fix it."

Now, my sister can be annoying, pushy, and over-confident at times, I'd be the first to say it. Kind of like Brooke, now that I think about it. But a poor mother and role model? Ridiculous.

"What in the world are you blathering about?" I took her by the arm and led her to the kitchen table. Letting me guide her spoke volumes.

"You need a cup of tea, and probably a good night's sleep."

"It'll take more than a cup of tea to fix this mess," she sobbed.

Oh, lordy. I'd never seen my sister like this, and that awful sense of helplessness swept over me again. I set down the teakettle and put my arms around her. She let me. A bad sign.

"Suze, what in the world is going on?"

"It's Nora. She's pregnant."

"And?"

"She refuses to marry Dave, insists she doesn't want to be tied down because of a sheet of paper."

"Well, if she doesn't love the man, it's a better choice. You of all people know that. Aren't you always harping that women need to be self-sufficient and not depend on a man to take care of them?"

At those words, she began to wail. "You sound just like Richard, and you're both right. It's all my fault. That's why it hurts so much."

"What are you talking about? How could it be

your fault? You're not making any sense. Nora's a thirty-five-year-old woman, for God's sake. She knows what she wants out of life. She's not your little girl anymore."

"Yes, but Richard says I'm the one who filled her head with all those ideas about not needing a man in her life and now our first grandchild will be born illegitimate."

"Oh, for Pete's sake. This is the new millennium. People don't even use that term anymore. Do you want to go back to the fifties and have her stuck in a miserable marriage with a man she doesn't love, just for convention's sake?"

"But that's the thing. She does love him. But she wants to make the choices in her life without interference from a husband."

Oh, boy. My sister's angst was beginning to make sense. "How does Dave feel about it?"

"He's angry and hurt, and he feels she doesn't think he's a good enough catch for her."

"Maybe when her hormones settle down, she'll change her mind. If she really does love him, that is."

"Dave says he won't wait forever, and at this point, they're not speaking. He's threatening legal action."

I didn't know what to say or do. Why did life have to get so damn complicated? But this was my sister, and I had to dredge up some pearl of wisdom.

"The truth is, Suze, it really isn't your affair. Nora and Dave will have to work it out."

"Easy for you to say. It's not your grandchild we're talking about. Everything is different when you're talking in the abstract."

Some of her spunk was returning. She took the tissue I offered and wiped her eyes and blew her nose.

"I was wondering..." she began, and a chill of dread climbed up my spine. Uh-oh. When I saw the pleading in her eyes, I knew it didn't bode well for me.

"Could you talk to her? Maybe tell her how important it is to have both parents in the home when you're raising a child? Especially when they're both working—to help carry the load. You being a teacher and now working with special-needs kids and all..."

What my job had to do with it, I couldn't quite figure out. Obviously, she was too emotional to make sense. "I'm sure you already told her that since you were the one who worked all those years. She must have been aware of how you and Richard worked together to raise the family."

"Yes, but it'll mean more coming from you."

"Why?"

She looked a little sheepish. "She may have heard me talking to Richard..."

"Why are you mumbling?"

She sighed. "All right, she may have heard me

telling Richard that you were wasting your education when you let Robert talk you into giving up your career to stay home with the kids. I think she's afraid it could happen to her." She looked embarrassed, as she should.

"You think I didn't know how you felt? It was written all over your face," I said. "Why would she think Dave would want her to give up her career? Has he said that?"

"No, but she—"

"Wait a minute—exactly where are you going with this?" I narrowed my eyes.

"It would mean a lot if you could tell her how glad you are that you put your children's welfare first and your career second." She raised her eyebrows with a hopeful look.

"Are you saying you *want* her to give up her career?" This was totally nuts and not at all like my sister. Maybe it was Suze's hormones that had gone wild. After all, she was of menopausal age. "I can't do that. I don't even know if it's the right thing for her to do. We all have to make our own decisions about raising kids."

"No, that's not what I want." Suze shook her head vehemently. "I just want her to realize how much easier her life would be if she was married. Her's and the baby's. It isn't as if she doesn't love Dave. She just seems to have this weird idea that the baby is her responsibility alone. I suppose it's because she didn't plan on getting pregnant."

"Do you know how Dave feels about the pregnancy?"

"He was quite surprised. Now, he wants to be part of it all."

"Maybe that's the problem."

"What do you mean?"

"Maybe she feels he thinks she trapped him into it."

She wiped her hands across her face. "God, you think when your kids are grown up your worries are over. Instead, they just get bigger and more involved."

"I hope you're planning to spend the night. You're in no condition to drive back to Milwaukee."

"I'd like to stay if it isn't too much bother," she said. "Richard and I had words before I left. Of course, he blames me for her attitude."

I could see the pain in her eyes as she sipped her tea.

I HAD JUST SAID GOODBYE TO SUZE EARLY THE NEXT morning when Riley called.

"Can you come over?"

"What's going on?" I asked half-heartedly, Suze's problems with her daughter still fresh in my mind. Nora's argument sounded good now, before the baby was born. But that was without factoring in croup, fevers, and just general angst that came with raising children. Just look at Riley's life as a single parent. But should I be the one to tell her that? And would she even listen?

"I've decided to let Jake spend some time with his mother. They'll be here in an hour to pick him up."

I surmised from his curt tone that he wasn't happy about the decision.

"You're doing the right thing." I thought again of Nora. If only she could see the possible problems that lay ahead. She could be walking into a minefield of disasters, all of her own making.

"Yeah, well, I really haven't much of a choice, have I?"

"I'll be there as soon as I can." I dressed and hurried out to the barn with Maeve in tow. Usually, I felt a calming there but not today.

My mind chewed up possible problems and spit them out one at a time. I had my own disasters to face. Riley had made up his mind to go through life alone, and I had to agree with his decision. After all, it was what we both wanted. Wasn't it? Why did he feel he needed my company for backup today?

After hurrying through the chores, I put Maeve in her crate and left.

When I got to Riley's, he and Jake were still waiting for Brandi to arrive.

"Maybe she's not coming," Jake said, looking on the verge of tears.

"Give them time, buddy." Riley put his hand on the boy's shoulder. I could see his irritation.

Finally, Brandi and her family arrived, and he ran out to greet them. Riley was a little slower, and I decided to wait in the house. It wasn't long before we were all in the small living room, jockeying for seats.

Jake's face lit with excitement every time Brandi spoke to him, and he hung on her every word. I watched the interaction between them with apprehension.

"We'll have a lot of fun, honey. There's a wonderful carnival in town with rides and clowns and special treats that you'll just love." She was trying so hard to impress him that my heart ached—for both of them.

Riley was right. The woman was living in dreamland.

Jake returned her smile with an adoring one reserved just for her. He wanted to please his mother more than anything.

"Wow, that sounds like there'll be a lot going on for a first visit. Maybe it'd be better to spend some quiet time getting to know each other again." Riley joined the conversation, his lowered eyebrows showing concern.

"Oh, stop being such a worrywart. It's time he was treated like any other eight year old."

"Brandi, you don't understand…"

Jake watched their back-and -forth conversation, his head swiveling like he was at a tennis match. He sent a pleading look to his father.

"I understand I want to spend a few days with my son and show him a good time. Is that so strange? After all, you've had him to yourself for most of his life. Don't I deserve some time with him?" She turned pleading eyes toward her husband, who held their daughter in his arms.

"Brandi's right. We'll take good care of him. It's only for a few days. It isn't as if we're going to run away with him."

Some of the color left Riley's face at those words. The man had voiced his worst nightmare. He slammed his fist into his palm in frustration.

"Do you have my cell phone?" he asked Jake. His hands rested on the boy's narrow shoulders as he looked directly into his eyes.

Jake shook his head, flipping the phone out of his pocket for a moment, without looking at Riley. He only had eyes for his mother at the moment. Riley gave his shoulders a gentle shake.

"You'll call twice a day, right, buddy?" Riley sounded almost desperate, so unlike him, a man always in control.

"I'll make sure he calls. Now, stop worrying." Brandi waved her palm, brushing aside Riley's worries as meaningless.

I could see Brandi's promise didn't do much to convince Riley. But he did help Jake with his bag and walked him out to the car. I gave him a lot of credit for that. He stood stoically, cracking his knuckles again as the car drove away.

I wanted to put my arms around him and hold him tight. What would happen to this gentle man if he lost custody of his son? I had the sudden perception that he'd withdraw so deep within himself that no one, including me, would ever reach him again.

"It'll be all right. She'll take good care of him."

His only response to my lame words was a look of derision. He turned back to the house, and when I followed him in, I understood how empty the place must seem, coupled with the fear of losing his son forever.

"Did you hear the way she talked to him?" He ran his fingers through his hair in that same frustrated way. "She hasn't a clue of how to manage him."

"If things go bad, she'll bring him home, you know that." I put my hand on his arm. "She does love him, Riley. It was written all over her face when she talked to him."

He gave me a grateful look and patted my hand where it rested on his arm.

There wasn't anything more I could say or do so I left. This was a problem he had to deal with on his own now. It was his choice after all. He'd shut me out.

WHEN I TALKED TO RILEY THE NEXT AFTERNOON, HIS mood hadn't improved much.

"Would you like me to come over and keep you company?"

"I wouldn't be good company."

"Has Jake called?"

"Yeah, he called this morning—didn't say much except he was having fun with his little sister."

"That sounds pretty positive."

"If you say so." His curt answer cut.

"Okay then, I'll talk to you later."

"Hey, I do appreciate everything. I guess I'm not too good at expressing my feelings," he said softly. "Don't take any of this personally. What was it Brandi called me, a worrywart? That's me when it comes to my son."

"I understand," I said. "I'm the same with my girls. Just know I'm here if you need me."

I GOT UP THAT FRIDAY MORNING, DETERMINED TO GET on with my own life. What else could I do? I'd laid my love and future on the line, and it wasn't enough. Riley was determined to go it alone, and I couldn't stop him.

Early that evening, I gathered up my newly spun yarn, knitting needles, and a Waldorf salad I'd managed to put together and headed off to the Wool Gatherers. We were meeting at Carol's that night, trying to keep things as low-key and easy as possible for her.

I hadn't realized how tight my jaw was clenched

until I entered Carol's kitchen and relaxed my mouth in a smile of greeting. Their easy acceptance of me, with no pretense or agenda on their part, made me want to hug each one of them. They'd never understand my gratitude. I'd never felt this closeness to other women since my college days.

It was especially welcoming tonight because doubts still plagued me since I'd told Riley my thoughts about Jake spending time with his mother. What if I was wrong?

We sat in Carol's family room among the comfortable but well-used furnishings and piles of video games and various pieces of sports equipment. She'd warned me before my first visit that living with three sons definitely impacted her décor. She wasn't kidding. This was definitely a man's room, evidenced by the way the family's golden retriever lounged so comfortably on the end of the couch.

"Did you hear the latest? My ex and his wife had a baby girl yesterday."

The collective intake of breath and stricken looks would've been funny if the news hadn't been so painful.

"Yeah, so I guess it'll be sleepless nights and diapers for those two lovebirds now." Not even sarcasm could hide the pain in her voice.

Joan rose and quietly put her arms around her.

"It's okay. I've had a day to adjust." She gave her usual smile, only a bit watery this time. "But it doesn't seem fair that it'd be a girl. We were hoping for one the last two pregnancies." A devilish glint came back into her eyes. "I can only hope she takes after her mother."

Maybe it was the wine I drank before dinner, I don't know. But it wasn't long before I was spilling my guts about Riley and his former lover's appearance. From what Carol said, everyone knew we were dating anyway. They also knew Brandi, since she was a local girl.

"I'll admit it," Nancy said grudgingly. "You're a much better choice for Reilly than I would've been. As much as I would've liked to be with him, I don't think I could handle Jake and his problems like you do."

"He asked for my advice, and I told him to let Jake go for a few days. Now, I'm having second thoughts. What if it just makes Brandi determined to gain custody? Riley may be headed for the fight of his life, and I may have been part of the cause."

"Hey, don't beat yourself up over it. He asked for your advice, and you gave it. The final decision was up to him," Nancy said.

"Yes, but what if something happens to Jake?" The thought of his mother carelessly wounding him emotionally tore me up inside. "I love that little guy so much it scares me."

I had no claim on him—morally or legally. I wondered again if I should've kept that option open, at least thought about it some more. Riley did say he loved me, and I knew I loved him. I would be the best mother in the world to Jake, even if there were no blood bonds between us.

"We don't always realize beforehand the ramifications of a split on the children. Sometimes, the need to just get out of a bad situation is too overwhelming," Carol said.

Lila rested her hand on my shoulder and gave it a squeeze. "Brandi has to see for herself that Jake's in the right place now that she's found hers before she can find her own peace of mind."

I picked up my needles again, finding a measure of comfort in their words and the twisting and turning of yarn into the symbolic Aran patterns: Celtic rope for Irish pride, fishermen's cable for safety on the waters, basket stitch for a plentiful catch, and diamond, the shape of a fishing net, for success.

What would the pattern of my own life be if I could knit it into a design? What stitch could show my joy at the birth of my daughters, the tears over my lost confidence, the anguish at Robert's death, and now the renewal of my spirit and love for Riley and Jake?

And what about Robert's gambling addiction? Surely, that must be what it had become. Robert never would've taken such chances if he'd had control over his actions. Why hadn't I questioned his frequent absences instead of accepting his easy explanations? And why hadn't I questioned his need for complete control over our finances? I would forever carry some blame for not recognizing any problem. Was there a stitch for that?

"Life is like a never-ending pattern, isn't it? Just going on, year after year, with its twists and turns," I said. I thought of my gram and my mother and sister. "Yet somehow, it all ties together to form a beautiful and unique design at the end."

"Wow, that was deep," Nancy quipped.

"It'll work out in the end, you'll see," Joan encouraged.

I wish I had her confidence. Even after what she'd been through these past years, she never seemed to lose faith in the human spirit. I marveled again how meeting these women had changed my life. A year ago, I never would've bared my soul to anyone as I'd just done—not even under the threat of pain. Yet here I was, so comfortable among these women that I could tell them almost anything. And I'd found Riley, a man who not only accepted me as I am, but also valued my opinion as an equal. I made up my mind then to stop at his place on my way home and see how he was faring.

18

RILEY'S GREETING WAS STRAINED AND BARELY welcoming when he answered my knock.

"Hi. I was on my way home and thought I'd stop in to see if you'd heard how things are going with Jake."

His hair stood in unruly tufts on his head, making his unshaven cheeks even more noticeable. He looked more like a street person than the L.L.Bean types I sometimes saw.

"You look like hell, by the way."

"Good to see you, too." He opened the door wider. "You might as well come in since you're already here. Just don't expect any scintillating conversation."

"How's Jake getting along?" I asked.

"How the hell would I know?" he said, pain carved in merciless lines across his face. "He hasn't called since early this morning. It's way past his bedtime now, so I don't suppose I'll hear from him anymore today."

The faint smell of wood shavings permeated the air.

"I see you've been busy."

"Yeah. I'm working on a new project. Want to see it?"

A trail of sawdust followed him from the front door to the kitchen and covered the front of his jeans with a fine powder.

I followed him through the kitchen and out to his workshop.

A four-poster bed stood in the center of the room, taking up most of the shop space.

"Wow." I reached out and touched one of the spiral-carved posts that ended with a delicately carved finial, also in a spiral pattern. "It's beautiful."

"I thought you'd like it. It's a reproduction of a late eighteenth-century New England antique. Only it's king-size, and the headboard, footboard, and posts are cherry instead of mahogany."

He looked over his shoulder at me. "It's a marriage bed. One that should last a lifetime. Like a good marriage."

"It must've taken you many hours."

"I lost count."

"Who's it for?"

"A very special lady."

His cell phone rang before I could ask any more

questions. I noticed his hand trembling slightly as he pulled it out of his shirt pocket.

He swore under his breath as he read the number.

It wasn't hard to figure out who was on the phone. The rigid set to his shoulders and the mono-syllabic tones confirmed my suspicions. That, and the way he cracked his knuckles and ran shaking fingers through his hair after ending the call.

"They're on their way here."

"What happened?" The bottom fell out of my stomach as I waited for his answer. It couldn't be good.

"Brandi was so hysterical I couldn't quite get things clear, but I'm assuming Jake had several meltdowns today and this last one was major. She doesn't know what to do, so of course she's bringing him back here. That's how she's always handled problems."

I put my hand on his arm, and he flinched.

"Don't be so hard on her. You know how difficult it can be to calm him down once he gets going."

"Didn't I try to tell her that?" He set his jaw. "If she's upset the kid so he backslides, I'll..."

"Hey, c'mon. At least she's trying to be a mother to him now. Cut her a little slack. Jake needs this."

His face melted into acceptance. "You're right, I'll try. It's just so frustrating when other people think they know Jake better than I do. Acting as if I'm the one making him 'different'."

Did he include me in that group? I know he did at first and could only pray we'd moved beyond it.

"Can you stay until they get here? I don't play nice when I'm frustrated and angry." His fists clenched at his sides. "You're the only other person I trust to know what's best for him."

My heart sang with relief at those words, and I moved closer. He opened his arms then, and I stepped into his embrace.

"I don't know how I made it this long without you," he said in a whisper against my ear. "It's been damn hard."

I wrapped my arms around him the way I loved to do, tightening the embrace.

"It's going to be all right. Whatever happened, we'll fix it—together." I tried desperately to believe my own words, but doubt clouded my mind.

It seemed we waited forever, clinging to each other, before we heard a car in the driveway. We ran out the door together, down the porch steps, and into the cool evening air. The car had barely come to a stop when Jake jumped out, a frantic look on his little boy face.

"My God, wasn't he even in a seatbelt?" I heard Riley's roar as he crossed the expanse of driveway.

"I couldn't call you," Jake quivered in a soft voice, his narrow shoulders heaving with sobs when he reached Riley's open arms.

"Shh, shh, it's okay. You're home now." Riley knelt down on the gravel driveway, clutching the boy to his chest as though he'd never let him go again. Once again, he'd managed to quell his own anger for the boy's sake.

"I'm so sorry," a shaken Brandi whispered, staying near the car and out of Riley's reach. "I had no idea he would get this upset." She was on the verge of tears herself.

I walked closer, seeing she needed support, too, and she grabbed my arm.

"I forgot to charge his cell phone and didn't bring mine. We were at the carnival, and all the noise and crowd upset Jake for some reason. He wanted to talk to Riley, and when we told him he couldn't, he just freaked out—screaming and thrashing around." She rambled on incoherently, trying to explain what she clearly didn't under-stand. "No matter what I said or did, he wouldn't stop. He was like some kind of wild animal caught in a trap."

I covered her fingers with mine. I knew how frightening the experience could be if one wasn't prepared. It was good for her to realize, as painful as the experience had been, what raising Jake would be like before she got embroiled in a legal battle.

"Mark had to pick him up forcefully and carry him to the parking lot. Luckily, he had his cell phone in the glove compartment. I told Jake then I'd call his dad, but it was too late. He was beyond rea-soning with." She swiped at her eyes, a defeated look crossing her face. "Mark's right. I can't handle this, and neither can he. It would be best for Jake if he stayed with his father, and we only had short visits. Maybe when he grows up…" She turned toward the car where her husband and small child waited, engine running.

"Be good to them. They deserve it," she said, giving my arm a squeeze before hurrying to the car. They drove off with a screech of tires.

Riley looked up at the sound and gave a sigh of relief. Jake had quieted now, sobbing softly into Riley's chest.

"C'mon, buddy. Let's go into the house." He put one arm around Jake and the other around me. We walked into the house, all of us subdued. It had been quite an experience, and hopefully, we'd all learned something from it.

"Let's get you cleaned up and into your pajamas. It's way past your bedtime." He directed Jake toward his bedroom.

Jake stopped and asked, "Is my mommy gone?"

I looked into his eyes and saw the regret there. "Yes, but she said to tell you she'll be back another time to visit. She doesn't live that far away." I didn't know what else to tell him. Hopefully, it was the truth.

He sighed like a weight had been lifted from his shoulders. What threw him over the edge? I had never seen him behave in the way Brandi described; it went way beyond his usual meltdowns. Had Jake tried too hard to be perfect in order to win his mother's love?

"Can you help us get settled?" Riley signaled me to come along while Jake prepared for bed. "Maybe you could read to him tonight."

"Would you like that?" I looked down at the child who smiled through his tears. The emotional storm had passed, and he was exhausted.

"That'd be good," he whispered.

"I'll get a book. Any one in particular you'd like?"

"*Goodnight Moon*."

"Oh, Jake, not again." Riley rolled his eyes. "It's been a nightly ritual for years."

"*Goodnight Moon* it is." I winked at Jake and went over to the bookshelf. The boy needed familiarity tonight.

I sat beside him on the bed after he was tucked in and read the story. His eyes were half-closed when he asked me, "Do you think my mommy loves me?"

"I know she does. She loves you very much. That's why she lets you stay with your daddy because she knows you're happier here."

"Yeah, I am," he whispered as he closed his eyes. "I love my daddy very much. And you, too."

Those words brought tears to my eyes. How would I ever be able to leave this beautiful child?

Riley had been standing in the hall, and I knew he'd listened to our conversation.

"There's a reason I wanted you to tuck him in tonight."

"Really?" I had thought he'd want to be the one to do it after the traumatic experience Jake had just been through.

"He needs to know we're a team now."

I looked at him incredulously. "What do you mean?"

"I've learned something through this whole mess. Something I've known in my heart for a long time but have been afraid to admit.

"I love you, Martha, plain and simple. I know we've decided on a relationship with no strings, but I can't accept that anymore. It's not good enough. I need to know you'll be here with me, always. No matter how crazy life gets."

"So, what exactly are you saying?"

"This is my inept way of asking you to marry me."

"I thought marriage was out of the picture?" My racing heart refused to believe what I was hearing. Why had he changed his mind?

"Now that I don't have to worry about losing custody of Jake, if your answer is yes, it's because you *want* to marry us. And it would be the two of us, for better or worse, forever. I'll understand if you turn me down. Jake and I are not exactly the poster boys for happy ever after. But we'll love you more than we've ever loved anyone else."

"Oh, Riley." My mind couldn't quite wrap

around the fact he wanted to marry me, and it had nothing to do with regaining custody of his son. This strong, loving man actually wanted me, at my age, graying hair, extra pounds, and all.

I was flummoxed. I didn't know what to say. The old Martha wanted to shout, *Yes, yes. This is what I've been searching for.*

But the new Martha whispered in my head, *Now, just hold onto your shirt here. You know what happened the last time you fell for happy ever after.*

"Well, do I get an answer?"

"I have to think it over." My God, I couldn't believe I said it. I knew the words would hurt him, but I had to be honest—with him and myself.

I left his place in a daze. What had I just done?

19

I CALLED SUZE THE NEXT MORNING. I NEEDED sisterly advice and confirmation that I was doing the right thing. For all of us. Jake, Riley, and me.

"You made it home," I said when she answered, as if I wouldn't have heard otherwise by this time. I've always had this annoying habit of stating the obvious. The fact that my sister let it pass without a cutting remark was a clue to her state of mind.

"Oh, yeah. But nothing's changed. I can tell Richard still blames me, even though he denies it."

"Oh, for cryin' out loud. You know he's just taking his frustration out on you. Tell him to get over it already."

"You know what? All these years, I've thought you wasted your education staying home to be at Robert's beck and call while I scrambled at dead-end jobs, resentful that I didn't have your education and opportunities. I wanted more for my daughter—"

I interrupted her. "Your family should thank you for it—you did a great job raising your kids to be self-sufficient."

"Yeah, right." She sniffed loudly. "Maybe I was wrong. Why is the grass always greener on the other side?"

"I wish I had the answer to that and a lot of other questions, Suze. On that note, I have some news."

"Okay, spill it."

Her voice lacked her usual enthusiasm, big-time, but I forged ahead. "First, you have to promise you won't breathe a word to my girls."

That caught her attention. I heard her sharp intake of breath. "Tell me."

"Riley asked me to marry him."

"What was your answer?" No squeal of delight or exuberant congratulations there.

"I told him I had to think about it."

"Oh, boy. I'll bet that didn't go over well. Have you made a decision?"

"I know what I want to do, but..."

"Well, if it helps any, I'm through harping to my daughter about a woman not needing a man in her life. Circumstances can change things right quick, can't they?"

I hung up the phone after she reassured me again that she'd keep my secret. Suze had always been my lifeline, only today, we seemed to be holding each other up. I had hoped talking to her would give me the answer I needed, but all it did was stir the pot more.

I had to admit, my love and admiration for my older sister had been part of my driving force toward independence. I'd always known she felt I'd wasted my education, and it had added to my guilt. What would've happened if she'd been the first one in the family to go to college?

Instead, she'd married right out of high school, lost in the romance of being a wife and mother in suburbia.

The romance of that life left when she'd had to work menial jobs for years to support the family while her husband attended college. I knew she blamed herself for her choices and was determined her daughter wouldn't follow in her footsteps. That wasn't to say she didn't love Richard. They had a strong marriage. Maybe the hardships had made it even stronger.

So, where did that leave me?

It was enough to make my head ache. I called Maeve and started down my favorite deer path with her at my heels. Summer would be over before I knew it, and I actually began to look forward to the fall, knowing the hardwoods would be turning their brilliant reds and yellows and the nip of frost would be in the early morning air. The change always gave me that extra burst of energy I lacked in the heat and humidity of summer.

Fall had always meant a new beginning—a new school year, new friendships, and so on.. Last year, it had been the beginning of a new life for me. Little had I realized I'd once again be standing on the threshold of change.

I wanted to be logical about my decision, but how could I be logical about these feelings in my heart? I knew what I wanted. I wanted to be with Riley—all day, all the time.

Did that mean I would fall back into my old habits? Was I ready to give control of my life over to another?

I thought about Robert and our life together. He was a good man and a good father. How had things gone so wrong? If we'd shared the financial burden, would it have prevented his gambling? I'd never know.

We'd started out as partners, but after the kids came along, it'd been easier to let him make the major decisions—less hassle all around. The girls were only two years apart, and I'd been overwhelmed with bottles, diapers, and lack of sleep. Robert had started traveling for business by that time, and he came home on the weekends to a zombie and a house pretty much in shambles.

Without any discussion, through the years we'd fallen into a pattern of job sharing. I took care of the girls, all their activities, and the household. He was in charge of finances and our social life. I didn't have the desire or the energy. Besides, he was the one who wanted to entertain. Good for his career, he'd said. I'd found it easier to just go along.

So, I was like my sister after all. Filled with misdirected anger. I really should've been angry with myself these past years and maybe, subconsciously, I was.

I had a chance now for a new relationship. I'd learned enough about myself and what I wanted to make one work. Things would be different with Riley; we'd already established a pattern in our relationship. If he valued my opinion on matters concerning Jake, I had no doubt we'd work as a team. Any man who could stay with his son through the ups and downs they'd been through would never leave a commitment. I didn't have to worry about that. Now, all I had to do was tell him.

I ARRIVED AT THEIR DOOR JUST AS THE SUN WAS setting. It'd turned into a warm and muggy evening, and they were both outside, sitting in lawn chairs and swatting mosquitoes.

Riley jumped from his chair when I got out of the Camry. "C'mon in," he said a little warily.

"We can stay outside." I was suddenly nervous. What if he'd changed his mind? Maybe my hesitation had turned him off.

"The bugs were about to carry us off anyway. Weren't they, Jake?" He patted his son on the head. "You go and get ready for bed, okay, buddy? I'll be in as soon as I talk to Martha."

"I want Martha to read to me tonight." He grabbed my hand with a pleading look. "Okay?"

"Sure, I will. You get ready, and I'll be there."

"Well?" Riley gave me a piercing look with his fathomless eyes. "I guess you've made your decision?"

"There's something I have to tell you first." Explaining Robert's past to Riley wouldn't be easy for me, knowing his history with women and secrets. But what choice did I have?

When I finished, he ran his hand through his dark hair in that familiar way. "Wow! And I thought Brandi was the expert at covering her tracks."

"You must think I'm really stupid not to have noticed things weren't right in our lives."

"I'm thinking maybe you and I are alike in that respect. We're honest and assume everyone else is the same until proven otherwise."

If I wasn't crazy in love with him before, those words sealed it. I put my arms around him, feeling secure and well-loved for the first time in a long time.

"Let's not change, either. I like the way the world looks through my rose-colored glasses," I said. "I'll only take them off when necessary."

"Well, say it already. You're killing me."

"Yes, I'll marry you." I put my hand on his arm. "And I'll thank my lucky stars every day that you and Jake came into my life."

He pressed his forehead to mine, closed his eyes, and let out his breath with a deep sigh, as though he'd been holding it for a long time.

"Let's go tell Jake."

We went into his bedroom, arm and arm.

"Does that mean I'll have a real mommy? One who lives with us all the time?" At the look of incredulous happiness on his face, I almost broke down into tears. Riley's arm tightened around my shoulder and kept me from collapsing into an emotional mess on Jake's bed.

"It sure does, buddy." Even Riley's voice had a crack in it.

"That went well," he said in his usual understated way when we were alone. He held me close and kissed the top of my head. "You smell so sweet, like someone put love in a jar just for you to wear."

That love spilled out of my heart and lit up my entire body like a roman candle, ready to explode at any moment with happiness.

. . .

I WAITED A FEW DAYS BEFORE CALLING MY DAUGHTERS.

Lexie gasped in surprise. "You're kidding. Oh, Mom, I wish I'd had the chance to meet Riley while I was there at Christmas. He must be quite the fella if he convinced you to marry again."

My knees went weak with relief. At least one of my daughters trusted my judgment enough not to question my choice of men. I laughed, my happiness spilling out in my voice. "Actually, it didn't take much convincing. When you meet him and Jake, you'll understand."

"I am so proud of you and the way you've handled your life this past year. It's like you've become this whole new person instead of just being my mom. You've given me a lot to think about."

"Honey, you'll never know how much that means to me." My voice choked with emotion. "Now, wish me luck. I have to call your sister with the news."

"I wish I could be there to give you moral support." Her voice hardened in a way that showed her new determination. "Don't let her intimidate you. She's awfully good at it, you know."

She spoke from experience. I couldn't begin to count the many times Brooke coerced or demanded the more compliant Lexie into following her lead during their youth. As a matter of fact, she still tried, but Donald quickly put the damper on any plans that didn't match his. Poor Lexie had two of them to battle for her independence. I wished again there was a way to counsel her without interfering in her marriage. As long as she was happy though, who was I to shake things up? I still remembered how torn I'd been when Suze and Robert were at odds.

"I can handle your sister. Lord knows, I've had years of practice. I just hope she can accept Riley because, no matter what, this wedding is going to happen."

"Good for you, Mom."

"We're planning an engagement party in a few weeks. I hope you can make it."

"Count on it. Let me know the details as soon as you have them."

I gritted my teeth and dialed Brooke's number next.

"Hi honey. This is your mother calling with a surprise announcement." For a moment there, I thought I had her voice mail and the wuss in me hoped to leave a message. It would give her time to adjust, I told myself.

No such luck. She picked up the phone at the sound of my voice on the recorder.

"Hello, Mother," she said in a droll voice. "Should I sit down? You haven't robbed a bank or decided to shave your head and pierce various body parts, have you? Nothing you do could surprise me these days."

I decided to ignore that and go right to the big announcement. "Riley and I are getting married."

The sentence was greeted with silence, but I heard her hyperventilating again so I knew she was still there.

"Please tell me this is a joke."

"It's no joke, and before you say anything else, I want you to know that I love him very much and nothing you can say will change that." Hopefully, I'd beaten her to the punch. "We're planning an engagement party in the near future. I hope you'll come. Lexie and Donald will be there." I harbored the dim hope it would sweeten the pot if she heard her sister wasn't putting up a fuss.

"I guess congratulations are in order then," she said quietly. Not exactly the exuberant reaction one would hope for, but at least she hadn't hung up on me or started slinging hateful barbs.

"Will you be able to come up for the party?"

"Oh, I'll be there. You can count on it. It's past time I met this Riley person." Now that sounded more like the Brooke of thunder and brimstone I'd expected.

Hopefully, she'd realize before she got here that Riley would soon be her stepfather and treat him with respect.

Oh, boy, I had to warn him. Even dealing with Jake's tantrums wouldn't prepare him for that meeting unless he was forewarned, and possibly forearmed.

THE FOLLOWING WEEKS PASSED IN A HAZE OF happiness. Riley, Jake, and I spent most evenings together, going over future plans. I'd never seen Jake so excited—in a good way.

The day of the party arrived way before I was emotionally prepared. My children and Riley were going to meet soon, and I was a physical and emotional wreck just thinking about it. Why hadn't I insisted they meet earlier instead of when we were celebrating our engagement? Putting off a problem never made it easier. I'd learned that years ago but still chose to ignore it whenever I could.

The doorbell rang at exactly 3 p.m.. That would be Brooke, of course, right on the minute. But why the doorbell? She usually barged right in.

Riley and Jake stood on the porch, early by two hours. Jake was spiffed up and polished to within an inch of his life, wearing a dress shirt, pants, and red bow tie. Riley stood behind him, dressed in a navy sport coat with gleaming silver buttons, blue-and-white striped shirt, and camel dress pants. I blinked in surprise. Wow. They looked way too handsome to be mine.

Only, the apprehensive look on Jake's face broke my heart. Was he afraid he wouldn't like my girls? Or they wouldn't accept him?

"Hey, buddy, don't you look gorgeous," I said, reaching over and deliberately mussing his hair a bit. My Jake didn't have to look like a model from a holiday catalogue to be loved.

"The girls are going to eat you up." At the frightened look on his face, I remembered that he took everything literally. "That means they'll fall in love with you on sight."

His shoulders relaxed at that, and a grin spread across his face.

"But why are you here so early?" The words came out before I had a chance to filter them through my social niceties. A trickle of nervousness ran down my spine. "The party isn't going to start until five."

"We couldn't stand it any longer. We're too excited," Riley said.

He nodded toward Jake, but he wasn't fooling me. He was as nervous as I was. The high color in his cheeks and the steel glint in his eye were dead giveaways. He wanted to get this first meeting over with as much as I did. My stories of Brooke must have shaken him up more than I intended. But I'd wanted him to be prepared.

"Have they arrived yet?"

"No. I expect them any minute." I wiped my sweaty palms down the sides of my cut-offs.

He put his own hands in his pants pockets and frowned. "I thought maybe we could meet before the other guests arrived."

Was he expecting fireworks?

Now what was I supposed to do? I needed time to get ready myself. I'd spent the day getting the house prepared for the big event.

When I'd told the Wool Gatherers of the engagement, they'd enthusiastically joined in the party planning, making lists and delegating jobs among themselves. When I declined their generosity, they answered back.

"Hey, if it weren't for us, you and Riley would never have connected," Lila said.

"And I take full credit for dragging you to the Christmas Arts and Crafts Festival." Carol put her hands on her hips in a no-nonsense gesture. She looked so cute with her new baby-soft locks coming in, how could I deny her anything?

"Just promise me you won't get carried away and turn this into the Shoreview party of the year."

My warning fell on deaf ears. A group of them had just left after dropping off food, drink, and decorations. My quiet little gathering had turned into a major celebration, just as I'd feared. Everywhere I'd gone these past weeks, I'd been met with congratulations and enthusiastic greetings. The guest list had grown proportionately. What was it about weddings that turned perfectly normal people into sappy romantics?

I hadn't wanted the party held at some hall. The thought of my family and friends intermingling for the first time in a strange place left me cold. I wanted them to meet in the intimacy of my new home where they could get a feel for the life Riley and I planned to lead.

He had already agreed to move in here. It would be a wonderful place for Jake to grow up—lots of room for him to run and play. And being with the gentle animals, learning to care for them would be an extra benefit. Riley was making plans for a new, bigger workshop.

Jake had stood quietly at his father's side during our discussion, and I finally came out of my own little world and noticed his bored expression.

I turned to Riley. "Why don't you take Jake out to see the lambs while I get dressed?" Hopefully, that would keep them out of my hair for a while. "Oh, but don't let him roll in the grass with Maeve. We want to keep those new clothes looking good until he meets all the guests."

As soon as they left the house, I ran to take a quick shower. I was in and out like a flash and was soon standing in my room with hair dryer and curling iron in hand.

I'd bought a new dress for the occasion. It was black and elegant and even showed a bit of cleavage. I knew it would take some time to get my hair fancy enough to do it justice.

Now that Jake and Riley were waiting, my fingers turned to all thumbs and I felt like crying with frustration. Just when I was about to give up and let it hang as usual, I heard the front door open and Brooke calling for me.

"I'm up here," I shouted.

"Aren't you ready?" She swept into the room, looking like she'd stepped off the pages of the Sunday *New York Times* style section, wearing a blue silk dress that draped in all the right places and red Manolo four-inch heels. Wait until Nancy got a load of that.

20

"Honestly, Mother, I swear you need a keeper."
One look at my face, and she grabbed the curling
iron out of my unresisting fingers. "Let me help. You
never did master this thing, did you?"

Brooke had just gotten a good start on my
hairdo when I heard Riley's voice calling up the
stairs. I had hoped to have a few more minutes
alone with Brooke to ask her to be my maid of
honor. Now it would have to wait.

"We'll be down in a second," I answered.

The moment I'd been dreading had arrived.
Brooke finished up in record time, an annoyed
frown marring the beauty of her face. I went down
the stairs first, and Riley's appreciative whistle
calmed my flutters a bit.

"You look beautiful," he said as he took my hand
in his.

"Riley, this is my eldest daughter, Brooke." I felt her breathing down my neck like a dragon.

"Hello," he said warmly, releasing my hand and extending his own.

He would have looked relaxed to anyone but me. She barely touched his fingers. They eyed each other like opposing bantam roosters.

I was so glad I'd finally gotten up the courage to explain Robert's past to Riley. How could I not if I was going to marry him? He'd have to understand how much I loved my children and wanted to protect their father's memory. And he did, reaffirming why I loved him as I did.

She narrowed her eyes. He narrowed his. I could see they were evenly matched. It was a battle of wills, and they'd have to prove their worth to each other if they were to get along.

"So you're Riley—the sheep shearer." Brooke threw the first salvo across the deck.

"I am," he answered with a *What are you going to do about it?* expression. His chin jutted out. "I'm also a father and a cabinetmaker."

"My father was a very successful businessman and left my mother financially independent. I'd hate to see her lose what he worked many years to achieve."

"Brooke, please—" I was aghast. I realized I'd made a big mistake by trying to shield her and not telling her the truth about my finances. I could see that now, when it was too late. Riley waved my concerns away.

"I wouldn't want that either. We've worked things out between us." His look softened when he looked my way. "I love your mother and only want the best for her. I happen to think that's marriage to me."

Brooke never took her eyes off him. "She's made up her mind so I have no choice but to accept it. But remember, I'll be watching."

"I'm glad she's had you looking out for her." Riley made the first overture. "You and your sister will always be her priority."

Brooke's shoulders relaxed a bit at those words. She finally put her hand out to clasp his. "Does this mean I have to call you Dad?" she said in a dry tone.

Jake came into the room then and peeked out shyly from behind Riley.

"Are you my new sister?" he asked.

Brooke smiled broadly, and the tension in the room lowered immediately.

"Well, I guess I soon will be if your name is Jake."

I had to ask her now, before the crowd arrived.

"Brooke, would you be my maid of honor?"

She looked a little stunned at first but then grinned again. "Wow, Mom. This is a lot for me to grasp. You're getting married for the second time, and I'm still single. Does that put me in the category of perennial bridesmaid?"

Then she did something very uncharacteristic. She gave me a great bear hug and said, "I'd love to be your maid of honor."

If I didn't know my daughter better, I'd swear there was a hint of a tear in her voice.

My sister and her husband arrived early, looking relaxed and cheerful. I hurried over to greet them.

"I'm so glad you made it. How're things going with Nora?"

"Things are looking up. As her time draws closer, she's starting to think things over. I have a feeling she'll marry Dave after all. Maybe it was the hormones, and I'm off the hook." The grin on her and Richard's faces said it all. I prayed things turned out well for all of them.

We were standing around the living room later that evening, discussing the upcoming wedding when the enormity of the situation I had gotten myself into hit me full on. The wedding plans could now become a living, breathing force of their own, in danger of taking over my life.

I remembered Lexie's wedding and the excruciatingly detailed planning by Robert and Brooke. They'd wanted a great social event for their friends and colleagues. Lexie had been her usual malleable self. She didn't care what they planned as long as she got to marry Donald. Even Donald was more interested in the planning than she ever was.

That's not what I wanted, and I knew Riley didn't either.

"I heard of a wonderful wedding planner out of Wilmet. I'll call her as soon as I get back to Chicago."

I could hear the excitement in Brooke's voice as the engine of her enthusiasm gathered steam. I had to head off that train before it left the station or there would be no stopping it.

But how to do it without blowing the closeness we'd just rediscovered after I asked her to be my maid of honor? I didn't want to break our fragile truce over something so petty.

Riley's eyes caught mine, and I could see my concern mirrored there. His lips parted, about to say something, when Lexie broke into the conversation.

"I don't think so." The decisive words cut through Brooke's enthusiastic plans like a machete. We both turned in amazement to face a very determined Lexie.

"Save all the hoopla for your own wedding. I think I know Mom well enough to guess that isn't her style. Right, Mom?"

I could have kissed her, bless her little heart. She got right to the crux of the matter without me having to say a word.

"My plan is to keep it simple and meaningful to us," I breathed into the silence with trepidation.

"Please don't tell me it's going to be a 'down home' wedding and that the Border collie is going to give you away."

I laughed at the picture that put in my mind— Maeve racing up the church aisle, pulling me behind her in my wedding gown. Anyone who knew the dog would shudder just thinking of the havoc she could create in ten minutes in a church.

"I promise it'll be elegant but simple. You won't even have to wear pink chiffon."

Some of the Wool Gatherers had joined the conversation by this time. "We're all here to help," Joan said.

"It'll be a beautiful occasion." Carol clasped her hands together, her eyes sparkling in anticipation.

Lexie put her arm around her sister's shoulders. "C'mon, buck up. You'll just have to put all that excess energy into running your own life from now on."

"Just what do you mean by that crack?" Brooke asked.

"Let's face it, sis. You're a major organizer of other people's lives. I know you mean well, but isn't it about time you started thinking about your own future and let the rest of us alone?"

I wished I had a camera to take a picture of Brooke's expression at that moment. Before she could give a snappy retort, Jake ran in, tugging on her hand. She looked down, her expression formidable, but it immediately softened when she saw who it was. I had forgotten how much she loved children and what a popular babysitter she'd been in her teens. I'd assumed the parents liked her because she had the house running like clockwork when they got home. But now, I could see she had a soft spot for children.

"Auntie Brooke, come see what I found in the bushes." He danced up and down with excitement.

She looked back at us with a frown. "We'll talk about this later."

As Brooke followed Jake out the patio door, I heard her saying in an unusually patient tone, "I'm not your aunt, remember? I'm your big sister."

"Okay, but it's a baby rabbit. Do you think we can keep it?"

THE WOOL GATHERERS STOOD TOGETHER AT THE door as the evening ended. We passed hugs all around, and I thanked them tearfully for their help with the party. But I knew I was really thanking them for all their help in getting my life back on track.

Soon after they left, I noticed Jake yawning and pulling on his ear. I'd learned months ago to pay attention to the signal. He would soon be overwrought if he didn't get home and into his bed.

Riley and I exchanged looks.

"Hey, buddy, I think it's time for us to get going." Riley put his hand on the boy's shoulder but looked at me. "Could you come along? There's something I want to show you."

What could be so important that he wanted me to leave my family and follow him home at this hour? Was there something going on with Jake that I'd missed?

"I guess so."

"It won't take long, I promise." The mischievous grin assured me it couldn't be anything too serious.

A few minutes later, I drove the Camry down country roads, following his truck. When we reached his house, we all hurried inside, Jake already half asleep in Riley's arms. I helped get him ready for bed. Tonight, he couldn't even stay awake long enough for his favorite story. I kissed him gently on the forehead and said goodnight.

"Can I call you Mom after you and Daddy get married?" he whispered in sleepy tones.

"I'd really, really like that," I whispered back, fighting tears.

Riley stood in the doorway. "C'mon, I have something to show you."

He led the way out to his workshop, reaching back for my hand. "Close your eyes," he demanded before opening the door.

"What's going on?" I giggled, feeling positively intoxicated with the evening's happiness.

"Just close your eyes and do what I tell you for once." His voice carried his own happiness.

He guided me into the room, stopping suddenly when we were inside. I could smell that familiar scent of fresh woodchips, mixed tonight with the odor of stain and varnish.

"Ready?"

"I guess so." Curiosity had me holding my breath.

"Open your eyes then."

I wasn't prepared for the sight in front of me. My breath caught in my throat. It was the four-poster bed he'd been working on the night Jake was with Brandi.

"Happy engagement."

"Oh, Riley, it's gorgeous."

"I knew that weekend Jake left with Brandi that I couldn't face life without you. I wanted to make you something special. Something to show you that I plan on us being together forever."

My heart overflowed with hope for our future at that moment. Not just for Riley and me, but for my new son and my daughters. I knew our lives would not be perfect. You don't reach my age without realizing life has its peaks and valleys. But it could be filled with more happy moments than sad. No matter what the future held, we could make it through, together.

As a family.

A family of individuals joined by love. I gave him a great bear hug.

"What's that for?"

"That's for us, forever."

WHEN I GOT HOME A SHORT TIME LATER, EVERYONE had already gone to bed. I was too energized to go up myself.

I sat on my red couch in the dimly lit room and pulled my completed sweater out of the knitting bag at my feet, filled with a sense of accomplishment. It had been a long journey but worth every step.

I ran my hand lovingly over each cable and knot. I'd give the sweater to Brooke as her bridesmaid gift, a tie to me and my grandmother and the ancestors who came before us. It would be up to her and Lexie now to continue the pattern of our family.

I looked forward to each step of the journey.

THE END

Thank you for taking time to read *The Spin I'm In*. If you enjoyed it, please consider telling your friends or writing a short review. Word of mouth is an author's best friend and much appreciated.

BONUS EXCERPT

It Never Felt So Good
For the Love of Fiber ~ Book Two

"Sometimes the one thing you want in life is the thing you can't have. That doesn't mean you give up. It means you change direction."

How often had Gram said those words? Often enough that they became my personal mantra, to be repeated nightly before falling into bed. But how many times would I have to change before I lost myself in the process?

I lay under the covers, those words echoing again when my cell phone rang so early on a Monday morning, along with a premonition of bad news. The only person ever to call me this early was Mom.

I let the phone ring three times before doing a log roll off the lumpy futon and turned half-closed eyes toward the bedside clock. I grabbed the phone and sat up.

I wasn't disappointed. It was my mother.

"Hi, Mom."

"Cara, you've got to get up to Shoreview right away to see Lucy. Something's happened to your grandmother."

"*What? How*?" Wide-awake now, I transferred the phone to my right ear and took a deep breath.

"Did she fall? Is she in the hospital?" Even though Gram was my Mother's mother-in-law, they'd always been close.

A picture of my tall, slender Gram, always so confident and sure of herself flashed through my mind, followed by the pictures I'd seen in TV commercials, of an elderly lady writhing on the floor in pain.

Or was it a car accident? She still drove her Buick like it was 1950 and everyone in town would get out of her way. But things had changed, even in her little corner of the world. Everything but Gram, I suspected.

"No, of course not." Mom clicked her tongue. She did that when she was annoyed. She'd always accused me of being a drama queen and jumping to conclusions.

"One of her friends called last night," Mom said.

"Some new woman I've never met. They found my number in Lucy's address book. They're worried about her. It seems she's been acting strange lately —not like herself at all."

"Strange how?" I got up from the edge of the futon and paced across the narrow room, phone in hand.

"She's getting forgetful, driving erratically— they're afraid she'll hurt herself. She drove that big Buick of hers into the side of her shop. Luckily there was only minor damage but someone heard the noise and called the police. The O'Brien boy was on duty and gave her a warning—said he'd be watching her driving. She was upset and embarrassed, according to her friend.

"I called Lucy as soon as I hung up with her friend but she didn't even seem to know who I was." She paused almost as if to let me know she was thinking things over. "Unless she was trying to make me feel guilty for not visiting more often?"

"Mom, I really can't do anything about it at this hour of the morning." I closed my eyes for a moment, immediately regretting my sharp tone with her. I loved my mother but sometimes her wish for me to run the family dynamics since her remarriage drove me crazy.

After pulling a double shift at the Daily Grind the previous evening, I'd stayed up for hours working on my latest art piece at the studio of my boyfriend-slash-mentor, Stefan. Too tired to drive back to my own place, I'd crashed here on his lumpy futon, not even bothering to undress. My head throbbed and my shoulder muscles ached. I'd need a double shot of espresso before my mind could even begin to function.

"Cara Eileen Olson, don't you get snotty with me. You're beginning to sound like that Steve person you're dating, or whatever you call him these days."

I decided to ignore the jibe about Stefan; we'd been down that road so often it had ruts. I raised my eyes heavenward in a silent plea. I'd be using a walker before Mom stopped talking to me like I was a teenager.

It wasn't that I didn't worry myself about Gram . . .I did, immensely. I couldn't quite put my finger on it, but when I had spoken to Gram last month there was something lacking in her voice; the spark was missing. Gram always showed an interest in my art work. But her voice had sounded flat, uninterested at times, and she kept repeating herself. I'd tried to dismiss it because I couldn't bear to think anything was wrong. Gram had been the one stable person in my childhood. The one who was always there, encouraging my dreams of success in the world of art when no one else cared.

Now I was feeling guilty. I should have called her last week to check in. I'd expected her to always stay the same. For a woman her age, Gram's clear skin wore the wrinkles well. As a child, I'd hoped I'd miraculously turn into the tall, athletic girl I saw in her family pictures. The girl with the straight, shoulder-length silvery blond hair, cool blue eyes and lanky Scandinavian build. But no, I was a definite throwback to my mother's Irish ancestors; short, a tendency to roundness with curly black hair. My blue eyes and fair skin were the only things Gram and I shared in looks. But we had our love of art in common.

"You'll have to go up to Shoreview and straighten things out," Mom continued. "Lord only knows what's going on in that shop of hers."

"Isn't it normal to be a little forgetful at her age?"

"Really, Cara. That's all you have to say? It isn't as if you'd be giving up some great career." She clicked her tongue again, putting me right back into teenage rebellious mode.

All during art school I'd worried about Mom's prediction I wouldn't be able to support myself with my art. Turns out she was right. But it would take slivers under my fingernails before I'd admit I'd made a mistake and give up painting for a more practical career. Art was my life. It had been since the first time Gram put a paintbrush in my four-year-old hand and guided it across the paper. Something came alive in my soul that day, something that has sustained me through all the ups and downs of my so-called career. Giving that up would be like stealing my very breath. I couldn't do it, even if it meant I'd be the oldest barista in Daily Grind history.

"I can't expect Dave to give up his life here in Florida to care for my former mother-in-law. His health isn't all that great."

That's the first I'd heard about any health problems and my chest muscles immediately tightened. Mom had finally found a new life for herself with Dave and I didn't want to do anything to jeopardize their happiness.

"What about the boys? Couldn't one of them check things out?" As if. Desperation made me reckless but I was in a tight spot here.

"Don't be silly. Lucy's always adored you and you know it. You're the only one she'll listen to. Besides, your brothers have wives and children to consider. They can't leave their jobs and families to fly across country to stay with their grandmother. It's only a four hour drive for you. At least you'll get free room and board there and Lord knows you probably need it."

Ever practical, my mother.

Her words hurt. Probably because they were so true. Seven years in Chicago and what did I have to show for it? A few showings in a minor gallery and a relationship going nowhere. If it weren't for the job at the coffee shop, I'd be panhandling.

"I can't stay long, Mom. Contrary to family opinion, I do have a life." Okay, so it wasn't much of a life, but it was still mine. "Besides, I'm sure Gram is just fine."

She had to be. I couldn't bear to think otherwise. I was tied to Chicago for the foreseeable future because my chance for success was here, with Stefan and his expertise. A dark cloud of doubt closed around me when I thought of my work. Something was missing. I felt it. I could almost taste it. Stefan was the only one I knew who could help me find what that was and he was more than willing.

"Remember how Gram took us in after your Dad died?" Mom asked, stabbing me again with that familiar dagger of guilt.

"I'll go up tomorrow and check things out," I sighed. The truth was, I didn't trust anyone else to look after Gram.

"Let me know what you find out, kiddo." Relief rang loud and clear in her voice. "I gotta' go. It's a beautiful morning here and we're going for a bike hike." So much for Dave's poor health. As always, Mom had manipulated me into doing what she wished.

I closed my cell phone with a snap and looked out the rain-drenched window at a grey Chicago day. As I watched from the third floor window, a CTA bus raced by, spewing sprays of water in every direction. A smartly dressed woman stood at the cross walk, shaking her fist in anger before brushing off the water dripping from her tweed suit jacket. I felt her frustration.

I dragged myself into the studio where Stefan was hard at work on his latest project, girding my loins for the upcoming flap. Monday morning and rain. Yup. It had *bad day* written all over it.

The bright white walls and fluorescent lights made my half-opened eyes blink in defense. Stefan worked with his back to the large windows, the grey light slanting through the rain-blurred glass of little help today.

"I have to drive up to Wisconsin to check on my grandmother tomorrow. Want to ride along?"

He stood back, eyes squinting as he stared at the paint-smeared canvas, lost in his usual myopic vision. His distracted, "Hmm...?" told me he probably hadn't heard a word I'd said.

"I have to drive up to Wisconsin tomorrow to check on my grandmother," I repeated, emphasizing each word. "One of her neighbors called Mom. They're worried about her."

"Tomorrow? But Frank has his opening at the Fitzgerald gallery in a few days." Stefan turned, paintbrush in hand, an annoyed frown crossing his narrow, esthetic features. "We can't miss that. It's a chance to mix with a lot of influential people. And Ted Beaupry will be there. It'll give you a chance to meet him on a social level before he judges your entry. Could give you an extra edge."

"I know, but Mom sounded pretty upset. She thinks Gram's in trouble. I can't just ignore it. I feel bad enough that it's been months since I've visited

Gram. You know how I feel about her. She's always been there for me when I needed her."

"I'm sure she'll be just fine without you. Didn't you say she had lots of friends?"

"We could be back in time for the opening," I said, running a hand through my out-of-control curls, smoothing my hair down. Why I bothered, I don't know. Stefan wouldn't have noticed if I wore a paper bag over my head at this point.

"For God's sakes, Cara, you can't keep putting your family before your work."

What? Where the hell had Stefan been all these weeks while I'd spent every spare minute in this studio? In la-la land?

"If you want to be a serious artist, you have to act like one," he said, the words followed by a heavy sigh.

"We could be there tomorrow evening, check on Gram and leave the next morning if all is well," I insisted. Only now did I realize how much I'd neglected Gram, always expecting her to stay the same and be there for me when I needed her. I had to get up to see her.

"But what if she isn't well?" He asked, widening his eyes and raising his eyebrows. "Then how long are we going to be there?"

"What's one lousy opening?" Leave it to Stefan to accentuate the negative. I raised my voice in frustration. "It isn't as if it's at a major gallery for Pete's sake."

"As usual, you just don't get it, do you Cara? Can't you see how your family manipulates you? You're never going to make it as an artist if you don't change that attitude."

"Oh, I see," I said, my fingers digging into my palms. "I'm supposed to be totally self-centered?" I bit my tongue before the, *like you*, comment slipped out. Not the best way to treat a mentor, the working part of my brain warned.

"Dedicated to your work is the way I'd put it," Stefan said.

"I put as much time as I can into my art. You know that."

"Sure, when you're not working that dead-end job at The Daily Grind or worrying over your family."

"I've hardly spent any time with my family this past year. Besides, we don't all have rich daddies to pay our bills."

"Cara, cut it out. I told you to quit that job and move in with me. I can pay the rent and buy the groceries."

"I know." It was true. He'd been after me for a long time to quit, but I wasn't about to give up my independence, even when things were at their bleakest with my artistic career. I needed to keep my own identity and freedom. And besides, I liked working at the coffee shop. If I didn't, I'd end up doing all the household chores out of guilt, taking over the responsibility for his everyday life, just as

I'd done for my brothers. But now my two brothers had wives to change those long established habits. I'd learned to my surprise just how well they got along without me. I guess I'd assumed Gram could too.

"Let's not argue again. It only upsets me and there's nothing I can do about it." I was torn between my feelings for the dark-eyed, brooding artist that appealed to the romantic in me, and the petty boy he became when thwarted. He was as determined to make me a protégé of his style as I was to prove myself worthy of his time, only it didn't seem to be working.

Frustration over my work and my life built up like a soon-to-erupt volcano. I knew if I didn't get out of here fast, words would come spewing out of my mouth like red hot ashes, burning up my feelings for him forever.

"Maybe time away will be good for me, help me get back on track." Oh, how I wanted to believe it.

"That isn't even logical." He curled his lip and turned back to his canvas. "What you need is more time spent on your art."

"Let's talk about it later. I have to go home and change before work." Grabbing my raincoat off the hook by the studio door, I pushed my arms through the sleeves. Being late for my shift at the coffee shop wouldn't help me get unscheduled time off.

"When will you get that piece for the contest finished? You only have a few weeks left," he shouted after me. "This could be your big break. You know Ted Beaupry is one of the judges. If he likes it, you're a shoe-in for national recognition."

I glanced back into the studio, my hand on the open door. My half-finished canvas sat on the easel, waiting.

What if Gram needed me for more than a few days? How would I ever get the piece finished in time? Would it ever really be finished to my satisfaction? I'd worked and reworked it so many times that I was beginning to despise the damn thing. It just wasn't right, no matter what I did. Suddenly sick of it all, I turned my back on the studio.

"Yeah, right," I murmured and shut the door behind me. *Oh, God. What if he was right and I missed this chance for success? Would I ever get another?* The thought burned a hole in my gut.

The familiar jingle of the coffee shop door jarred me back to the reality of my life as I entered, almost overpowered with the sweet nirvana of freshly ground beans, brewed coffee and cinnamon. Was there another place on earth that smelled as good? Not to the caffeine addict in me. I hurried behind the counter and grabbed a mug, sighing with pleasure as that first jolt of warm caffeine streamed through my blood. It was a relief to get away from the studio and the constant reminders of my failure.

My thoughts were foggy the rest of the day, consumed with fear over Gram and the argument with

Stefan. I'd called Gram on my lunch break to tell her I was coming, but she had that same distracted air about her and cut me off after a brief conversation.

The dinging of the cash register, the grinding coffee beans and the loud chatter of customers seated at the bistro tables didn't afford me quiet brooding time. Probably a good thing, because the more I thought about the forthcoming conversation with my manager about time off, the more I dreaded it. Maybe it was the coffee I'd sipped all day, or maybe it was something else.

I finally caught her alone at the end of my shift. Things had been dicey between us lately because I had been offered the manager position first—a job I turned down because of the time commitment.

"Could I talk to you for a minute?" I asked.

"What about? It's been a long day and I want to get home." She pulled the hair net off her dull blond hair and narrowed her pale blue eyes.

"I need to take some time off to visit my grandmother in Wisconsin. She's ill." I took a deep breath and tried to keep my cool.

"How much time are we talking here?" She snapped her gum in my face. "We're pretty short-handed and the owners say I can't hire anyone new."

"I'm not sure. Hopefully only a few days, a week at the most," I mumbled, rubbing my hands together.

"You can take the time off but I can't guarantee to hold your job, especially if it's more than a week. It isn't fair to your coworkers. There are a lot of people looking for work right now."

"Thanks, I appreciate it."

"Just don't make a habit of asking for favors, Olson." Another snap of her gum and she turned away.

I swallowed what was left of my pride, promising myself I would someday mimic the words of that old song and tell her to "take this job and shove it."

When I returned to his apartment that evening, Stefan was still at work in the studio. He finally set down his brush and looked my way. Fatigue lines were etched around his deep-set, dark eyes. Running his hand through his too-long black hair, he glanced down at his other hand at his watch. "Is it that late already?" he asked, surprised. "Whew!"

The artist in me couldn't help but admire his dedication. And the romantic in me recognized him as every young girl's fantasy of the struggling artist in need of loving care.

"I hope you brought food. I forgot about dinner again." He flashed his lost boy look.

"No, I didn't. I had to wait to talk to my manager about leaving tomorrow. She was pretty ticked and said she couldn't promise to hold the job for me."

"So, did you tell her you'd stay?"

Looking at Stefan, the view through the rose colored glasses I usually wore in his presence faded even further. How many years would it take for this man to know me?

"Of course not. Didn't you hear me this morning? I said I had to check on my grandmother."

"And you're going to go, even if it means losing your job."

"What did you expect?" He was too clueless to understand when it came to relationships. That had always been part of his charm, too involved with his art to be bothered with the mundane problems of the masses. But it wore thin today.

The phone rang and as usual he let it go to voice mail. "Stefan, please call and let me know your decision about the Fitzgerald opening. I'd like to get my plans confirmed." The throaty feminine voice brought up images of satin, chocolate and wine, everything sexy in my mind.

"Who was that?" I asked.

"A new graduate who wants mentoring. Not important." He shrugged, suddenly interested in a canvas propped against the wall.

"Why was she asking about the Fitzgerald opening?" It was only this morning I found out I might miss it.

"I guess she heard I might be going alone and wanted me to introduce her around." Color rose up the back of his neck. I'd never seen him blush before. Something was up. If I had the time or energy

I'd try to weasel it out of him. But it would have to wait.

"Stay the night, Cara. We can talk more about your plans after dinner," he cajoled.

"You can't talk me out of going. I have to go home and pack. I came by to see if you'd changed your mind about coming with me. Obviously you haven't, so I'll just leave."

I slammed the door behind me with a burst of satisfaction and ran down the steps before he could follow. He never opened the door.

Early the next morning I threw the last of my personal belongings into my car. Who would've thought they all would fit into the trunk of my ancient Ford Escort? How depressing. But then, the life of a struggling artist and barista didn't call for an extensive wardrobe.

I came to Chicago filled with plans of great adventures and artistic success. Those plans had shattered like most of my dreams with the slamming of the trunk. Wait. Do broken dreams make a sound when they shatter? Or is there just this silent aching deep in your soul?

My life had taken a U-turn and I could very well end up exactly where I started, back in small town Wisconsin with a head full of dreams and not much else.

I refused to obsess about it. This was just another bump along the road to success. I'd be back

soon. And to prove it, I'd leave all my work and sup-
plies at Stefan's studio.

I drove over there to say goodbye and make one
last plea. Maybe I hadn't given him enough credit.
Maybe he *did* care.

A part of me still hoped I was wrong about him.

I stood in the doorway and shouted into the studio. "Stefan, I'm leaving for Wisconsin now."

He was painting of course, probably had been at
it all night, oblivious to the rest of the world. I imagined the argument we'd had hardly ruffled his
feathers. I'd always envied that quality of detach-
ment before, but right now it annoyed the hell out
of me.

"Okay, Babe. Give my regards to your
grandmother."

His distracted voice kept me from crying and
begging him to come along. Three years together
and he couldn't come to the door to see me off?
Most likely he wouldn't miss me until he got hungry
and I wasn't there to prepare a meal.

Or maybe it had something to do with that
phone call that I wasn't supposed to hear. One more
thing to add to my list of worries.

"Goodbye, Steve." Now I was imitating my
mother's earlier dig. A childish retaliation, but I
knew he hated his oh so ordinary given name. It felt
good.

I made it to the Wisconsin border before the tears

started to fall, not even sure why I was crying. I had so many reasons. The stormy weather of yesterday had passed and varying shades of green could be seen in the frequent fields now visible along the highway. I rolled down the window and sucked in a deep breath of the fresh, clean air. It made me feel better.

Was I really going to miss out on the chance of a lifetime? Or should I be more concerned with Gram?

Whichever it was, it didn't matter at the moment. I knew I had to pull myself together to face my future and Gram's—so I continued the long drive toward my hometown of Shoreview, Wisconsin.

I slowed the car to a near crawl as I reached the crest of a hill leading into town and my nerves started jumping. *What would I find?*

The town of Shoreview spread out below me like a picture postcard, like one of those on the racks in every drugstore in tourist country. So perfect it made my teeth hurt. No litter, no panhandlers and not a Starbucks in sight.

What would Gram say when she saw me? Was she upset that I'd gone so long without a visit?

Would he *be there? The one person I'd carefully avoided on my previous visits?* I managed to keep him out of my thoughts while busy in Chicago, but whenever I came home, painful memories of him returned like a newly ripped off scab.

"You can do this, Cara," I whispered. I took a deep breath and plunged my car down into the deep abyss of small town living and my never to be forgotten insecurities over a young love lost before it ever had the chance to blossom.

Coming Soon from Kate Bowman

ABOUT THE AUTHOR

Born in Wisconsin to an original Brady Bunch, I had the dubious honor of being #14 in the family. As a result, I'll never run out of characters. The early years of my marriage were spent moving around the country with my engineer husband, collecting interesting stories and characters along the way. I picked up my first romance after a particularly stressful shift at a suburban Chicago hospital where I worked as an RN. Hours later, bleary-eyed and exhausted, but able to sleep because the story affirmed that good things can happen to good people, I was hooked. After seventeen years in the Chicago suburbs we returned to Wisconsin and a new life of country living. After a local class in spinning, I decided it would be fun to have my own source of wool. Several years and many animals later, I found a new source of humor for my stories. I've always loved animals and you'll find many of them populate my books. My stories are about real people trying to make it in this crazy, sometimes funny, sometimes sad world—but always with an ending that will renew your faith in love and life.

When I'm not writing, you'll find me with my family or out walking in my fields, spinning wool, knitting or weaving, but always listening to the interesting stories of those characters living in my head.

For more information about me and my books, visit www.KateBowmanAuthor.com.

Thanks for reading *The Spin I'm In.*

~Kate Bowman

"Fill your paper with the breathings of your heart."
—William Wordsworth